He'd never heard
a less convincing lie

"I don't believe there's another man, Vicky." Justin gripped her arms firmly. "Now why don't you just tell me what's got you so upset, why you don't want to see me."

"The police warned me to stay away from you. They...they think you're the chain-letter killer."

"What do you think?"

"Oh, Justin, I don't know. I'm so scared! I received another letter. It said I only have seven more days, and then...then I don't know what's going to happen."

"Nothing's going to happen to you," Justin said gruffly, wrapping her in his arms.

"But Theo was killed and then Eve, and I'm next on the list."

"No one is going to kill you," Justin declared, "because I'm not going to let them!"

ABOUT THE AUTHOR

Elaine Stirling lives in Toronto with her two children, Nicholas, age seven, and Benjamin, age four. The idea for this book came to her when a friend received a chain letter. "She was so furious," says Elaine, "that I started wondering if someone might actually kill over a chain letter. And that led to other ideas.... After that flash of inspiration, it took two years of hard work before *Chain Letter* saw the light of day. But for a book as brilliant and original as this one, the wait was well worthwhile.

Books by Elaine K. Stirling

HARLEQUIN INTRIGUE
28–UNSUSPECTED CONDUCT
35–MIDNIGHT OBSESSION
53–FOUL PLAY

HARLEQUIN TEMPTATION
139–ALMOST HEAVEN

HARLEQUIN SUPERROMANCE
261–THIS TIME FOR US

Don't miss any of our special offers. Write to us at the following address for information on our newest releases.

Harlequin Reader Service
901 Fuhrmann Blvd., P.O. Box 1397, Buffalo, NY 14240
Canadian address: P.O. Box 603,
Fort Erie, Ont. L2A 5X3

Chain Letter

Elaine K. Stirling

Harlequin Books

TORONTO • NEW YORK • LONDON
AMSTERDAM • PARIS • SYDNEY • HAMBURG
STOCKHOLM • ATHENS • TOKYO • MILAN

This one's for my mother,
Ann Maki.
If not for her thousands of hours
of free child care,
I'd still be working
on my first book.

And also for my sister,
Lisa Bobechko,
owner of the real Nick Nack Nook,
who generously pitched in with her time
whenever mine was running out.

Special thanks to special friends,
Candy and Tom Mooney,
whose tireless legwork
brought Madison to my doorstep.
I couldn't have done it without you!

Harlequin Intrigue edition published March 1988

ISBN 0-373-22085-5

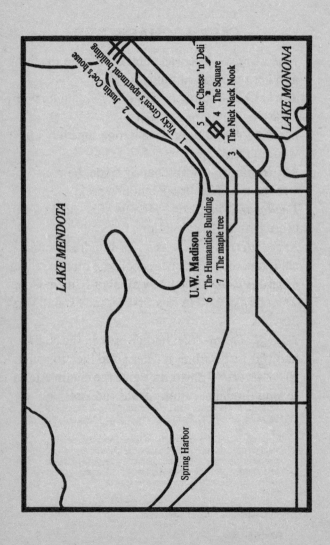

LAKE MENDOTA

LAKE MONONA

U.W. Madison
6 The Humanities Building
7 The maple tree

the Cheese 'n' Deli
The Square
The Nick Nack Nook

Justin Coe's house
Vicky Green's apartment building

Spring Harbor

CAST OF CHARACTERS

Vicky Green—She was number four on the list, and her time was running out.

Justin Coe—Number seven. He was a man with a past.

Mother—She'd been dead a long time but still wouldn't give up.

Mr. Rubinoff—A butcher by trade, he was strong enough to break a man's neck.

Lieutenant Simmons—He was after Justin for more than traffic violations.

Rick Paterson—He was a two-hundred-pound child and didn't like being called a moron.

Maeve Wilson—She knew all about Justin Coe.

Theo L. Dalta—He was first on the list and very nervous.

Rosa N. Shoon—She hadn't broken the chain and was just waiting for her good luck to roll in.

Eve Lamorth—She didn't give the chain letter a second thought . . . until it was too late.

Chapter One

Hunched over an ancient typewriter, the man laboriously pecked out the seventh name on the list: Justin Coe. An inspiring name, he thought. It sounded like justice, although he knew better than anyone that there was no such thing.

Donning a pair of rubber gloves, he carefully rolled the paper out of the carriage. Then he rose from the kitchen table, removed the gloves and picked up a photograph from the nearby hutch.

There were pictures of her in every room, but this one was his favorite. With her eyes so soft and gentle, she looked like a saint from one of those old religious paintings. Amazing, he thought, how a camera could lie. But then, she was good at deceiving people. She must have fooled the photographer, too.

He was the only one who knew what she was really like, the only one who had to live with her rages, her unpredictable moods. What choice did he have? She was his mother.

He would never forget that horrible night she came back to him. He'd awakened from a sound sleep thinking there was a draft in the room. But the window was shut tight. He'd rolled over, and there she was, standing beside the bed with a strange smile on her face. She was wearing a long white robe, the kind an angel wears, and he could see clear through her as if she were made of smoke.

"Thought you'd gotten rid of me for good, didn't you?" was the first thing she'd said.

He shuddered now at the memory, his fingers gripping the photograph until his nails turned white. "I've finished typing the letters, Mama."

"Well, it's about time. What in blaze's name took you so long?"

"I had to find the right people," he said. "It wasn't easy."

Her reply came, as it always did, from somewhere deep inside him. "What right people? I told you to pick seven names, that's all. You always make such a production out of things."

He made an effort to appear submissive. "I know, Mama. But I'll be mailing the first letter tomorrow morning. Shouldn't be long before you have that nice little place in the sun."

"I certainly hope not," she muttered. "There isn't enough room for the two of us around here."

Dutifully the man kissed the portrait before setting it down. Then he shambled into the living room and picked up the needlepoint he'd been working on.

The quotation, taken from an old epic, was one of his favorites. Mama had read him the story long ago, a rip-roaring adventure full of black magic and treachery. But what had stuck in his mind all these years were the opening lines.

Mother, love a son's honor.
Life is pain, no justice.
Revenge, destruction, death to all!

Funny how those few words had come to mean so much to him lately. Pushing the needle through the mesh, he drew it out the other side. Maybe now things were going to work out for both of them. Mama would finally have what she wanted, and he would find some peace.

"Look at those disgraceful stitches!" Her voice shrieked through him, while the needle plunged deeply into his finger.

"Dammit, Mama, now look what you made me do! I'm bleeding all over the sampler."

"Don't you curse at me, you ungrateful creature! Remember, I'm the one who brought you into this world."

"Yes, I know, but..." He gave up defending himself and sucked on his finger instead. He didn't want to arouse her suspicions. She had to continue believing he was the same obedient son he'd always been.

When the bleeding stopped, he began ripping out the soiled stitches. For a long while, the room was silent. He worked on the floral border until his shoulders ached and his eyes blurred. Then, setting the project aside, he got up and headed for bed.

"You're doing a much better job on the needlepoint now, son," the man heard her say.

His feet came to a halt at the doorway to his bedroom. He couldn't have been more astonished if the sky had fallen. "Thanks, Mama. I'm glad you like it."

"Why did you choose that quotation? As I recall, the story terrified you as a child."

He loved how it felt to keep secrets. "Yes, well, I've grown up since then. Nothing scares me anymore." *Not even you.*

"Don't overestimate yourself, son. Where are you going to hang the needlepoint when it's finished?"

He pointed to a spot above the bed. "Right there, I think."

"Yes, that should look quite lovely. Now get a good night's sleep. We have a lot of work ahead of us."

"Yes, Mama. Good night."

The man shut off the lights and allowed himself a small grin of satisfaction. Everything was going to be all right. Mama didn't suspect a thing.

Chapter Two

After a disastrous day at the store, Vicky Green was looking forward to a quiet evening at home. She refused to think anymore about the shipment of porcelain Easter baskets that had gone missing, or the two-hundred-dollar vase that seemed to fling itself off the stepladder while she was arranging the window display. All she wanted tonight was to be alone and up to her elbows in mulch. Happily, at the moment, she was both.

It didn't matter that the kitchen of her apartment resembled a tree nursery in the aftermath of a tornado. Plants uprooted and lying on their sides, bags of potting soil spilled across the tiles, the place was a blissful contrast to the artful tidiness of the Nick Nack Nook. Vicky was in the midst of fertilizing Calliope the coconut when there was a knock on her apartment door. The front double doors of her three-story brick condominium were quite often left ajar with visitors ignoring the doorbell.

"Go away," she mumbled. But the caller continued to knock incessantly. Vicky threw down her towel. "Okay, okay, I'm coming!"

She yanked open the door and found herself face-to-face with a short, dark-haired man. No words emerged from his mouth, but his jaw kept moving up and down as though he were priming a pump.

Vicky tapped her foot impatiently. "Is there something I can do for you?"

"Are you, er, V-V-V. E. Green?" he finally managed.

Vicky hoped the man was not trying to sell her something. In response to his abysmal stuttering delivery, she'd probably end up buying his entire stock out of pity. "I might be," she answered cautiously. "Who are you?"

"M-M-My name is Theo Dalta. I was wondering if you'd received this yet." He shoved a piece of paper in her face.

"Is it one of those notices from the condo association?" she asked, thinking he might be a new neighbor.

"No, a chain letter."

Vicky began to close the door. "I'm afraid you'll have to excuse me—"

He lunged forward and grabbed her arm. Then, just as quickly, he released it. "Sorry, didn't mean to seem bold. I just . . . just needed to talk to someone on the list."

"What list?"

"D-Didn't you get your letter?"

"No."

Theo poked at the paper rattling in his hand. "It's right here. See for yourself."

Keeping one eye on the unwelcome visitor, Vicky skimmed through typical chain letter drivel until she came to the seven names. Theo Dalta's was first; hers was fourth. She recognized none of the others. With a shrug, she handed back the paper. "So, it's a chain letter. Nobody pays attention to these things."

"I wasn't going to, but like the letter says, I had two weeks to follow the instructions, and my two weeks are nearly up."

"Yes, well?" She watched a bead of sweat trickle down Dalta's receding chin.

"Some w-weird things have started happening to me."

"What kind of things?" Vicky could have kicked herself. Why didn't she simply slam the door in his face?

"I'm pretty sure someone's been following me. And this morning, someone tried to j-jimmy the lock on my front door."

Perhaps an exaggerated sigh would get the message across. "Mr. Dalta, even if what you say is true, I'm sure it had nothing to do with the chain letter. But if you're really worried, go to the police."

"They won't do anything. They'll just think I'm paranoid."

"No." She shook her head emphatically. "I'm sure they'd be more than cooperative. Chain letters are supposed to be illegal, aren't they?"

Dalta finally must have realized he was getting nowhere. His shoulders drooped. "Okay, Ms Green, don't help. But just you wait and see. Once your letter arrives, you'll change your tune quick enough." He pulled out a business card and handed it to her. "When you get your letter, give me a call. Maybe then you'll be willing to take me seriously."

Vicky had no intention of calling the man, letter or no letter, but if taking his card would get rid of him, it was worth the trouble.

"I'm a dental hygienist," he added, "with my own clinic on Washington Avenue. If you ever need your teeth cleaned—"

"Yes, thank you, Mr. Dalta. Good night," she said and shut the door. Returning to the kitchen, Vicky plunked herself in front of the coconut palm. "You should've seen the way that man's hands shook, Calliope," she told the sad-looking plant. "I'd never let him anywhere near my teeth!"

SEVERAL DAYS LATER, Vicky had all but forgotten Theo Dalta's visit. With Easter on its way, the Nick Nack Nook was doing a brisk business—at least brisker than its usual customer or two a day. This morning, Vicky was finally giving Rick Paterson a chance to open the shop on his own, something he'd been begging to do for months. Most of her friends thought she was crazy to entrust him with the responsibility, but they didn't know Rick the way she did.

Collecting her mail from the hall by the front door, Vicky brought it upstairs and into the living room, where she sat down beside the avocado plant. Proudly she brushed a bit of dust off its leaves. "I must say, Arthur, you're looking good. You really have earned your regal name."

Humming contentedly, Vicky sorted through her mail. There was nothing exciting—a gardening magazine, a few bills and a legal-size envelope for V. E. Green.

Curiosity soon turned to disgust after Vicky tore open the envelope and recognized the chain letter. Not that it should have bothered her. She'd already seen Theo Dalta's copy, and hers appeared to be identical.

Still, if only to determine who the sender might be, she couldn't help but read it.

Dear Number Four,
This is not your typical chain letter. You and the six people named below have been specially selected to take part in a unique opportunity. Follow the instructions carefully, and no harm will come to you.

First of all, make a copy of this letter for seven local friends, in each case deleting your name from the list and adding theirs before mailing. Then, prepare a list of the seven names and addresses, put the list in an envelope marked with your number (4), along with ten dollars

There is a maple tree at the front of Memorial Union on Langdon Street. About five feet up, you will find a knothole. When no one is looking, deposit the envelope containing the new list and the money into the tree.

You have precisely fourteen days from the receipt of this letter to carry out your instructions. Do not break the chain. I repeat, do not break the chain. The consequences of ignoring this letter can not be overstated.

1. Theo L. Dalta
2. Rosa N. Shoon
3. Eve Lomorth
4. V.E. Green
5. Sean Filipi
6. Curtis Donet
7. Justin Coe

There was no signature, and the names meant no more to Vicky now than they had the other night. Oddly enough though, reading Dalta's letter, she'd found it easy to disregard. Now, the undertones seemed much more threatening. And, of course, that was exactly what Theo Dalta had said would happen.

Irritated, Vicky crumpled the letter and tossed it into the kitchen trash, determined to put it out of her mind completely. Chain letters were silly, annoying, and not worth the time it took to read them.

To her dismay, in the shower she could think of nothing else. Theo Dalta had been genuinely worried. What about his claim that someone had tried to break into his house? No, it was preposterous for him to assume the letter had something to do with a burglary attempt. He was probably the kind of person who kept six locks on his door and never stepped on sidewalk cracks.

Vicky put on a silky lavender blouse and pastel-flowered skirt. The more she dwelt on the little man's intrusion into her life, the more annoyed she became. It was only because of him that she'd even given the letter a second thought.

What she really ought to do was phone him and give him a piece of her mind. But Vicky knew she wouldn't. Blaming him wasn't entirely fair. She'd worked herself into a tizzy quite nicely on her own.

Now there were more practical things to worry about, such as catching the Metro bus that was due to go by any minute. Vicky was halfway out the door when the telephone rang. Stopping to listen, she considered letting it ring; curiosity prevented her.

"Is this V. E. Green?" said the man on the other end. His voice was not familiar, but Vicky recalled it was precisely the way Theo Dalta had addressed her the other night.

A faint shudder ran through her. "Who wants to know?"

"Lieutenant Simmons, ma'am. Madison P.D."

Vicky sank into the nearest chair. "The police? Why are you calling me?"

"To ask you a few questions. Are you acquainted with someone by the name of Theo L. Dalta?"

Oh, great. This was all she needed. Dalta was probably wanted for armed robbery and now trying to implicate her. She hoped the disgust in her voice was obvious. "I've only spoken to him once."

"How long ago was that?"

"A few days. Tuesday evening, I think." Somehow Vicky worked up the nerve to ask the next question. "What's Mr. Dalta done, lieutenant?"

"That's what we're trying to figure out."

"What do you mean?"

A pause crackled through the receiver.

"Theo Dalta is dead, ma'am."

Chapter Three

"Dead? He can't be! I just saw him the other night!"

A short while ago, Vicky had never even heard of Theo Dalta. Now the police were calling to tell her he'd died! What business was it of hers? Didn't he have any next of kin who . . .

Guilt nipped at the heels of Vicky's anger. The poor man. She had no right to be so callous. "Was it sudden?" she asked, filled with remorse.

"Looks that way. Think you could come and answer a few questions for us?"

She gasped. "Me? Why?"

"Your name and address were found in the pocket of the deceased."

"But I couldn't tell you anything. I don't even know the man."

"I can appreciate that. It's just routine, ma'am. Won't take long."

Glancing at her watch, Vicky bemoaned her bad timing. If only she had left a few minutes earlier, this might have been a perfectly normal day. "Actually, lieutenant, I was on my way out when you called. I'm the proprietor of the Nick Nack Nook, you see, and I've left a new employee there by himself. I really should check up on him." Rick Paterson wasn't exactly a new employee, but this was hardly the time or place to discuss his limitations.

"Ms Green, a man has died from something other than natural causes. I think in this case you should make the extra effort to help us out." The officer's deep monotone did not encourage dissent.

"All right," she said with a sigh. "Do I go to the police station?"

"No, I'm here at Dalta's place. Know where it is?"

"He gave me his business card, but I don't remember what I did with it."

The officer gave her the address. "How soon can you be here?"

"In about half an hour, I think. Is that soon enough?"

"It'll do."

As soon as she hung up, Vicky called the store, hoping Rick would understand why she had to be late. She knew he was capable of violent behavior, but so far she had been lucky. Ever since Rick came to work for her, he'd been as docile as a lamb.

At first, she wasn't worried when no one answered the phone. Rick might have been with a customer, and she had taught him that a customer in the store took precedence over the telephone. Then again, he could have been unloading boxes in the back room.

But after more than twenty rings, Vicky began to fret. Maybe he hadn't even arrived at the store that morning—no, someone would have let her know. Rick lived in a basement apartment in his sister's home, and whenever he couldn't come in, Diane made a point of calling Vicky.

Perhaps some emergency had forced him to leave the shop. All sorts of possibilities raced through Vicky's mind, but there was little she could do about any of them. The police were expecting her, and she'd already missed the first bus. It would be best that she get the questioning over with, then head for the Nick Nack Nook as soon as possible.

Sunshine sparkled off the waters of Madison's Lake Mendota as Vicky boarded the bus across the street from her condo. Usually she loved watching the colorful boats sailing across the city's largest lake, but today she stared out the window and saw nothing.

A tangle of hair blew across her face, and Vicky realized that in her haste she'd forgotten to pull it back into her usual disciplined twist. It now billowed about her shoulders and tickled her nose, an unruly mass that was neither blond nor brown, but some nondescript shade in between.

She changed buses near the domed Capitol Building, jostled by commuters who didn't know or care that Theo Dalta was dead. Vicky wished she was one of them.

Finding Dalta's house in the serene, tree-lined neighborhood wasn't difficult. It had to be the one behind the police barricade with the two squad cars parked in front. Vicky approached a uniformed officer by the stairs of the two-story house. "Excuse me, my name is Vicky Green, and I'm looking for Lieutenant Simmons. He's expecting me."

"Yes, ma'am. Go on up. You'll find him inside."

Vicky climbed the stairs and opened the door to a reception area. No one was there, so she walked through an office with steel cabinets and a dentist's chair. Two men in blue were on their way out.

"Lieutenant Simmons?" she asked, glancing from one to another.

The large man gestured over his shoulder. "He's in the apartment, ma'am."

Thanking him, she went through an inner doorway to a living room. The apartment was small and dingy, with the back entrance open to reveal a rickety porch and a neighbor's brick wall. At first, no one seemed to be there. Then a man in a plaid shirt and green polyester sports coat appeared from another room.

"Ms Green? Lieutenant Simmons."

"How do you do?" Vicky smiled nervously. The man might have smiled back, but it was difficult to tell, since his face contributed little to the effort. He reminded Vicky of a basset hound—droopy eyed, stocky, short limbed.

"Have a seat," he said, waving in the direction of a Naugahyde chair. Then, sitting across from her, he pulled out a notepad. "Okay, Miss Green, might as well get right to it. The men and I have been up all night, and we're feeling a little punchy."

"I understand."

"First of all, what's your full name?"

"Victoria Elizabeth Green."

"Age?"

"Twenty-eight."

"Where do you work?"

"I own the Nick Nack Nook on State Street."

He looked up. "What's that?"

"A gift shop."

"Had it long?"

"About five years." Vicky found his line of questioning odd, but then what did she know about police investigations? He was probably trying to put her at ease by posing simple questions first.

"How long have you known the deceased?" he asked next.

"I don't know him at all. He showed up at my door three nights ago, we talked for a few minutes, then he left. That was it."

Crossing his legs, the lieutenant hunched over the pad. "What time did he show up?"

"Around seven." As she waited for him to take notes, Vicky decided she didn't care much for this place. It was gloomy and depressing. So was Lieutenant Simmons, for that matter, but who could look good after staying up all night?

"Lieutenant," she said when he'd finished writing, "you mentioned that Theo Dalta died suddenly. How did he die?"

The officer scratched his head with the eraser end of the pencil. "Broken neck, far as we can tell. Must have fallen down the back porch stairs. His body was discovered by a neighbor letting out the dog."

Vicky leaned over to peer through the back entrance. "We're only two stories up. Could a person really break his neck in such a short fall?"

The policeman shrugged. "Guess it depends which way you take the dive." He stabbed at his notebook. "Okay, back to business. What did you and the deceased talk about?"

She wished Lieutenant Simmons would stop referring to Theo Dalta as "the deceased." For all his other shortcomings, he'd been very much alive the other night.

"We talked about a chain letter."

No reaction registered on the officer's face, but then he'd no doubt heard stranger things in his day. "Go on," was all he said.

"He wanted to know if my letter had arrived and what I was going to do about it. Both our names, you see, were on the list."

"Had your letter arrived?"

"Not until this morning."

"Mind if I take a look at it?"

Panic rose and fell in her stomach. "I didn't bring it. Was I supposed to?"

He gave her a plainly exasperated look. "Might have been a good idea under the circumstances, don't you think?"

"Gosh, I...I'm sorry. I didn't...I mean, nothing like this has ever happened to me before. I just wasn't thinking."

"Never mind. It's no big deal, but I'd like to drop around to your place and pick it up, if that's okay with you. Would later today be all right?"

"I work until six, but I'm going straight home after that."

"Good enough." Lieutenant Simmons got up from the chair. "Come with me, Miss Green. There's a few things I'd like you to see before we bring them into the lab."

Vicky followed him into a tiny kitchen. The place was cluttered with dirty dishes, but a space had been cleared on the counter for a pair of transparent plastic bags containing bits of paper.

"Don't take the papers out of the bags," the lieutenant said. "Fingerprints. But take a look and tell me what you think."

Vicky picked up one of the bags to examine its contents more closely. She recognized a few words, including her surname and the name Justin Coe. "It looks like this might be the chain letter."

"Is that right? Tell me, Miss Green, did Dalta seem worried or depressed about getting the letter?"

"I wouldn't know about depressed, but he was definitely worried. He was convinced someone had been following him and had tried to break into his apartment." Once more, Vicky became acutely aware of the silence surrounding them. She couldn't wait to leave. "You don't really think there's a connection between the letter and...the accident, do you?"

The lieutenant shrugged. "Not likely, but we gotta cover all the bases." He slid the second plastic bag across the counter. This one contained a single sheet of white bond paper. Block letters from magazines had been clipped and pasted to read, 'Death to all.'

Vicky began to feel cold. "Where did you find this?"

"The same place we found your name and address. In the pocket of the deceased."

Vicky grabbed the edge of the counter to steady herself. Death to all. Rational people didn't carry notes like that in their pockets. And to think she'd actually opened her door to the man! "Is he...was he a..." The polite words for what she wanted to ask escaped her.

"Was he some kind of psycho?" The lieutenant almost, but not quite, touched her arm to steady her. "Even if he was, there's no need for you to worry. He can't hurt you now."

"N-no, I don't suppose he can."

"I do have one more question before you go."

"Yes?" Vicky continued staring at the note.

"What were you doing last night around ten o'clock?"

"I was at home potting plants."

"Is there anyone who could verify that?"

She looked up, and an odd sensation scurried along her nerve endings. "Not that I can think of. Why? Am I supposed to have an alibi?"

Obviously much less concerned than she was, the officer picked up the second bag and held it to the light. "Nah, it's nothing like that, Miss Green. Just thought I'd ask."

VICKY DIDN'T STOP for her ritual coffee and newspaper at Mr. Rubinoff's Cheese 'n' Deli. It was already past noon, and she was in a hurry to get to the store. Sprinting the last few blocks from Madison's Capitol Square to the Nick Nack Nook, she was relieved to see that the outside of the shop, at least, was still standing.

Inside, she was further comforted by the tinkle of the bell announcing her arrival. Everything appeared to be in order. There were no customers, but there was nothing unusual about that.

"Are you here, Rick?" Vicky called out. There was no answer.

She checked the stockroom and found it empty. Then, hearing the bell, she returned to the front. There was Rick, wearing an expression of total innocence, like a two-hundred-pound, six-foot-three-inch child.

The morning's trauma had taken its toll on Vicky's patience. "Where on earth have you been?" she demanded sharply.

"I was hungry. I wanted lunch."

"But I phoned nearly two hours ago, and there was no answer. Where were you then?" Although Rick's mental capacities were limited, Vicky made a point of treating him as she would any friend or employee. But at the moment she felt more like a parent.

He raised his arm as if to ward off a blow. "I . . . I don't know. Maybe I was in the bathroom. Don't yell at me, Vicky. You know I don't like it when people yell at me." His face contorted as he groped for an explanation that would satisfy her.

"I know that," Vicky said, trying to regain her composure, "but when people get angry, they have a right to express their anger."

"Even when it makes others feel worse than they already do?"

Despite her best efforts, Vicky smiled. "Point taken, Rick. But listen to me. This is important. Whenever you go out, you have to remember to lock the store."

"But I was only gone a few minutes." He held up a small paper bag from the Cheese 'n' Deli. "You know Mr. Rubinoff always has the sandwiches ready at lunchtime."

"How long you were gone is not the issue. You still have to lock up."

The dark-haired man stared at his feet. "You must be awfully mad at me."

"Not mad, Rick, disappointed."

"You won't fire me, will you? You're the only one, except for Mr. Rubinoff, who doesn't think I'm a moron."

"You're not a moron," she countered. "Don't ever say that about yourself." Feeling like a beast, Vicky went over to hug him. "I won't fire you, but if you *ever* leave the store unattended again, I'll have no choice. Is that understood?"

He nodded. "I promise I'll always lock the door—no, I won't even leave, no matter how hungry I get."

Vicky had to chuckle. "That's quite a sacrifice. Now let's get to work. I want to show you how to make a bank deposit."

There were enough pre-Easter customers to keep Vicky reasonably occupied that day, but the time between sales dragged. Rick, though a conscientious worker, was not a great conversationalist. Vicky's thoughts kept wandering back to that brief and bizarre encounter with Theo Dalta.

His death couldn't have had anything to do with the chain letter. He fell off his porch—sad, tragic, but that was all. As for the strange note in his pocket, well, who could say what it meant? Theo Dalta's sudden death was no reason to take on the paranoia Theo Dalta had felt when he was alive.

Nevertheless, to be on the safe side, Vicky called a locksmith and arranged to have a strong dead-bolt lock installed on her apartment door that evening. It wasn't until the locksmith had been and gone that she felt secure enough to retrieve the letter. Cringing, she lifted it out of the garbage. The letter had landed on last night's potato salad and carried with it the undeniable aroma of curdled mayonnaise and onions. She hoped the lieutenant wouldn't mind.

Suddenly curious, Vicky took the phone directory and looked up a few of the names. Sean Filipi lived on Crestwood. Rosa N. Shoon, second on the list, was also in the book. Vicky was listed as Green, V. E., which confirmed where the letter writer found the names.

She toyed with the idea of calling one or two people to find out if they'd received their copy. She might even ask if Dalta had contacted them. Then, thoroughly annoyed with herself, Vicky shoved the directory aside. Calling strangers about a chain letter bordered on insanity.

Ten minutes later, Vicky told herself it was the debilitating effect of living alone that forced her to dial Sean Filipi's number, despite earlier good intentions.

There was no one at home. An image of Mr. Filipi lying dead in his living room flashed through Vicky's mind, but that, she knew, was nothing more than imagination working overtime. She had never been the least bit clairvoyant. The second number she tried, a woman answered.

"Is this Rosa Shoon?" Vicky asked.

"Yes, who's this?"

"My name is Vicky Green. I hate to bother you, but I was wondering if you'd received a chain letter recently."

"Why? Did you send it?"

"No, certainly not. I received one, too. I just wanted to know whether you'd...well, you know, done anything about it."

"I did what the letter said, if that's what you mean. You never know about these things. I have a friend in California who followed the instructions in a chain letter, and a few weeks later, her mailbox was stuffed with dollar bills."

This was not the response Vicky had anticipated. "I don't recall the letter saying anything about getting money."

"Not in so many words," the woman pointed out huffily, "but people usually do get something. I hope you're not thinking of breaking the chain. That would ruin it for the rest of us."

Vicky decided not to tell Rosa that the chain had already been broken—permanently—by Theo Dalta. She gave the woman some noncommittal answer and hung up.

Staring at the tree-lined avenue outside her window, Vicky wondered if she was the only rational person on the list. One had heard footsteps behind him; another was willing to throw hard-earned money into a tree, for heaven's sake. All Vicky really needed was one kind soul, someone slightly more reassuring than the lugubrious Lieutenant Simmons, to tell her she was not crazy for ignoring the letter.

For a change, she went to the bottom of the list. The phone book contained two numbers for Justin Coe, a home number on Sherman, which wasn't far from her place, and a business number at the Humanities Building on the University of Wisconsin campus. A professor; that sounded promising.

No one was at home so she tried his office number. A man answered right away.

"May I speak to Justin Coe?" Vicky squeezed her eyes shut, telling herself the conversation would be over soon.

"This is he."

She was already beginning to breathe easier. Justin Coe spoke with the eloquent timbre of a professor emeritus. She could almost visualize his silver hair, half glasses and tweed jacket.

"You don't know me," she said, "but my name is Vicky Green. Have you, by any chance, received any strange mail lately?"

There was a pause. "Perhaps you could be more precise. What do you mean by strange mail?"

Vicky cleared her throat. "A chain letter."

"Are you one of my students?"

"No, I'm..." She tried to think of a reasonable explanation for who she was. "I'm just...Vicky Green. This must sound like a crank call, but I promise you it's not. You see, Mr. Coe, you and I are both on the list. There are seven of us—or rather, there *were* seven until last night."

"What happened last night?"

"Theo Dalta died."

"Who?"

Now she had definitely piqued his interest. "Theo L. Dalta, the first one on the list."

"What list?"

"The list in the chain letter!" Vicky drew in a great lungful of air and forced herself to exhale slowly. "Sorry, I didn't mean to scream in your ear. It's just that I've had an awful day. I shouldn't have bothered you...."

There was silence for a moment, then he said, "No need to apologize. We all have days like that."

A silly tear of gratitude trickled down Vicky's cheek. "I really appreciate your listening to me, Mr. Coe. I've never paid any attention to chain letters before, but when people start dying and policemen start calling—"

"Did you say the police?"

"Uh...yes, this morning. I had to answer questions about Mr. Dalta. Not that I knew anything..."

"You said that both our names were on the list."

"Yes, I have the letter right here. Let me read it—"

"No, don't bother. Vicky, I was uh...planning to go out for a bite when I finished this paperwork. Would it be convenient for you to join me? I must say, you have my curiosity aroused."

Vicky glanced around, as though searching for a place to hide. "I don't really know if I should . . ."

"I am quite respectable, I assure you."

Justin made the claim with a dash of humor, which only made Vicky feel foolish. "I didn't mean to imply you weren't, Mr. Coe." She was the one who'd called; she had no one to blame but herself for getting into this mess. "Where do you want to meet?" she asked, deciding she would nix any place that wasn't well lit and teeming with people.

"Why don't you name a place? Somewhere central, near the Square, perhaps."

Vicky thought a moment. They could, she supposed, meet at the Cheese 'n' Deli. Mr. Rubinoff worked long hours; he'd keep an eye on her while she was in the company of Mr. Coe. "There's a restaurant on Hamilton Street called Rubinoff's Cheese 'n' Deli," she told him. "It's nothing fancy, but the food is good."

"Perfect. Shall we meet at, say, seven o'clock?"

"Seven o'clock is fine."

Her pulse was pounding frantically by the time Vicky hung up. Three times she picked up the receiver with the intention of calling Justin Coe and canceling their evening. But being the basically timid creature that she was, the thought of phoning him back was twice as excruciating as the prospect of meeting him for dinner.

Chapter Four

Mr. Rubinoff's swarthy face, sweating from the hot stoves, lit up when Vicky entered the Cheese 'n' Deli. "I missed you this morning, Victoria!"

She walked past shelves of imported delicacies to the cluster of tables at the rear. "I missed you, too. I had a...an appointment." Mr. Rubinoff would be terribly upset if he knew she'd spent the morning with the police, so she didn't elaborate.

So far, the only patrons in the restaurant were a young couple and a woman alone with a book. None of them looked like a potential Mr. Coe.

"You were very kind to let Rick open the store on his own this morning," Mr. Rubinoff said. "So few people are willing to give the young man a chance."

Unfortunately Vicky knew that what he said about other people was true. "Rick did quite well on his own, all things considered," she said.

"Are you staying for dinner?"

"Yes. I'm supposed to meet someone, but he hasn't arrived yet."

"Oh, ho! A man, is it?" The proprietor pulled out a chair with a flourish.

"Yes, but he's not a—"

"I shall bring up a bottle of our finest Yugoslavian Bordeaux."

She waved her hand through the air. "No, you don't understand. This is just a—"

"On the house, of course. And if you deny me, my heart will shatter."

Vicky sank into her chair with a sigh. "Okay, Mr. Rubinoff, you win."

"Certainly I win. No one wins an argument with a Gypsy, except another Gypsy." Humming a soulful lament, the man lumbered off.

Vicky was wondering idly whether Justin Coe was the type to appreciate Yugoslavian Bordeaux when she remembered that Lieutenant Simmons was supposed to have dropped by her apartment to pick up the letter.

She couldn't leave the restaurant now; Mr. Coe was due to arrive any minute. *Nice going, Vicky, standing up a policeman.* Digging through her purse for change, she hurried to the public phone at the front of the restaurant and looked up the number for the Madison Police Department.

Lieutenant Simmons wasn't in, but Vicky left a message to say she'd be home in a couple of hours. Then, turning around, she saw a man studying the display of imported chocolates. Spellbound, Vicky stared for what must have been a full minute.

He had the blondest hair she'd ever seen—not wheat colored or sandy, but snow blond, a shade one associated with Sweden and the midnight sun. A trim beard in a darker shade of blond framed his lean face, giving him the look of a well-heeled skipper.

The image was enhanced by the white cotton pants and the navy sweatshirt he wore with the sleeves pushed up to his elbows. Casual, refined; urbane, jaunty. All of those adjectives seemed to apply.

He turned to her with languorous ease. "Are you Vicky Green?"

Her hazel eyes widened. The eloquent baritone was the same, but on the telephone he had sounded decades older. There were no half glasses to detract from his incredible sil-

ver-blue eyes, and nothing about his bronzed complexion
that suggested airless lecture halls.

"You're Mr. Coe?" she asked, struggling with an unsettling mixture of anticipation and helplessness.

"Justin, please. I'm on my own time now." He stepped
closer and took her hand. "I was expecting someone
older . . . and not nearly as pretty."

"Me, too," she blurted. "That is, er, you're younger than
I expected." With an inadvertent swirl of her skirt, Vicky
gestured across the room. "Our table is over there."

Good grief, she'd very nearly called him pretty—a description that was not so much inappropriate as inadequate. Justin Coe was, in the finest masculine sense of the
word, beautiful.

He took a seat across from her, shifted the cutlery slightly,
then rested his forearms on the gingham-covered table.
Every movement he made was fluid, effortlessly smooth,
reflecting a confidence Vicky couldn't help but admire. Her
own tummy at the moment was threatening to growl, which
meant she had to say something quickly to cover up the
noise.

"Do you come here often?" he asked in the nick of time.

Vicky pressed her hands discreetly to her stomach. "Every
morning for coffee."

He looked around, his eyes taking in every detail. "Looks
like a cozy place."

"It is," she assured him.

Justin Coe, Vicky decided, was too much of everything.
He was too blond, too handsome, too tall, too perfect. Personally, she'd always felt more comfortable with average,
non-threatening men who'd come to terms with a few extra
pounds or their receding hairlines. They helped keep
Vicky's own shortcomings in perspective—her fly-away,
dirty-blond hair, more or less controlled in a single knot at
the back of her head; her too slight figure that hadn't
changed much since she was a fourteen-year-old tomboy;
and her milky complexion that had gone out of vogue de-

cades ago. From the curious way Justin was looking at her, Vicky was convinced he'd already sized up the glaring differences between them.

"Aha, I see that your guest has arrived!" Mr. Rubinoff's voice boomed through the restaurant as he placed the wine on the table.

Vicky couldn't have been more grateful for her friend's timing. From the way he rearranged the centerpiece and fussed over the condiments, she knew he wouldn't leave until he got an introduction. "Mr. Rubinoff, I'd like you to meet Justin Coe. Justin, this is my good friend, Mr. Rubinoff, owner of the Cheese 'n' Deli."

The men shook hands, the older one bowing in European fashion. "Good evening, sir. Welcome to my humble establishment."

"Thank you. It's a pleasure to meet you."

"Have you been acquainted with Victoria for very long?"

Justin gave him a puzzled look. "You mean Vicky?" He slid her an amused glance. "Nearly five minutes, I'd say. But from what I've gathered, she seems like a lovely lady."

Good for you, thought Vicky, silently awarding him a few extra points. If Justin had been anything less than utterly gracious, Mr. Rubinoff would have hovered at their table all evening, making sure that Vicky was duly appreciated. Her parents and brothers lived hundreds of miles away in northern Wisconsin, but she could always rely on her old Gypsy friend to assume a familial role.

"I have known Victoria for years," he said, as though it was some kind of personal accomplishment. "She is like a daughter to me."

"I see." Justin's reply was polite. For no particular reason, Vicky tensed.

"Are you a native of Madison, Mr. Coe?" the older man asked in his thick eastern European accent.

"I was born in the Midwest."

Now Vicky knew why she was tense. Mr. Rubinoff was about to launch into a full-scale interrogation.

"I know a Coe family in Middleton," the Gypsy went on to say. "You are, perhaps, a relative of theirs?"

Justin's eyes flickered. "I have no living relatives."

Okay, Vicky decided, time for the third degree to come to an end. "Could we see the menus, please?"

Mr. Rubinoff looked at her blankly. Then he offered an apologetic smile and handed them the menus. "The special this evening is smoked ham, an old family recipe. I recommend it highly."

Justin scarcely perused the selection before deciding on the special. Vicky chose the same, and the proprietor lumbered off with their orders.

"You'll have to excuse Mr. Rubinoff," Vicky said. "He means well, but he can be a bit overprotective at times."

"So I gathered." Justin no longer seemed the least bit perturbed. He turned the bottle of wine and examined the label. "Yugoslavian. How about that? It's been years since I . . ." He let the sentence drop and looked up. "Shall I pour?"

"Please." Sipping the wine, Vicky wondered when to broach the subject of the chain letter. Again, Justin deftly made the decision for her.

"I'd like to see the letter now, Vicky."

"Of course," she said, reaching for her purse.

He took it and was about to read, when he stopped and held the letter up to the light. "What's this? A watermark?"

Vicky gave him a sheepish grin. "Mayonnaise. I had to dig it out of the garbage."

He looked at her with intense silver-blue eyes, then chuckled. But the chuckle dwindled to a smile, then faded altogether as he read the letter. "Which one died?"

"The first one. Theo Dalta."

"How?"

"A broken neck. He fell off a porch."

"Was it suicide?"

Vicky shrugged. "They don't know yet."

Justin studied the letter a while longer. Then he took out a pen and copied down the names on a paper napkin.

"Are any of the names familiar to you?" Vicky asked.

He shook his head. "Not offhand, but I do intend to find out more about them."

"I looked them up in the phone book," she announced, as though she'd done something quite courageous. "They all live in Madison."

Something must have amused him. His face crinkled into a smile, but not a condescending smile—a nice one. "Have you spoken to anyone besides me?"

"I met Mr. Dalta briefly a few days before he died, and I talked to Rosa Shoon on the phone."

"How did you learn about Dalta's death?"

"From the police. Remember I told you? They called me in for questioning this morning." She felt her cheeks color incriminatingly. "My name and address were in his pocket, but I swear I don't know why he had them." She wondered if Justin had noticed the panic in her voice; it sounded painfully obvious to her.

Incredibly he reached across the table and touched her hand. "Don't let it upset you, Vicky. The police have to be thorough when someone dies accidentally. But just because this Dalta fellow was unlucky enough to receive a letter before he died doesn't mean the two incidents are connected."

That was precisely what she'd been waiting to hear from someone other than herself. "So you don't think there's anything to worry about?"

"I don't think so."

Suddenly Justin, for all his outward perfection, no longer seemed intimidating. He was actually quite kind. "Thank you for being so sympathetic," she said.

Tucking the list of names into his pocket, he returned her smile. "My pleasure. Now that the unpleasant business is out of the way, why don't you tell me about yourself, Vicky?"

"There's not much to tell. I was born and raised in northern Wisconsin, came here to attend college and decided to stay."

"Is there a Mr. Green who influenced your decision to stay?"

She laughed. "No, I'm not married.

"What do you do?"

"I own a small gift shop on State Street. It's called the Nick Nack Nook."

"The Nick Nack Nook. Clever name."

"How about you?" she asked, preferring to steer the conversation away from herself. "What attractions does Madison hold for you?"

"Offhand, I can think of three terrific attractions. The sailing, the people and my job. I'm an associate prof at UW. English Literature."

He really was a professor. Now that she'd had a few minutes to observe him, Vicky realized that it wasn't so inconceivable. Justin did have an air of authority about him, a self-confidence that evolved from something deeper than mere physical charm. And he wasn't as young as she'd first thought him to be. Strands of silver ran through his pale hair and beard, the creases near his eyes suggesting not so much age as a life lived to the fullest. Vicky guessed he'd be somewhere in his late thirties.

She glanced at his hand; no wedding ring. Too bad she wasn't forward enough to ask about a Mrs. Coe.

"I take it from your reaction that English Lit is not up your alley?" he said.

Vicky stared a moment, then realized Justin couldn't possibly have known what she was thinking. She grinned. "How could you tell?"

"I think it was your lack of enthusiasm when I proudly announced what I teach."

"I must admit, my taste in reading is limited to financial papers and whatever can be read comfortably in the bathtub."

Justin's gaze swept over her, as if he might be contemplating the image of Vicky in bubbles. Reflexively she folded her arms across her chest.

"Shakespeare can be enjoyed in the tub," he insisted, "as long as it's a paperback edition."

Vicky managed a slightly breathless laugh. "No doubt, but I've always blamed my lack of interest on my teachers. Their methods managed to suck the lifeblood out of literature for me."

Justin leaned closer, and she caught a whiff of his clean, citrusy cologne. "Then we'll have to remedy that."

His remark and his proximity gave Vicky the feeling one gets when riding up and over the top of a ferris wheel—which was, of course, perfectly understandable. What woman wouldn't feel giddy at the prospect of seeing Justin a second time? But she couldn't possibly manage it. It wasn't Justin's fault, but in his presence, she could never feel like anything other than twenty-eight-year-old wallpaper.

"Here we are—two specials!" Mr. Rubinoff showed up as if from nowhere carrying two plates heaped with food.

For the next little while, Vicky's and Justin's conversation revolved around the pleasures of gastronomy, and she found herself laughing and chatting, amazingly close to forgetting her self-consciousness.

Phoning Justin may have been the most impulsive thing she'd ever done, but who cared? Even if she never saw him after tonight, she could look back and recall that a silly chain letter had resulted in the most fascinating date she'd ever had.

Except that this wasn't a date, and the chain letter wasn't silly. Ever since she'd put the letter back in her purse, Vicky had felt a strange sensation gnawing at her stomach. At first, she'd attributed it to guilt for enjoying herself so soon after Theo Dalta's death. Laying down her fork, she knew what it was that she'd tried to suppress.

"Justin, the police showed me something at Mr. Dalta's this morning. I think I've been trying to ignore it, but I can't."

"Then don't ignore it. Tell me."

"They found a note in his pocket, a poison-pen note. You know, with letters cut out of magazines."

"I know the kind you mean. What did the note say?"

She swallowed hard, trying to dispel the sense of dread creeping along her spine. " 'Death to all.' "

Her knife chose that moment to ricochet off her plate and clatter to the floor. As soon as Vicky bent to retrieve it, Mr. Rubinoff appeared with a replacement.

She sat up, prepared to mumble some apology. But when Vicky looked at her dinner partner, she forgot her embarrassment.

Justin Coe's face had drained of color, a fact that had not gone unnoticed by the hovering Mr. Rubinoff.

"Mr. Coe, is something wrong?" the proprietor asked. He topped up Justin's water glass and slid it toward him.

Justin shook his head. "It's just that 'Death to all' sounds pretty ominous. I just hope it isn't connected to the chain letter."

The Gypsy, scowling, continued to hover at the table. Vicky touched his arm. "It's okay, Mr. Rubinoff."

He seemed reluctant to leave, but another customer required his attention, so he had no choice. "Let me know if you need anything." He directed the offer specifically at Vicky.

When she and Justin were alone, Vicky leaned across the table. "Does the note change your opinion about Theo Dalta's death? That maybe his death is connected to the chain letter?"

"Who knows? I'd have to know more about it. What did the police say?"

"They didn't. I'll ask the lieutenant tonight if they've come up with anything new."

Justin straightened. "The lieutenant? He's coming here?"

"No, to my place."

"Oh, okay." He sat back in his seat. "Not that I have anything against the police, mind you. It's just that…well, I have these outstanding parking tickets. You know how it is."

Vicky, although she abhorred driving and refused to get her license, did know how it was. She had three older brothers for whom life was a constant battle with the law in their hometown. They never committed any serious wrongdoings, but their disdain for anyone in uniform was legendary. As a child, Vicky, too, used to avoid the police, but only so she wouldn't have to admit her kinship with the "wild" Green boys.

"I promise not to breathe a word to Lieutenant Simmons about your tickets," she teased.

His grin was disarming. "I'd appreciate that."

Vicky lost the argument over the dinner tab. As they got up to leave, she felt a twinge of regret that the evening had come to an end so quickly. Only a short time ago, she'd been wondering how she would ever get through it.

"Can I give you a lift home?" Justin asked as they walked past colorful shelves of local and imported gourmet foods.

"I wouldn't want to take you out of your way," she protested, not with total innocence, since she knew from the phone book that they were practically neighbors.

"I'm on Sherman Avenue," he said. "Is that anywhere near you?"

"I live at Gorham and Livingston."

"Perfect, right on my way." He offered her his arm. "Shall we go?"

The combination of wine, food and Justin's charming company dispelled the last of Vicky's hesitation. "Let's," she said, taking his arm happily.

Before they could leave, Mr. Rubinoff called out from the cash. "Victoria, a word with you, please?"

Inwardly she moaned. Why now, of all times? Justin was already holding the door open for her. "I'll be out in a minute," she told Justin with a sigh.

He nodded. "I'll have the car out front."

Mr. Rubinoff stood at the counter, glaring at Vicky as though she'd broken a curfew. "I trust you have enough sense not to go anywhere with that man."

Accustomed to his directness, Vicky answered easily. "He's giving me a ride home. What's wrong with that?"

"Your Mr. Coe is hiding something."

"How can you possibly know that?"

Mr. Rubinoff tapped his chest. "I feel it—here."

"Oh, come on, he's a nice man. You haven't given him a chance." Vicky wouldn't have believed it, but she was using the same wheedling tones on Mr. Rubinoff that as a teenager she'd used on her parents.

"I overheard what you were discussing, and I have bad feelings about it." He tapped his chest again. "I tell you, Justin is not what he appears to be."

Vicky's mouth dropped open. "You were eavesdropping?"

"But of course."

"That's an awful thing to admit to."

"Not at all. If you had wanted privacy, you would have gone elsewhere for dinner. You came here so that I could keep an eye on things, no?"

Vicky felt herself shrinking. "Well, maybe...in a way." Mr. Rubinoff was right, as usual, and Vicky was not really upset because he'd eavesdropped. She was upset because he didn't approve of Justin.

Folding his arms across his broad chest, her friend smiled triumphantly. "I knew it."

"But I still don't understand your reservations about Justin. He's a college professor. I phoned him at his office."

"There is more to a man than his profession, Victoria."

"Mr. Rubinoff, Justin's only giving me a ride home, and I doubt that I'll be seeing him again after tonight."

"That is good news, but why not take a taxi? I'll give you the money."

Vicky waved the offer away. "Don't be silly. I'll be perfectly safe. Thanks again for the wine, and I'll see you in the morning."

The old man watched Vicky leave, his rheumy eyes filled with concern. "*Ja develesa,*" he murmured in the Gypsy tongue. Go with God.

Chapter Five

Grateful as Vicky was for Mr. Rubinoff's concern about her, when it came right down to it, her personal life was her own business. So, as she walked out the door of the Cheese-n-Deli, she reassured herself that she was indeed a grown woman, a woman able to look after herself. Besides, why should she have any reason to fear Justin Coe? She had called him for this meeting, after all....

A low-slung silver sports car was waiting by the curb, its sleek lines gleaming like pewter beneath the streetlights. Vicky looked both ways, up and down the street, thinking for a moment that Justin had driven off without her.

Then she heard the voice. "I'm right here, Vicky."

She looked down to find Justin grinning at her through the window of the sports car. "This is yours?" she gasped, noting the gilt emblem of a jaguar on the hood.

"Yes, do you like it?"

Vicky's stomach clenched. "These things go fast, don't they?"

"Depends on the driver. Hop in."

People, Vicky soon discovered, did not hop into a Jaguar XJ-S. Instead, they hunkered down and snuggled into it, something like cozying up to a beast in his lair. After bumping her head on the frame and catching her skirt in the door, she managed to settle herself in the leather seat with a modicum of dignity.

"Are you all right?" Justin asked while the engine growled in feral anticipation.

Vicky wiped the perspiration from her brow. "I think so. I don't know much about cars, but aren't Jaguars terribly expensive?"

He revved the engine, seeming to derive great pleasure from the sounds it made. "Terribly."

"But you're only a professor...." She stopped just short of being rude.

Justin looked at her with a mixture of curiosity and amusement. "You're wondering how I can afford it?"

She reddened. "I guess I am, sort of. Not that you owe me any explanations or anything."

"It's no big mystery," he said, depressing the clutch and shifting into first gear. "Plain old family money."

They pulled away from the curb with a squeal and Vicky lost all interest in pursuing the topic of Justin's financial state. Her only concern at the moment was survival.

Mercifully there were no policemen in sight and traffic after dark was minimal. Otherwise, they never would have made it, Vicky was certain. The lights of downtown Madison whipped past her window in a blur, and by the time they shrieked to a stop at her three-story brick apartment, the knot of hair behind her head was in abysmal disarray. She recalled that, at some point, Justin had suggested she close her window, but she'd been much too busy clinging to the seat.

Now he was holding the passenger door open for her. She stepped outside, wobbling, until Justin steadied her with a hand at her elbow.

"Thanks for dinner," she mumbled. "And the flight home too, I suppose."

He laughed gently. "Don't mention it. By the way, I appreciate your agreeing to see me about the letter. Not many people are willing to take chances with strangers these days."

His comment reminded Vicky of something Mr. Rubinoff had said. He, too, had commended her for taking a chance—but on Rick Paterson. Funny, she had never considered herself the "chance-taking" type.

"I appreciate your not hanging up on me," she replied. "I must have sounded pretty hysterical on the phone."

His hands cupped her shoulders lightly. "You didn't sound hysterical, Vicky. You sounded like a nice lady. This evening confirmed it."

She felt the heat of his palms through the fabric of her blouse. The glow from the streetlight cast his face and beard into tawny golden shadows. "Thank you," she murmured.

Justin squeezed her shoulders briefly. Then he released her and stepped back. "Take care, Vicky. I hope we'll see each other again sometime."

As Vicky walked toward the front door of her apartment building, she heard the tires of the Jaguar screech their farewell. So much for that, she told herself. Justin had issued the classic male send-off, a variation on the proverbial, *I'll call you.*

A MAN STEPPED OUT from the dense shrubbery surrounding the property. After taking one last drag from his cigarette, he tossed the butt on the sidewalk, not bothering to crush it. Then he opened his note pad and methodically jotted down the license plate of the silver Jag, which had just departed.

Nice car. He wouldn't mind owning one of those someday. Whistling softly, Lieutenant Simmons tucked the notebook into his pocket and headed up the sidewalk to the red brick building.

The teapot was nearly boiling when there was a sharp rap on her apartment door. Vicky pulled the plug and ran to answer it, deluding herself into thinking it might be Justin.

All thumbs, she fumbled with the new lock before the door finally opened. "Lieutenant Simmons!" She shouldn't have been surprised. But then, she shouldn't have been disappointed either.

"You were expecting someone else?" As he stepped inside, the lieutenant tried to rearrange his jowls into a smile. His clothes were a disgrace. Either he hadn't slept in twenty-four hours, or his green sports coat had slept with him.

"Yes," Vicky said. "I mean, no. Actually, I'd forgotten you were coming." She motioned toward the kitchen. "I was just making myself tea. Would you like some?"

The lieutenant peered over her shoulder as though he was expecting an ambush. "No, thanks. I'll just take the letter and be on my way."

"It's in my purse." Vicky went into the kitchen and dug out the letter. Turning, she nearly collided with the lieutenant who, unbeknownst to Vicky, had followed her into the kitchen. "Good grief," she said. "You startled me."

This time, he almost managed a grin. "Sorry. Army training. Had to sneak through enemy lines in Korea. Hellhole of a place."

"I can imagine." She handed him the letter. "Sorry if I kept you waiting this evening."

"No problem. I had plenty of paperwork to keep me busy at the station."

Vicky walked him to the door. "Have you come up with anything new on Theo Dalta's death?"

"Not a thing. Looks like it'll be ruled accidental."

She wished she could feel more relieved. "Then you don't believe the chain letter had anything to do with it."

"Doesn't look that way. 'Course, now that I've got your copy to work with, I'll check a few things out." The lieutenant raked his hand through salt-and-pepper hair. "Uh…Miss Green, I couldn't help noticing that fellow you came home with tonight."

No one could help noticing Justin Coe, she thought drolly. "Yes, what about him?"

"He's a little heavy on the pedal, isn't he?"

It would have been unkind to snicker. Vicky bit her tongue. "I suppose Justin might appear a little reckless behind the wheel."

"Justin, you said?"

"Justin Coe. His name is included in the chain letter."

The officer scanned the sheet. "So it is. Listen, I don't want to tell you how to run your life, but if I were you, I wouldn't get too friendly with the people on this list, if you know what I mean."

She looked at him askance. "I'm afraid I don't know what you mean."

"Let me put it this way. If there is something to this chain letter business, the perpetrator could very well be one of these people right here. I've seen scams like this before." He slapped the letter with the back of his hand. The noise made Vicky jump.

"You mean someone on the list might actually be... dangerous?" she asked.

"You never can tell."

Vicky thought back to the qualities—excluding his driving habits—that impressed her about Justin. His air of refinement, his sense of humor, his riveting good looks. "I don't know, lieutenant. Justin may have his faults, but I have trouble believing he has anything to do with the chain letter."

The officer shrugged, his hand on the doorknob. "Believe what you like, but I'd still be careful if I were you. I see you got yourself a good dead bolt."

"I got it today, just for my own peace of mind."

"Glad to hear it. Our job is easier when people use common sense. There's no such thing as a foolproof lock, but if you can slow the burglar down, it's better than nothing."

Vicky had to remind herself that Lieutenant Simmons, all good intentions aside, was simply not the reassuring type. "Thank you for coming," she said. "You will let me know if you find out anything more?"

"Sure will. G'night, Miss Green."

THE MEMORIAL UNION was dark at this hour, unlike the way it was during the day when the students flooded in and out by the thousands. With its arches and parapets and ornate windows, the building looked like a huge granite castle right in the middle of campus. The man approached the building cautiously, glancing over his shoulder now and again to make sure he was alone.

The maple tree was easy to find. It stood off by itself, proud and majestic, and was probably years older than the Union building. He'd discovered the knothole months ago and figured it'd be a great hiding place. Who would ever think of looking in there?

The half-moon was tucked behind a puffy cloud. The streets were quiet, like a tomb. The man chuckled to himself. *Like a tomb.* Strange how his mind worked sometimes. He should have been a poet.

Pushing up his sleeve, he poked his arm deep into the knothole. At first, his fingers encountered wet slimy things—dead leaves, bugs, nests. But he didn't care. As long as there was—

An envelope! He felt the damp smoothness of the paper, glued seams, sharp corners. For a minute or two, he reveled in the feeling of success between his fingers. Then some instinct made him wary. Just because it was an envelope didn't mean it was his.

Nervousness made his movements awkward, and he dropped the envelope. For a moment, he was afraid it had fallen deeper into the tree, but no, it was still there. Sweat trickled inside his shirt as he carefully lifted his arm.

Now, at last, the envelope safe, he could see that it was marked with the number two. That'd be Rosa N. Shoon. He had a good memory for names.

"Hey, Mama, we did it!" He waved the money in the air, jumping up and down like a kid. "Our first ten bucks."

"Ssh!" she countered. "What do you think you're doing, yelling out loud in the middle of the street?"

His enthusiasm shaken, he said, "Sorry, Mama. I forgot."

"You forgot. Tell that to the men in the white coats when they come to take you away. They'll think you're a loony for sticking your arm into trees and yelling to yourself in the middle of the night."

Her remark slashed at his insides like claws on raw meat. But it was okay, he told himself. He wouldn't have to put up with her insults much longer.

"It won't happen again," he said, "I promise. But look, we got money, and a list of seven new people. It's just like we figured. If everyone gives us ten dollars and sends seven letters to their friends, in a few months we'll be rolling in money."

His mother's laughter gurgled through him. "I told you it would work, didn't I? We should have thought of this sooner."

The man lifted a calloused hand to his cheek and stroked it with affection. But, to his mind, the palm felt soft and smooth, because, of course, it was Mama's hand....

Chapter Six

Justin was hunkered down on the deck of his sleek racing sloop when he heard his name being called. Annoyed at the intrusion, he lifted his head.

The man standing on the pier looked familiar, but Justin couldn't place him right away. Swarthy and balding, he was built like a bull moose, a slight stoop the only concession to his age.

"Is there something I can do for you?" Justin asked. He had long since learned to hide wariness behind a cool, utterly courteous, detachment.

The man stood a few feet from the boat, the morning breeze lifting sparse gray hairs off his head. "I am Rubinoff, proprietor of the Cheese 'n' Deli. We met several days ago."

The accent should have given him away. Justin laid down the paint brush and stood up, shielding his eyes against the sun. "I remember. Nice to see you again." He reached across to shake the man's hand.

"Your sailboat is quite impressive," Mr. Rubinoff remarked, as his eyes skimmed the lines of the hull.

"Thanks."

"Rather expensive, no?"

"Yes."

"Where does the money come from, Mr. Coe?"

Justin looked up at him. "At the risk of sounding rude, it's really none of your business, is it?"

The older man shrugged. "Do your colleagues not wonder why you do not share their state of indigence?"

"They used to, but once they found out that I'd inherited the money, their curiosity seemed satisfied." *Does it satisfy yours?* he added silently. The man's penetrating gaze suggested that it did not. "Have you ever sailed, Mr. Rubinoff?"

"Me?" There was a cautious edge to the man's respondent laugh. "No, I've never had the stomach for it, but I can understand a man's passion for sailing. They say a boat is like a woman. Learning to handle them is straightforward enough, but the danger lies in becoming complacent, no?"

Justin picked up his brush and resumed painting. "I suppose there's a parallel there somewhere. If you're not a sailor, then what exactly brings you to Spring Harbor?"

A seagull landed on the dock beside Mr. Rubinoff, its head cocked as if it, too, wanted to hear the man's reply.

"You do, Mr. Coe."

Justin flinched, but continued to apply smooth strokes of white paint to the hull. "I gathered as much. How did you know where to find me?"

"From your complexion, I surmised that you were either a sailor or a skier, and this is not the season for skiing."

The younger man looked up at him with grudging respect. "How observant of you. But there are many places in this city to moor a boat. What made you decide to come here?"

Mr. Rubinoff waved in the direction of the nearby campus skyline. "You work at the university. Spring Harbor seemed a logical place to start." He looked around. "Is there somewhere I could sit down? My legs are not what they used to be."

Since this was obviously not a social call, Justin was reluctant to let the old man get too comfortable. Still, it would have been unkind to make him stand. "You're welcome to come aboard, but be careful of the paint."

The man looked dubiously at the blue-and-white boat rocking in the slip. "Well, I suppose I could try."

When he reached out to help him, Justin was impressed by the strength of Mr. Rubinoff's grip. His handshake had been no less powerful, but then the man had probably been butchering meat and kneading dough for fifty years.

Sitting down across from Justin, the old man laughed nervously and wiped the sweat from his brow. "This isn't so bad." Still, he gripped the seat as if they were actually about to launch.

Justin smirked. "You're a natural, I can tell. Now, why don't we get to the real reason for your being here?"

"All right. I came to warn you not to cause more trouble for Victoria. She does not need complications like you in her life."

"I didn't realize I was causing her any trouble."

"Perhaps you haven't—yet. But I don't like this business of her talking with strangers about chain letters and unexplained deaths."

"You may not be aware of this, Mr. Rubinoff, but Vicky was actually the one who phoned me. I didn't know anything about the letter until she told me."

"But you were on the list. Surely you've received one."

"I haven't."

Mr. Rubinoff looked as though he thought Justin was lying. "Then why would you bother to meet with Victoria about her letter? Surely a man like you has more important things to do."

"My reasons, sir, are my own concern, but if you must know, I was curious. I wanted to see the letter and hear what Vicky had to say." Annoyed, Justin saw the doubt cross the old man's face. "Look," he said. "As for causing Vicky trouble, I might as well tell you I haven't seen her since the night we met, nor have I made arrangements to see her in the future. Is that what you want to hear?"

Mr. Rubinoff seemed unimpressed. "What people say and what they do are often two different things. But rest assured, I will keep my eyes and ears open. You would be amazed at what old Gypsies like me can surmise."

"Surmise what you like. I have nothing to hide." Justin immediately regretted his glibness. He *did* have something to hide. Judging from the way the old man's eyes were boring into his, the Gypsy knew it, too.

Mr. Rubinoff stood up shakily, and Justin assisted him out of the boat. The sun rising over Lake Mendota was blinding, so Justin reached under the seat for dark glasses.

Mr. Rubinoff watched him, then looked down and pointed to the name on the bow. "Who is *Che Sara*?"

"It's not a she. It's Italian for 'What will be.'"

The man squinted at him. "An odd name for a sailboat."

Justin couldn't hold back a half smile. "It suits the temperament of the skipper."

"Yes, I assumed as much. Very well, Mr. Coe, I have said what I came here to say."

"Does Vicky realize you've been out crusading on her behalf?"

"Absolutely not. If she knew, she would accuse me of being a meddling old man."

"Which, of course, you're not."

This time, it was the Gypsy's turn to smile. "Which, of course, I am. Good day, Mr. Coe." He strode off, shoulders back, hands held stiffly at his sides.

Justin watched the receding figure with a mixture of awe and resentment. There was something to be said for Mr. Rubinoff's protective attitude toward his friends, an all too rare commodity these days. On the other hand, Justin didn't care much for people who felt entitled to answers simply because they had the gall to ask questions.

It might be wise to steer clear of Vicky after all, at least until the foofaraw of the chain letter wore off. In spite of his assurances to Mr. Rubinoff, Justin had indeed planned to call Vicky. But there were plenty of other attractive women in Madison, women who didn't have a psychic Gypsy in attendance.

Justin moved the brush along the smooth grain of the hull. He had hoped his wandering years were finally behind him, but maybe his hopes had been premature. It was still possible the chain letter was a fluke, a one-shot prank that had nothing to do with him personally; and if so, he had nothing to worry about. But if it wasn't, if the chain letter was somehow connected to his past—not for the first time since his evening with Vicky the phrase "Death to all" came to mind—well, there were plenty of other places in the world to moor the *Che Sara*.

THERE WAS DEFINITELY something to be said for routine. Vicky couldn't understand why people complained about the predictability of their lives. She thrived on predictability.

Six gloriously uneventful days had passed since she'd received the chain letter, been questioned by the police and met Justin Coe. The first two events she'd virtually managed to put out of her mind. As for the third, she was making progress.

It didn't surprise her that Justin hadn't called. College professors had busy schedules. Ones who looked like him, no doubt, were busier still, what with eager coeds looking for extra tutelage, swank faculty parties, and heaven only knew what.

Besides, it didn't really matter. She had nothing in common with a man who probably read Chaucer over breakfast and whose second language was Elizabethan English. Vicky had the Nick Nack Nook to keep her busy, and that was enough.

Breezily she stepped into the Cheese 'n' Deli for her morning coffee and paper. The place, she could have sworn, never looked so good. The coffee urn snoring contentedly, the cheese Danish enticing, regular customers at their regular stools. Even the predictable sight of Mr. Rubinoff solving the daily anagram was enough to bring tears to Vicky's eyes.

The man looked up from the newspaper folded on the counter. "Good morning, Victoria. How are you?"

"Good morning, Mr. Rubinoff. I couldn't be better."

"My, you are chipper this morning."

"Why shouldn't I be? It's a beautiful day! The sun is shining, the birds are singing...." Vicky trailed off when she realized other customers were staring. Not everyone was a morning person.

"Are you sure you're all right?" her friend inquired.

"Certainly I am." Vicky poured coffee into a Styrofoam cup and helped herself to a Danish. "How's the anagram coming along this morning?"

Sighing, Mr. Rubinoff tucked his pencil behind his ear. "Terrible. I have been struggling with it since five o'clock and have deciphered only two letters."

Vicky leaned over to look, though she needn't have bothered. Anagrams ranked with Shakespeare on her list of things to ignore. "At least you've finished the crossword and the jumble."

"That is no consolation," he muttered, ringing up her order without even looking at the cash register.

Humming the last song she'd heard on the radio that morning, Vicky gathered her breakfast and newspaper, and headed for the door. Yes, indeed, routine was wonderful.

The last stanza of Vicky's song died in her throat when she rounded the corner onto State Street. There were still a dozen small shops and restaurants between her and the Nick Nack Nook, but even from this distance, she recognized Justin Coe standing outside her store.

No one could mistake a fellow who looked as though his yacht should be moored within whispering distance. Monte Carlo, she decided, would probably suit him better than Madison.

Unconsciously Vicky slowed her pace. Justin's attention was diverted elsewhere, so she was able to observe him unseen. It was odd how, in the space of a few days, she'd managed to forget how tall and lithe he was, how well he fit his clothes. Today he wore a navy blazer, white pants and shirt, hands tucked casually in his pockets as he leaned against the storefront.

She came closer. He turned to her as calmly as he'd done the other night. "Hello, Vicky."

His snow-blond hair she'd remembered, but her mind had relinquished the details of its texture. Close cropped and silky, it contrasted appealingly with the chiseled contours of his face and the bristly cut of his beard.

And his eyes. How different they were in the morning. So bright, crystalline, the rare color of raindrops against a blue sky.

"Hello, Justin." She was surprised that the greeting came so easily, surprised also at how good she felt seeing him again.

"You're twelve minutes late," he said with a grin. "The sign says you open at ten."

She tore her gaze away long enough to glance at her watch. "It's okay. I've trained the hordes to stay away until a quarter past ten at least."

He laughed, and she laughed with him while she took out her key ring and opened the door. As always, entering the Nick Nack Nook pleased Vicky. The shelves were crammed with myriad handmade treasures, both local and from places as far-flung as the river valleys of Mongolia. The store smelled of earthenware and dried flowers, plank floors and herbal teas.

"This place looks like you," Justin said, his gaze roaming the shelves appreciatively.

Vicky set her breakfast on the counter. "Shall I take that as a gibe or a compliment?"

Folding his arms across his chest, he stepped back to study her. "A compliment, I assure you. Your lace blouse, the cameo, your hair in that delightful bun. Turn around, so I can see how it looks in the back."

Feeling utterly feminine when she ought to have felt silly, Vicky did as she was asked.

"Beautiful," Justin murmured. "You and your store would have been right at home in the last century."

It would be much too easy, Vicky told herself, to get caught up by his flattery. "My accountant says the same thing when he sees my income statements."

Justin appeared amused by her remark. "I've been meaning to call you, but things get really hectic at the end of a semester."

"It's all right. I've been quite busy myself what with Easter coming up."

"I haven't forgotten how enjoyable our evening was last week."

The sun must have come out from behind a cloud, for the room grew suddenly brighter. "Would you like to share my Danish?" Vicky asked. "I'm sorry I didn't bring an extra coffee, but I have instant."

"No, thanks, I just had some, but there was something I wanted to talk to you about."

Lifting the coffee lid, Vicky breathed deeply of the rich aromatic brew. "Go ahead. I'm listening."

Just then the front door opened, and Rick Paterson walked in. "Hi, Vicky."

"Morning, Rick. How are you?"

"I'm okay." He turned his head slowly and stared at the visitor.

"Justin, this is my friend and indispensable co-worker, Rick Paterson. Rick, this is Justin Coe."

The two men were approximately the same height, but that was where the resemblance ended. Justin was lean, streamlined, while Rick still displayed the lumpy muscular brawn of his football years. Justin regarded Rick keenly while the dark-haired man's stare was heavy lidded, less focused.

"Are you a friend of Vicky's?" Rick asked.

Justin smiled. "I'd like to be."

Vicky had not told Justin about Rick, and she was amazed to hear Justin lower his voice to a regular tone. Rick's speech was a bit slow, but otherwise he appeared quite normal. Most people on first meeting didn't realize there was anything wrong with him.

Rick did not respond to Justin's remark. "I'll be in the back room if you need me, Vicky. I'm gonna put one of those wooden ships together so our customers will know what they're supposed to look like."

"That's a fine idea," Vicky said. "I'll look forward to seeing it."

Head hanging, the young man shambled off. After a great deal of practice, Rich had learned how to be pleasant and cheerful with customers. But when meeting people on an informal basis, he often became shy and self-absorbed.

Vicky cast a quick glance at Justin who gave her a look of understanding. For that, she was grateful. There would be time enough later on to explain about her employee—if there was to be a "later on" with Justin.

He picked up her copy of the *Wisconsin State Journal.* "Have you read this?"

"Not yet."

Opening the first section, he ran his finger down a column, then stopped. "This is what I came to talk to you about. The obituary of Eve Lomorth."

Vicky, who was starving, tore off a piece of Danish and chewed it slowly. "Who's Eve Lomorth?"

"Number three on the list."

The list. She hadn't given it a thought for days. But now Vicky realized Justin was right. Eve Lomorth had been third on the list. The pastry slipped down her throat like a lump of wet cotton. "My gosh, how did she die?"

"It doesn't say. Only that she was forty-two, unmarried and died suddenly in her home."

Vicky scanned the notice herself. "It could have been a heart attack or a stroke."

"Could have been."

"It's probably just a coincidence."

"You're probably right," he replied, still staring at the paper.

Vicky was even willing to grasp at straws. "It may not even be the same Eve Lomorth."

"That's entirely possible."

They both looked up at the same time. "It isn't a coincidence, is it, Justin?"

"I honestly don't know."

"What do we do now?"

"I thought you might want to show this to your friend at the police department and see what he has to say."

"My friend? Oh, Lieutenant Simmons. I'd hardly call him a friend."

"But he knows about the chain letter, and he could find out the cause of death. If Eve Lomorth died naturally, we'll know it was a coincidence, however bizarre, and we can forget the whole thing."

Her appetite suddenly gone, Vicky rewrapped the remainder of the Danish. "I would like nothing better than to forget the whole thing. I'll call the lieutenant now."

As she reached for the telephone, Justin placed his hand over hers. "Wait a minute, Vicky. I don't really think this is a topic that should be discussed over the telephone."

"You think I ought to go personally to the police station?"

"In this case, yes. I'll come with you, of course."

"But I can't leave the store unattended."

"You don't have to," a voice said from behind her. "I'm here."

Vicky whirled around to find Rick Paterson at the doorway to the stockroom, strips of balsa wood in one hand, an Exacto knife in the other, its tiny razor-like blade glinting in the light. "Yes, I know you're here, Rick, but—"

"I've been alone before. Don't you trust me?"

"Don't be silly. Of course I trust you...." *Careful, Vicky, you're not handling this well.* Worried that Rick might misinterpret her agitated state, she took a deep breath and forced herself to smile. "You wouldn't mind if I went out for a little while?"

"I don't mind. Who died?"

"No one you know." This whole business of the chain letter was not a topic Rick would understand. The less he knew about it, Vicky decided, the better.

"Then why are you going to the police?" Before Vicky could reply, Rick turned to Justin. "Why did you come here and upset her?"

"I didn't come to upset her," Justin explained. "In fact, I'm going with Vicky to the police station to make sure that she's all right."

Rick said nothing. He stared at Justin long and hard, as if willing his sluggish brain to comprehend. Vicky felt the room grow prickly with tension.

"If you can give me a few minutes, Justin," she said, "I'll be ready to leave."

"That's fine."

Avoiding Rick's eyes, she fidgeted and fussed behind the counter. "Don't forget to count the money in the till and change the date on the register—"

The sound of splintering wood stopped her. Vicky stared dumbfounded at Rick's fist, now full of useless scraps of balsa.

"Why did you do that?"

He looked down as though he was looking at someone else's hand. "I...I don't know. I didn't mean to. I must have squeezed too hard."

She went to his side. "It's okay, Rick. That type of wood breaks easily. Why don't you leave it for now? We'll see what we can do later."

Rick didn't answer, but he continued to stare at the wood in his hand long after Vicky and Justin had gone.

"I DIDN'T THINK you'd want to come along," Vicky told Justin as they walked through the cool, tiled corridors of the police station.

"I didn't," he admitted, slipping an arm protectively around her waist, "but no gentleman sends a lady alone to the police—no matter how much the gentleman may want to."

Vicky laughed at his martyred expression. "You're handling it very well, so far."

"Thanks."

Lieutenant Simmons sat behind a desk heaped with paperwork. He looked up when the visitors walked in. "Miss Green. Wasn't expecting to see you so soon."

"Hello, lieutenant. This is Justin Coe. I think I mentioned him to you the other night."

"Sure, I remember." He waved toward a couple of chairs. "What can I do for you folks?"

Justin unrolled the newspaper he'd brought with him and spread it out atop the clutter. "Were you aware, lieutenant, that Eve Lomorth passed away yesterday?"

"Who's she?" He peered at the article. "Oh, yeah, I know the one. I wasn't the investigating officer, but I heard about it this morning. Real pretty woman, I hear."

"How did she die?" Justin asked bluntly.

The officer cast a curious look at the younger man. "Why do you want to know?"

"Her name is on the chain letter list."

"Ya don't say." The springs in his chair squawked loudly as he leaned back. "How about that?"

"Now that you know our reason for asking," Justin said, "would you mind pulling the file and telling us what happened to her?"

"Sure, why not? But I don't have to pull the file. It was one of those stupid household accidents that never should have happened. She was in the bathtub, and her electric radio fell into the water. You'd think people would know better by now."

Although Vicky heard the lieutenant's words, a small part of her refused to accept the possibility of a second accident. Yet what else could it be but one of life's little flukes? A fluke that caused two people from a list of seven to die within days of each other.

"Did the investigating officers come across the chain letter?" Justin asked the lieutenant.

"Where? In the tub?" The officer gave a derisive snort of laughter. "Mr. uh . . . Coe, if the deceased did get one of those letters, she sure as hell didn't have it in the water with her. And if there'd been signs of forced entry or foul play, you can be sure our guys would still be working on the case."

"So you're not planning to follow up on it at all?" Vicky asked in a shaky voice.

"I didn't say that, Miss Green. Your friend asked me if the officers found a letter, which they didn't. For the simple reason that they weren't looking for one." Grumbling, the lieutenant swiveled his chair around to a filing cabinet and brought out a manila folder labeled Dalta, Theo. When he opened it, a copy of the chain letter was on top. "Well, I'll be damned. She's number three, all right."

Justin rolled his eyes. "That's what we've been trying to tell you, lieutenant."

The seasoned veteran ignored Justin's sarcasm and continued to study the file. "Tell you what. I'm gonna talk to the officers who investigated Lomorth's death, and then I'll pass this new information on to the FBI."

"The FBI?" Vicky gasped.

"Chain letters are a federal offense, Miss Green," the officer explained, "and they're also out of our jurisdiction. If there is any connection between these two deaths— and I'm not saying there is—we're gonna need a lot of help."

"Thank you, lieutenant," Justin said. "That's what we were hoping you'd say."

"Yes, thank you," Vicky echoed.

The policeman stood up, tucking in his plaid shirt. "Don't mention it."

"Would you keep us posted?" Justin asked.

"That's not for me to say. Depends on how the FBI wants to handle the case."

Vicky noticed the strained look on Justin's face as he got up to go. He was clearly uncomfortable in the presence of Lieutenant Simmons.

"One more thing, Mr. Coe," the lieutenant called out when the two of them had reached the door.

Justin stopped abruptly. "What is it?"

"It's about a few outstanding traffic tickets. Since you're already here, we don't need to bother with a warrant, do we?"

"HOW DID HE KNOW?" Rotating the glass of Kentucky bourbon in front of him, Justin shook his head, perplexed.

Vicky had been trying to think of the right way to confess ever since they'd left the station. "Actually, Justin, I didn't want to tell you this, but the night you drove me home from the Cheese 'n' Deli, Lieutenant Simmons saw your car. He must have taken down your license plate number."

"Why? Were you and your friend Mr. Rubinoff trying to set me up?"

She didn't think Justin was seriously upset. In fact he'd seemed almost relieved to pay the tickets. She risked a tiny smile. "I'd never do anything like that. But remember I told you that the lieutenant was coming over that night to pick up the letter? Can I help it if your checkered past finally caught up with you?"

Justin's tone was short on humor when he muttered, "Let's just hope that's all he catches up to."

"I beg your pardon?"

"Nothing," he said. "Let's look at the menus."

The restaurant Justin had chosen for lunch was halfway between the campus and Vicky's shop. They had both decided they could use an hour's relaxation after their visit with the police. "Was everything all right when you phoned the store?" Justin asked, setting aside his menu.

"Yes, Rick's had twelve customers this morning, and said everything's fine. He also told me not to hurry."

"Good for him."

"Sometime I think he likes working without me—"

"Well, well, if it isn't the illustrious Professor Coe!" A plump, middle-aged woman suddenly appeared at their table, beaming at Vicky's companion.

Justin looked up. "Maeve, how're you doing?"

"Couldn't be better, dear boy."

"And your research trip? Did it go well?"

"Splendidly. There's nothing like the Big Apple to reaffirm one's faith in the arts. And the parties, my word, the parties!" She turned and planted a look of acute interest on Vicky. "Now who might this be? I don't believe I've seen you on campus."

Vicky laughed and held out her hand. "That's because I haven't been a student for some time. I'm Vicky Green."

"How do you do, I'm Maeve Wilson."

"The venerable *Doctor* Maeve Wilson," Justin added. "They say that when this lady delivers a lecture on the dramatic arts, the muses weep."

Maeve waved a fleshy hand through the air. "Please, love, you do embarrass me so. Would either of you mind terribly if I joined you? I see no one here over the age of twenty. Most disconcerting."

Vicky caught Justin's hapless look and took it to mean they'd be hard pressed to refuse. "Please do," Vicky offered, saving him the trouble. She would have preferred to have Justin to herself, but Maeve seemed like a rollicking sort of person, a pleasant addition to lunch.

"Thank you. You're too kind."

Vicky watched with interest while Maeve settled her considerable girth into a chair. She was dressed in a tweed suit that looked too warm for January, let alone April. Her face was as plain as porridge, but her eyes that stared boldly from behind thick glasses were large and expressive.

The first thing Maeve did upon sitting was to pull out a packet of thin brown cigarettes. When she lit one, Vicky nearly gagged. It smelled vile.

"Since you're not a student, Vicky, and I assume you're not an instructor, how did you meet our Justin?"

Thankfully, "our Justin" came to Vicky's rescue.

"It was one of those charmed accidental meetings," he said to his colleague. Unable to improve on his reply, Vicky simply smiled, trying not to cough.

Maeve folded her hands at her chin. "How lovely. You must excuse my inquisitive manner, but I've always had a certain soft spot for Justin. Mustn't let him gad about with the wrong sort of woman." She cast a glance at Justin, then laughed uproariously.

"Actually, I owe Maeve quite a debt of gratitude," Justin pointed out. "She was responsible for the university's hiring me a few years ago—no small honor, considering Dr. Wilson has been an esteemed member of the faculty for over twenty years."

"How fascinating," Vicky replied.

Smoke billowed from Maeve's nose as she leaned closer to Vicky. "But do let me tell you how I met Justin. He was at the Library Mall near one of those marvelous vegetable stands, reading a map of the city and looking quite lost. I thought to myself, how could a lady of a certain age such as myself possibly be of assistance to such a stunning young male? The opportunity was too great to resist."

Vicky cast a curious glance at Justin who was ignoring Maeve's gushing in favor of getting another drink. She didn't blame him. The woman had a tendency to overwhelm.

"So your assistance resulted in a job offer?" Vicky concluded.

"Yes, quite. As it turned out, he had a degree from Oxford, can you imagine? The boy's knowledge of English literature was nearly as astounding as mine." She laughed, but her laughter soon dissolved into a fit of coughing.

Justin reached over and pounded her on the back. "Are you all right, Maeve?"

"Certainly, love. It's these damned cigarettes. And for heaven's sake, stop beating me." When she'd regained her composure, she resumed the story. "So I pulled a few strings, threw my weight around—if you'll pardon the pun—and lo and behold, you now see before you a man about to obtain full professorship and a position as department head. Isn't it marvelous?"

Modestly Justin said, "Well, I think you're much more qualified for the job."

"Nonsense, dear boy. I shall continue to teach, which is what I do best. Administrative hog wallow holds no appeal for me."

Lunch in Maeve's company continued for the most part along the same boisterous vein. In the course of an hour, the woman had cleaned her own plate and finished off what Vicky couldn't eat of hers.

"I really should get back to work." Although Vicky had enjoyed Justin and Maeve's witty repartee, she'd long since given up trying to get a word in edgewise.

Justin drained his coffee cup. "I'll walk with you."

"That's not necessary," Vicky said. "You haven't finished your dessert."

"I don't intend to." He turned to Maeve as if by reflex. "You go ahead." His friend put up no argument. Eagerly she brought his plate closer and dug into the cheesecake.

"Where do you work?" Maeve asked between mouthfuls.

"I own the Nick Nack Nook, a few blocks from here."

"Oh, yes, I've seen it from the outside. Looks like a lovely place. I must come in one of these days."

"Please do."

Vicky suspected that Justin was as anxious as she to escape Maeve's company, but whatever the reasons, she was pleased to prolong the time they had together. State Street glistened with the spring hues of trees and flower boxes. Vicky loved the civilized bustle of Madison, a far cry from the small logging town she'd grown up in. Surprisingly enough, Justin, in a short space of time, had added a dimension to her enjoyment of the city. If only it would last, she thought wistfully.

"Tell me about Rick," he said as they walked along the busy sidewalk.

If there had been any hint of challenge in Justin's question, any mockery, Vicky would have given him a stock answer about her employee's condition. But she heard the way he'd spoken to Rick that morning and sensed his empathy.

"I first saw him about three years ago on the Square," Vicky explained. "He used to huddle on the corner with the winos and the panhandlers, but he never approached anyone for money. I always thought he seemed different from the others."

Justin glanced at her. "What do you mean by different?"

"I don't know, bewildered, frightened, as if he couldn't quite understand how he'd ended up there. One day I needed help lifting heavy inventory, so I asked Rick if he'd be interested in a few hours of work."

"You took quite a risk, hiring him on your own."

Vicky shrugged. "I didn't think so. In spite of his size, he'd always appeared gentle. Anyway, he turned out to be so conscientious and eager to work that I gave him more odd jobs and finally hired him part-time."

"What's the matter with him?"

"Rick was in a car accident during his sophomore year at UW. The day it happened, he'd injured his ankle in football practice so his mother was driving them home."

They stopped outside beneath the dark green awning of the Nick Nack Nook. "Was his mother killed?" Justin asked.

"No, she was hardly injured at all. But Rick suffered extensive brain damage. They didn't think he would ever walk or talk again."

Through the display window, Vicky caught a glimpse of Rick chatting with a customer while he packed her purchase into a box. He really was doing well these days.

Justin watched him, too. "What a horrible tragedy. Does he have any recollection of the accident?"

"He never mentions it. Everything I've been told is from his sister—that's who he lives with now; his parents are retired and living in Arizona. Anyway, apparently he was a brilliant student, an economics major on a full athletic scholarship. The sad thing is, at times he does seem to recall how intelligent he used to be."

Just then, Rick saw Vicky through the window and waved at her excitedly. Then his eyes shifted to Justin, and he quickly looked away.

"I'd better get inside," Vicky said.

Before she could go, Justin captured her hand. "I have something to ask you."

Looking up at his handsome face, she felt her stomach tighten in anticipation. "Yes?"

"Are you doing anything tomorrow?"

"No, it's my day off."

"Would you be interested in spending some time together?"

She controlled an urge to squeal with joy. "That would be nice," she replied calmly. "What did you have in mind?"

"A funeral."

Chapter Seven

Vicky stared at him, aghast. "What did you say?"

"It's probably not the most romantic invitation you've ever had, and I do intend to make it up to you. But Eve Lomorth is being buried tomorrow, and I think we should go."

"I can't imagine why."

"There are a few things about the chain letter that are bothering me, and since the cops aren't likely to tell us anything, it wouldn't hurt to do some digging ourselves."

Vicky stared at him in amazement. With the sleeves of his white shirt rolled up, his blazer tossed over one shoulder, Justin looked utterly refined and self-assured. No one could have guessed that his sense of curiosity bordered on the ghoulish.

"Why invite me? You could go on your own."

"I could, but a couple is less conspicuous than a man on his own, and secondly, I think it would be good for your own peace of mind."

She laughed mirthlessly. "Don't kid yourself. I'd have considerably more peace of mind if I could forget I ever heard of Eve Lomorth."

He massaged the back of her hand with his thumbs, an erotic and highly irrelevant gesture, thought Vicky. "I won't beg you to come with me, but I really would appreciate your company. We can do whatever you like tomorrow evening—dinner, a movie...the choice is yours."

Vicky cast a wistful glance at other couples passing by on the street. She was willing to bet none of those women attended a funeral on their second date.

Still, a small part of her identified with Justin's curiosity. She needed to know more about the bizarre circumstances that had thrown them together.

And there was one other, far more basic motive for considering Justin's request. Vicky simply wanted to see more of him. She also knew that formal dates exaggerated a person's attributes; sometimes, they even deceived. She would much rather spend time becoming acquainted with the real Justin Coe, no matter what that entailed. A sort of crash course on togetherness.

"All right," she said at last. "I'll go with you."

For an instant, Justin's cool reserve fell, and Vicky saw a look of sheer gratitude in his eyes. "I'll pick you up at ten," he said. Then, kissing her lightly on the cheek, he left.

THE MAN LIFTED the thick, black anthology from the bookshelf and opened it to a page halfway through the book. He didn't need to use the index anymore; he practically knew the story by heart.

The hero of the tale was a knight, born illegitimate, who grew up constantly defending his mother's behavior to those who scorned her. As a child, he believed she was an angel, sent down from heaven and disguised as a sinner to teach people humility and brotherly love.

But as the child grew, he came to realize that his mother was a mere mortal after all, and that the filthy drunken men who shared her bed learned nothing of humility, even less of love.

He fought in the Crusades and came home wounded and bitterly disillusioned. The knight knew by now that his aging mother was nothing but a harlot. As defender of all that was good and noble, he knew there was only one recourse.

The man slammed the book shut.

Only one recourse.

It hadn't worked the first time, but this time he knew he wouldn't fail. What the man didn't realize, as he sat there alone in the room, was that Mama had read the end of the story right along with him.

VICKY WAS PAINSTAKINGLY removing seeds from a kumquat while awaiting Justin's arrival at her apartment the next morning. Some people smoked when they were nervous; other people drank coffee or tea by the gallon. Vicky puttered with plants.

A feeling of peace came over her whenever she held a tiny seed in her hand. When she buried the seed in rich moist soil, she experienced a small sense of giving life. It was a feeling she needed this morning in particular.

Vicky stayed where she was when the doorbell rang. "It's open."

From the kitchen table, she could see Justin as he stepped inside the entryway. He looked marvelous in a dark suit, subdued tie and a crisp white shirt. No, strike that, he looked mournful, she told herself firmly, the way people ought to look for a funeral.

She had changed clothes six times that morning, finally settling on a pale gray Laura Ashley dress with lace at the collar and cuffs. At the moment, she was also wearing a full-length butcher's apron. "I'm over here," she called out.

Justin came into the kitchen and stared at the sodden heaps of rind and pulp on the table. "What are you up to?"

"What's it look like? I'm seeding a kumquat."

"Why?"

"I had to do something to kill time." Vicky went to the sink, rinsed the stickiness from her hands and lifted the apron over her head.

"What do you do with the seeds once you've got them?"

"Come with me, I'll show you."

Justin followed Vicky into the living room, a room she'd decorated over the past few years with total self-indulgence. The walls were painted a soft pink and the furniture was cream-colored with pastel floral cushions—the perfect backdrop for the myriad greenery. Expecting high praise for her tasteful decor, Vicky was devastated when Justin looked around and merely chuckled.

She planted both fists on her hips. "What's so funny?"

"Well, your place is really quite pretty, but come on, confess—it's actually a plant hospital, right? And you were performing emergency surgery on that kumquat." He smiled hugely at his joke, apparently thinking she, too, would see the humor.

She did not. But she had to admit, however reluctantly, that smiling suited him. His eyes sparkled; frown lines vanished from his face. "What's wrong with my plants?" she demanded, still not terribly impressed with his source of amusement. "I happen to have grown every one of these from seed myself."

Justin pointed to the coconut palm near the sofa. "Okay, let's take that one, for instance. It looks as though it's gone through a forest fire."

Vicky went over to the small tree whose leaves were splotchy, yellow and curled up at the edges. "I know. Poor Calliope, she's been fertilized and repotted three times, but I think what she really needs is horse manure."

Justin's face muscles twitched in an obvious effort to maintain a straight expression. "Horse manure? I'm sure your neighbors would be impressed. What did you call her? Calliope? Do you actually name all your plants?"

"Certainly. I talk to them, too. It gives them a sense of identity." Vicky pointed to the only healthy plant, the avocado near the picture window. "He's named Arthur, and the lemon tree beside him is Lindy. Over there is Perry pineapple, Oscar orange, and my three date palms, Dotty, Donald and Desiree."

Justin smiled again as he took Vicky's face in his hands. "You know something?" he said. "I have the strangest feeling that I'm going to enjoy getting to know you."

Though they might not find the same things funny, Vicky felt the same way about Justin.

EVE LOMORTH'S FUNERAL was held in a chapel near the cemetery grounds. Only about twenty people showed up to mourn her passing. Vicky felt like a real hypocrite as she sat in a back pew beside Justin, pretending bereavement and listening to the clergyman's eulogy. Justin was busy observing the other mourners, jotting notes in a pad concealed not too discreetly on his lap.

After the burial, Eve's companion, a woman in her fifties, approached Vicky and Justin. "Thank you so much for coming," she said, dabbing her eyes with a handkerchief. "I know Eve would have been delighted. Are you relatives...?"

Vicky felt a sudden urge to bolt, but before she could, Justin pulled her sharply to his side. "I'm the son of an old friend of Eve's, though we hadn't seen Eve for a while. Moved to another state," he said to the woman. "You must excuse my wife. Vic—Veronica took the news of Eve's death very hard."

The woman issued Vicky a look of deep sympathy. "I know how you feel, dear. It was a great shock to all of us. Would you do us the honor of coming to the house for coffee? You may feel better if you spend some time in Eve's home."

"Oh...no-o-o, I don't—" Vicky began, shaking her head vehemently.

"We'd love to, thank you," Justin cut in with incredible aplomb, pinching Vicky to keep her silent.

"Wonderful," the woman answered. "The cars are just starting to leave now. Feel free to follow."

"Are you crazy, Justin?" Vicky was sitting in the front seat of the Jaguar, too incensed to worry about his driving. "We can't go to that woman's house!"

"Why not?"

"Because... because we don't know her and we don't know Eve. What if people start asking questions?"

"Don't worry, I'll do all the talking. You can go on with your grief-ridden role." He gave her a guileless grin. "You're pretty good at it, you know."

With a look of disgust, Vicky sank lower into the seat. Never again would a pair of crystal blue eyes and a killer smile persuade her to do something so idiotic.

As promised, Justin did all the talking, and he did it well. He moved through the crowd easily, offering and accepting condolences, asking discreet questions, occasionally patting his distraught "wife's" arm. At least, he didn't bring out his notepad, Vicky thought with grudging relief.

After they'd nursed a cup of coffee and nibbled on tiny sandwiches, Vicky pulled Justin to a corner of the living room. "Let's go," she whispered.

"Not yet," he replied and promptly caught the hostess on her way to the kitchen. "Excuse me, but I wonder if I could ask a big favor of you?"

The woman who'd invited them smiled pleasantly. "By all means."

"Have you gone through Eve's belongings yet?"

"No, I'm afraid I haven't been able to face that task yet."

Vicky stood by a huge potted palm. It was all she could do not to crawl behind it.

Justin, however, suffered from no such inhibitions. "My father, who as I mentioned was too ill to come, sent Eve a letter with some old family snapshots. They mean a great deal to him, and now that Eve is no longer with us, I wonder..."

"Oh, but you must have them back, of course. Come with me." The woman led Vicky and Justin down the corridor to a bedroom at the far end of the house. "Her recent correspondence is still on the dresser. Eve wasn't a terribly organized person, may she rest in peace, so I imagine the mail goes back several days at least."

Justin thanked the woman, but stood where he was at the bedroom door. Finally the woman took the hint and stepped into the hall. "I'll leave you two alone," she said, eyeing Justin intently. "Call me if you need anything."

"She suspects something," Vicky whispered when they were alone, refusing to leave her post by the door.

"No, she doesn't." Justin wasted no time in getting started. He was already halfway through the clutter of paper on Eve Lomorth's dresser. Soon, he held up a legal-size envelope with no return address, the top neatly ripped with a letter opener. "This looks promising."

It took him only a moment to read the message inside. He held the paper up for Vicky to see. The letters, cut from magazines, read simply, "Mother, Love."

She swallowed hard. "It's set up just like the note Dalta got," she said, her voice hoarse with fear. "Let's get out of here."

"Just a few more minutes." To Vicky's consternation, he began to open drawers. "The chain letter's got to be around here somewhere."

"Justin, please."

"Did you have any luck?" The hostess appeared in the doorway, her tone polite but insistent. Clearly she was not going to allow anyone unlimited rummaging privileges in her late friend's bedroom.

Still remarkably composed, Justin showed the woman the envelope before tucking it into his jacket pocket. With his other hand, he discreetly slid the bureau drawer shut. "Yes, thank you, I found them. My father will be very grateful."

"I'm so pleased." The woman's gaze moved from Justin to Vicky who took a step backward into the dim light of the hallway. But it was too late. The woman had to have noticed the spread of perspiration stains along the underarms of Vicky's gray dress, all the more conspicuous because the house was nearly frigid with air-conditioning. No wonder cat burglars wore black, Vicky thought with an inward grimace.

"There is one thing I'm curious about," Justin said, stroking his beard thoughtfully.

"What's that?" asked the woman.

"The day Eve died. Did anything unusual happen that day, something that might have triggered the . . . accident?"

She tipped her head and smiled tightly. "Why do you ask?"

Good grief, Vicky thought, she doesn't only suspect; she knows we're up to something.

Justin didn't miss a beat. "We had a similar tragedy in our family a number of years ago, which is probably why my father couldn't bring himself to come here today."

Vicky noticed that he hadn't really answered the question, but the woman was obviously too courteous to press for an explanation. "How sad for your father. Now let me think, what happened that day? Nothing much, as far as I can recall. A telephone repairman called that morning to tell us the circuits were out of order, even though there seemed to be nothing wrong with the phone. He was going to drop around that afternoon, but whether or not he did, I don't know. I was out for the rest of the day." Fresh tears spurted from her eyes. "Poor Eve, she was all alone when it happened . . . If only I could have done something . . ."

Justin, the insufferable con, opened his arms and invited the woman to sob on his shoulder. "Now, now, you mustn't blame yourself. It's just one of those inexplicable twists of fate that leaves us feeling helpless . . ."

Not to mention nauseous. Let's get out of here, Justin. Vicky hoped her grim expression conveyed the message. Perhaps it had, for Justin winked at her as he gently pried the woman from his chest. He thanked her again, offered further condolences from his father and escorted his grieving—and sweating—wife out the door.

In the car, Vicky leaned back and squeezed her eyes shut. "That was, by far, the most humiliating experience I have ever gone through in my life."

"Why? I thought everyone was quite nice."

Her eyes sprang open. "That's just it! How could you stand deceiving such nice people?"

"We weren't doing anything so terrible. Eve's friend seemed quite pleased to have us there."

"She was the hostess. How else could she seem?" Vicky tried to peel the soggiest parts of the dress from her body, shifting in the seat to take advantage of air vents.

Justin chuckled. "You're not cut out for amateur sleuthing, I take it?"

"Are you kidding? I fall apart if I have one item too many in the express line at the supermarket."

"Tell you what. I'll drop you off at home, then deliver this note to Lieutenant Simmons. There's no point in both of us going to the station."

In her haste to escape Eve's home, Vicky had forgotten about the note. "What did it say again?"

"Mother, love."

"That doesn't sound very threatening. Not like the other one."

Justin continued to stare straight ahead. "No, but unfortunately, it does prove there's a connection between the two deaths."

Her flicker of optimism vanished. "I guess it does."

Ever the perfect gentleman, Justin insisted on walking Vicky right to the door of her apartment. "Are we still on for dinner and a movie this evening?" His gaze roamed her face with surprising tenderness.

"I am if you are." Crazy as it seemed, Vicky was glad now that she had accompanied Justin. She had a sneaking suspicion that his aura of confidence was enhanced by her being there. Even if it wasn't true, it felt good to think so.

He slid his arms around her waist and kissed her on the lips. Lightly, effortlessly, Justin took Vicky's breath away.

A long cool shower did wonders for her perspiration-drenched body and tense frame of mind. As she towel dried her hair, Vicky even managed to look back on the day with a certain élan. Quite a pair she and Justin made, like Tommy and Tuppence, the private detectives in Agatha Christie's short stories. Except, of course, Tommy and Tuppence had been married to each other.

But then again, so had she and Justin been—for a while, anyway. What name had he given her at the funeral? Veronica? Straight out of an *Archie* comic book. Oh, well...

Vicky slipped into a comfortable pair of cotton slacks and a T-shirt. She still had the whole afternoon ahead of her, plenty of time to run errands and relax before her date this evening.

Her date.

The words so often carried with them unpleasant associations: forgettable faces, banal conversations, awkward good nights. But she sensed that tonight, with Justin, would be something else entirely.

His face, for one thing, was far from forgettable; his conversation was always a delight. And as for an awkward good night? With a man like him, it was hard to imagine.

Contentedly Vicky drew up a list of things she needed from the nursery—peat moss, pots, dusting powder. The groceries could wait until another day. She couldn't manage bags of peat moss and milk on the same bus trip.

On her way outside, she checked the mail. One of the envelopes was obviously hand delivered since it bore no stamp, probably a notice from the condo association advising her the fees were going up again.

Vicky waited until she was on the bus before opening her mail. The doors were closed, the wheels of the bus turning, by the time she realized she was dead wrong about the letter. After "Dear Vicky," it began:

Seven days have passed, and so far you have not followed the instructions laid out in the chain letter. You were specifically warned against breaking the chain. Remember, you are to make a list of seven local friends to whom you've mailed copies, and include it with ten dollars in an envelope marked with your number. Drop the envelope into the maple tree in front of Memorial Union.

You still have one week to comply. But should you be tempted to ignore this reminder, consider what happened to number one and number three when they broke the chain.

Remember, Vicky, you are fourth on the list.

Chapter Eight

Horrified, Vicky stared at the letter, unconsciously making comparisons to the first one she'd received. Then, the salutation had read "Dear Number Four"; now it was "Dear Vicky." Then, there had been the reassuring distance of the postal service between her and the sender; this time, the writer had delivered in person. He knew her first name. He knew where she lived. And from all accounts, he intended to kill her.

She looked around at the other passengers on the bus. Could it be one of them, someone from her neighborhood? Her eyes caught those of an elderly man in the front seat who quickly looked away. Had she embarrassed him by staring, or did he know something? Vicky shook her head, disgusted by her paranoia.

She turned to the people behind her. They were looking out the window; no one was paying her the slightest attention. Their silence, their indifference induced something like a roaring in her brain. Didn't they realize what she was going through? Didn't anybody care?

She had to get off the bus at once. Pulling the cord, Vicky bolted for the front exit, stumbling when the bus lurched. The driver turned to her and smiled. "Miss your stop, ma'am?"

She stared at him. Why did he ask? What did it matter to him? Was he the— *Get a grip on yourself.* Just because she'd been on the bus when she'd read the letter did not mean she was suddenly surrounded by enemies. "No, I, uh, I thought I missed it, but I didn't. The next stop will be fine."

She hurried down the steps and onto the sidewalk. As the big white vehicle drove away, Vicky realized she'd given no thought to where she was headed. Certainly the trip to the nursery no longer seemed to matter.

She looked over her shoulder. Had anyone seen her get off? Was she being followed?

Indulging in panic, as tempting as it was, would get her nowhere. She had to force herself to calm down and think. The bus had dropped her off at Madison Park, halfway between her place and the Square. She found a park bench facing Lake Mendota and sat down.

Gulls swooped over the sun-dappled water. To the west lay the UW campus, a picturesque cluster of old and new architecture. Beyond that, a finger of greenery reached out into the lake to form University Bay.

After a minute or two, Vicky's breathing returned to normal, and her mind, though still anxious, cleared. She had to tell someone about the letter. The police, certainly. But she also needed to talk to somebody.

There was Justin, but he would be tied up with classes all afternoon. And besides, it hardly required great deductive powers to realize that he'd been the most recent visitor to her apartment. Maybe he— *No, it wasn't him!* She couldn't allow herself to think it might be.

Mr. Rubinoff. She would talk to him. He'd know what to do.

Feeling better now that she had at least a short-range plan, Vicky got up and began to walk. Although tempted to look over her shoulder to see if anyone was following, she resisted. It was, after all, midafternoon on a busy street. She was safer here than in the silent confines of her apartment. And besides, like the letter said, she still had seven days.

By the time she reached the Cheese 'n' Deli, Vicky was out of breath. She'd been walking quickly, almost running. The lunch rush was over, and when she went in, Mr. Rubinoff was sitting calmly behind the cash register, reading the paper.

"Victoria, what are you doing here? Isn't this your day off?"

Vicky had never seen anything quite so welcome as her friend's swarthy, weathered face. She gave him a trembling smile. "Hi, Mr. Rubinoff. I hate to bother you, but something...something awful has happened. I need to talk to someone."

He picked up on her frantic state of mind at once. "Wait here," he said. "I will call Sophie from the kitchen to look after things." He disappeared to the back, then returned a minute later with the plump and friendly cook in tow. "Come upstairs to my apartment," he told Vicky. "Have you had lunch?"

She had to think about it as she walked through the kitchen to the narrow set of stairs. "No, I haven't eaten."

"Then you will join me for homemade soup."

In all the years she'd known him, Vicky had never been inside Mr. Rubinoff's home. Yet, the place looked just as she'd imagined it would. Small, cozy, crammed with books and magazines and European knickknacks.

He invited her to sit at the kitchen table while he sliced a loaf of dark Russian rye. Just being here, Vicky felt better already. On a nearby sideboard was a collection of old photographs in ornate frames. There were pictures of grandparents, parents, and children ranging from infants to teens.

Though he often spoke of his Gypsy heritage, Mr. Rubinoff never talked about his family. She'd always assumed he was something of a black sheep bachelor with only distant ties to the old country.

He set two steaming bowls of vegetable soup on the table and sat down. "Tell me what happened, Victoria."

Vicky told him about her morning with Justin and showed Mr. Rubinoff the latest letter. There was no need to backtrack to earlier events since he had eavesdropped on her first dinner with Justin.

"How do you feel now about Justin?" he asked when he'd finished reading the letter.

"Why? What do you mean?" She tensed, knowing exactly what he meant.

Mr. Rubinoff slapped the letter on the table. "For goodness' sake, Victoria, this man takes you to a funeral, drops you off at home and then you discover the letter. Does that not strike you as something more than coincidence?"

Perhaps, at some point, she would have come to the same realization herself. But because the conjecture came from Mr. Rubinoff who had castigated Justin the moment they met, she bridled against it. "Justin is on the list. He is as much a victim as I am."

"Except that he has not gotten a chain letter, so that he does not have this fourteen-day deadline hanging over his head."

Vicky's eyes widened. "How do you know he hasn't gotten one?"

His gaze flickered only briefly. "I have spoken to him. I know."

Vicky was too caught up with her own problem to wonder why or when the two men had spoken. "You know, Mr. Rubinoff, now that I think about it, it seems like none of us got our letters at the same time. Theo's two weeks were nearly up by the time I got mine, and Eve died a week after he did."

"How convenient."

"What is?"

"That Mr. Coe is at the bottom of the list."

"Oh, come on," Vicky argued. "I was trying to point out that if he's at the bottom of the list, it explains why he hasn't received a chain letter yet."

The Gypsy shrugged. "You could be right. The only thing of which I am certain is that something evil is going on. Tell me again, Victoria, about the two notes. What did they say?''

'' 'Death to all,' and 'Mother, Love.' ''

He opened a drawer and pulled out a pad of stationery. "Who were the other people on the list?"

"I can't remember. One of them was Rosa something, Rosa Shoon. She was second on the list, but she didn't break the chain. I imagine she's all right. Do you think I should . . . should do what the letter says?''

Mr. Rubinoff scratched his thinning hair. "I am almost tempted to say that you should, only because I care about you. This madman obviously possesses a highly disciplined set of values, no matter how twisted they may be. If you follow the instructions, you live. If not, you die. But to give in to his madness—no, no, you must not.''

He shut his eyes, as if to retreat and ponder the dilemma in privacy. Except for the rhythmic dripping of a faucet, the room was silent. Vicky finished her soup while she waited.

At last, Mr. Rubinoff opened his eyes. "I wish I could offer the perfect solution to your problem, but my mind is too feeble to work the way it once did. I have only three suggestions for you.''

Vicky laid down her spoon. "I'll gladly listen to whatever you suggest.''

"First of all, you must put your trust in God. He knows everyone's thoughts at all times. Nothing is beyond His power.''

Vicky felt a twinge of guilt. How long had it been since she'd gone to church? Too long, she realized. "I think I can handle that," she said.

"Good. Now, secondly, do not allow fear to take control of your life. Fear is this person's sharpest weapon. You must go about your daily business as if nothing is wrong. Take special care to lock your doors and windows, avoid being alone with strangers, but otherwise, behave normally.''

"That might be a little hard to do at the store.''

"You have Rick. He will protect you.''

She nodded. "You're right. I guess I'm lucky to have him. What's your third piece of advice?"

"You must have faith in those who are trained in bringing criminals to justice. The police know how to handle these things. Even I can tell, from the clues this person has dropped, that he is practically begging to be caught. I am certain it will not be long before the man is apprehended."

Vicky wished she could share her friend's optimism. But two people were already dead, and according to the schedule, she was next. Perhaps Mr. Rubinoff was right. It might not be long before the police caught the killer, but when it came to one's own survival, Vicky realized, time was painfully relative.

"Why don't you call the lieutenant from here?" he suggested, lifting the phone from the nearby counter.

Vicky dialed the number with a growing sense of calm. Thank heavens for people like Mr. Rubinoff. If she'd been home alone, she'd probably still be tearing her hair out.

Luckily Lieutenant Simmons was at the station when she called. She told him about the letter, and he promised to come over right away.

Ten minutes later, there was a knock on the door of Mr. Rubinoff's apartment. The lieutenant entered the kitchen, declined an offer of coffee and sat down to hear Vicky's story.

Not surprisingly, he wasn't happy to hear that she and Justin had attended Eve's funeral. But before he could protest too much, Vicky asked his opinion of the note Justin had found, thinking that even the lieutenant could hardly deny it was a fine piece of detective work.

"What note?" the lieutenant asked, to her surprise.

"The one in Eve Lomorth's bedroom. Didn't Justin bring it to the station? He said he was going to."

The lieutenant shook his head. "I've been in the building all day. Haven't seen hide nor hair of anyone out of uniform. What did this note say?"

"'Mother, Love.' It was the same kind as the one found in Theo's pocket, with letters cut from a magazine."

"Where did he find it?"

"On her dresser, mixed in with other mail."

"No sign of the chain letter?"

"No, but we didn't have much time to look."

The officer let out a deep breath. "Sure is some funny business going on. So why do you suppose your investigative partner didn't bring it in?"

Vicky only wished she knew. She specifically remembered Justin saying he would go to the police that morning. "I'm sure he intends to," she replied lamely. "He may have forgotten or had something else to do first."

The officer offered no retort, but pulled an evidence bag from the pocket of his sports coat. "Let's drop the letter in here, for what it's worth. I suppose you got your fingerprints all over it, huh?"

Vicky tried not to sound defensive. "Sorry, but I'm not accustomed to opening my mail with tweezers."

"Doesn't matter. There were no usable prints on the chain letter anyway." He read the letter once more through the plastic. "Well, at least this is something more to go on."

"Is that all you can say, lieutenant, to put Victoria at ease?" Mr. Rubinoff remarked. "Her life is being threatened, and you sit there as if this were another clue to a crossword puzzle."

"We're working on it, Mr. Rubinoff, just as quickly as we can. Beyond that, there's nothing more I can say."

The two men locked stares until the Gypsy looked away in frustration. Everyone sat in uncomfortable silence for a minute or two while the lieutenant unhurriedly looked around the room. His gaze wandered to the pictures on the hutch. "This your family, Mr. Rubinoff?"

"Yes," the older man replied as he cleared the dishes from the table.

Lieutenant Simmons picked up one of the photographs. "I've always liked these old tintypes. Are you in this wedding picture?"

One of the plates fell from Mr. Rubinoff's grip and clattered in the sink. "Yes, I am the groom. The others in the photograph are my bride, my parents, my five brothers and sisters and their children."

Vicky leaned over for a closer look. "You were all very handsome."

His reaction to her praise was slight. "I was only twenty-six when the photograph was taken. It was in Budapest, 1941."

From what he didn't say, Vicky assumed the Gypsy was a widower. "Are your brothers and sisters still living in Europe?"

He didn't reply right away. Vicky looked up and noticed the pained stoop of his shoulders as he stood at the sink. A sudden feeling of dread ran through her. Lieutenant Simmons, too, sat waiting motionless for his reply.

"They are dead," Mr. Rubinoff said at last. "Everyone in the photograph, except for me, was murdered in Auschwitz."

"Oh, my God." Vicky got up from the table and threw her arms around her friend. "I had no idea. I'm so sorry."

He turned and clung to Vicky for a moment, then released her. "Life goes on. One does not forget, but one adjusts." He turned to the lieutenant, summarily dismissing the subject of his family. "You will, I trust, do everything in your power to solve this chain letter case quickly?"

"Absolutely," the officer assured him. "The FBI is already working on it, and I've been burning the midnight oil myself."

"What about the other people on the list? Have you questioned them? Do you know anything about them?"

"Just the usual, so far. Social security numbers, credit ratings, that sort of thing."

"Is it possible that one of them might actually be involved in the crime?" Mr. Rubinoff asked.

Vicky knew where the questions were leading, but she was in no mood to defend Justin. She was in no mood for anything right now.

"It's possible," the lieutenant replied, "and we are looking into it."

"Good. Now, I must return to work. Sophie has not had a break since breakfast." The three of them descended the narrow stairs together. "Lieutenant, you and your men must look after Victoria. She is very special to me."

Vicky turned red, while the officer managed one of his halfhearted smiles. "I've got cruisers patrolling the area around Miss Green's apartment, and we'll continue to do everything we can."

The Gypsy lumbered to his usual place behind the counter. "That is better than nothing, I suppose. Do you like cigars, lieutenant? You could take a box back to the station with you."

"No, thanks, I'm trying to quit. Besides, we're not allowed to accept gifts." The lieutenant turned to Vicky. "Are you going home? I'd be happy to give you a lift."

Vicky considered refusing his offer. The thought of staring at four silent walls was terrifying. But then she remembered Mr. Rubinoff's advice: *Go about your daily business as if nothing is wrong.*

Vicky forced herself to smile. "Yes, I'd appreciate a ride home, thank you."

She didn't mind the lack of small talk in Lieutenant Simmons's car. Engaging the man in conversation wasn't worth the effort, and she had too much on her mind anyway. When they pulled up to the curb in front of her apartment, Vicky turned to thank him.

"It was the least I could do," he replied. "Say, Miss Green, about that funeral you went to with Coe..."

They weren't going to get away with it after all, she thought. "Yes? What about it?"

"You ought to know by now that playing detective is not a smart thing to do."

"I know, but if we hadn't gone, no one would have found the—"

"And I've warned you before about associating with other people from the list."

"You're referring specifically to Justin, I take it?"

"Well, lemme put it this way. If you expect the police to solve this case and look out for your safety, then you've got to be willing to use some common sense too."

"I know, but..." She let the argument drop. No matter how much she might want to, it was impossible to defend Justin, a man she'd known less than two weeks, with any certainty.

"As for that note your buddy found in Miss Lomorth's bedroom, didn't it occur to you that maybe Coe didn't want anyone else to find it?"

She stared at him blankly. "No, that didn't occur to me at all."

"It might explain why he wanted to find out about the police investigation, and why he was in such an all-fired hurry to go to the funeral."

"That's ridiculous." Wasn't it? Again, she could do little more than deny the allegations on Justin's behalf. The trouble was, Vicky wasn't sure whether she was attracted to Justin because she believed in him, or simply because he was attractive. The possibility that it might be the latter was frightening.

"I may be one hundred percent wrong, Miss Green, but at least bear it in mind, okay?"

Vicky agreed to bear it in mind. She got out of the car, then the lieutenant drove off, leaving her alone and more confused than ever.

A SMALL FADED SNAPSHOT lay on the desk in Justin's office. He sat and stared at the only reminder of his past he dared carry in his wallet. The picture showed a beautiful young woman and a ten-year-old boy relaxing on the deck of a seventy-foot yacht called the *Che Sara*. The beach in the background was part of the Italian Riviera, where he and his mother used to go off-season to escape the crowds.

Those were wonderful times, when the two of them could be a real family. But if he were to add up the days they actually spent together, it would amount to scarcely two years of his life. Two years. He might as well have had no mother at all.

But at thirty-seven, he was a little old to think of himself as an orphan. He'd long since grown accustomed to having no past; he'd even learned to relish his anonymity. Tucking the photo into his wallet, Justin stared out the window and didn't hear the rap on the door.

"Ah, you are in here, after all," Maeve declared as she strode into the office. "I was reluctant to barge in. I thought you might be sleeping."

"You're the only one who nods off at her desk, Maeve."

Sinking into a chair, she pulled out a long brown cigarette. "Office catnaps can be quite refreshing. You ought to cultivate the habit. Anyway, I've come to hear the latest. What happened at the funeral this morning?"

"I don't feel like talking about it."

"Oh, dear boy, do tell. You know I won't stop pestering you until you do." She opened the desk drawer nearest her and brought out an ashtray.

Justin watched Maeve light the cigarette. Her large eyes peered through the billow of smoke with candid curiosity. He wasn't surprised that a situation like this would appeal to Maeve's sense of the dramatic.

"All right, I'll tell you what little I know. As I've already told you, Eve Lomorth was electrocuted..." His friend listened with utter fascination as he related the latest facts.

When he finished, Maeve sat back as though she'd just ingested a gourmet feast. "I must say, it's the most bizarre thing I've ever heard, not to mention a fascinating literary allegory."

"What allegory?"

"The notes, dear boy. Haven't you heard those words before?"

Justin shrugged. "When Vicky first told me about 'Death to all,' I thought it sounded familiar, not just threatening. But I haven't been able to place it. The whole thing is so weird." He walked to the window that overlooked the Elvehjem Museum of Art. "Do you feel like a coffee?"

"Sounds delightful. Your treat?"

"My treat. I'll be back in a minute." Justin left his office and returned shortly with two Styrofoam cups. Handing one to Maeve, he sat down across from her.

"I've been doing some thinking," Maeve said. "Have you ever thought that your new companion might have something to do with the chain letters? I mean, not just a recipient, but a . . . perpetrator."

He raised an eyebrow. "Vicky? Not really. Why?"

Maeve ran her fingers through hennaed curls. "You must admit, my dear, that her appearance in your life can be directly attributed to the letter. I wouldn't be at all surprised if she was involved."

"I thought it was possible at first, but the more I get to know her, the more I'm convinced Vicky has nothing to do with what's happened."

"Aren't you making a rather hasty judgment?"

"No. I've always thought I was a fairly good judge of character, and Vicky doesn't strike me as the least bit devious."

Maeve smiled sagely. "The truly devious types seldom do. But just for curiosity's sake, how *does* she strike you?"

Justin leaned back in his chair. "Let me think. How would I describe Vicky? Refreshing . . . pretty . . . clever . . . shy. How's that for starters?"

Maeve snuffed out her cigarette and reached for another. "Impressive. The very qualities I would have died to hear at her age. Unfortunately, clever was the only term ever ascribed to the young Maeve Wilson."

"Come on, Maeve, I'm sure you're exaggerating." Justin was accustomed to his friend's jaded view of herself, but today he wasn't in a sympathetic mood. His thoughts were fully occupied with Vicky.

He couldn't wait to see her this evening. Granted, they'd been together all morning at the funeral, but that was hardly a happy occasion. He'd been preoccupied; she'd been a nervous wreck. He was looking forward to seeing her laughing and happy—

"Did you know your mother would have turned sixty this month?"

Jarred by the sudden change of topic, Justin sat up in his chair. "What brought that on?"

"I saw you putting her picture away when I came in."

"And you remembered her birthday? Of course, you'd remember. You've always said you were one of her biggest fans."

"I was. Maija Justason was a fabulous actress—alluring, mysterious, every man's ideal, every woman's dream."

Justin's lower lip curled. "On-screen, maybe."

"Now there you go again. Honestly Justin, considering how well you turned out, she can't have been that dreadful a mother."

"As a mother, she meant well. As a person, she failed miserably."

"Failed? You call your mother's life a failure? How, pray tell, could she have done better? A suburban bungalow with a chain-link fence? A beer-swilling husband and ten raggedy brats? Maija Justason had beauty, a glamorous lifestyle, and a wonderful career—things most of us would give our eyeteeth for."

"Those were the things that killed her, Maeve."

She slid her hand along Justin's arm. "I know, dear, and I shouldn't keep harping about her, but it does seem such a shame not to let the public know that Maija's son, at least, is alive and well."

He and Maeve had had variations of this conversation ever since they'd met. She had approached him that day at the Library Mall and said, "Did anyone ever tell you that you could pass for Maija Justason's son?"

Nearly twenty years had gone by since his mother's death, and not once, until his encounter with Maeve, had anyone confronted him with his real identity. Justin was so startled that he'd inadvertently blurted that he was Miss Justason's son. It was the only slip he'd ever made, but, thankfully, it resulted in a strong friendship.

"You know I could never go public with her story," he said, "even if I wanted to. That part of my life is gone for good, and anyway, I've grown accustomed to being Justin Coe, Associate Prof."

"Soon to be full professor."

"Whatever."

Maeve pushed herself out of the chair. "Well, dear boy, I must toddle off. But do keep me posted on the chain letter . . . and your fledgling romance."

Justin chuckled. "I haven't been able to keep a secret from you yet. No reason this should be any different."

He was glad to see Maeve leave, glad to have his solitude once more. When the telephone rang, he snatched it up, resenting the intrusion. "Hello?"

"Justin? This is Vicky, Vicky Green."

His anger melted, and he smiled. "No need to be so formal. You are the only Vicky in my life."

"Oh."

Puzzled, Justin glanced at the receiver. Admittedly, it hadn't been his wittiest remark, but he'd expected at least a halfhearted chuckle. Then something twigged in the back of Justin's mind. Vicky didn't sound like herself. "What is it, darling? Is something wrong?" The endearment had slipped out without him realizing, but strangely enough, he didn't regret it.

He heard a small noise—half sigh, half sniffle.

"The reason I called was to tell you that I, uh, won't be able to see you this evening."

"Why not? Has something happened?"

"No, I just . . . Well, something has come up, and I have to cancel our date. That's all."

Vicky was lying. Something *was* wrong. *Come off it, Coe. Your well-entrenched ego couldn't handle the possibility that a woman might actually choose not to go out with you. You dragged her to a funeral, for pete's sake! What did you expect?*

"Okay, Vicky." He hoped his nonchalance sounded more convincing than hers. "Do you want to set a new date or shall I call you later?"

There was a brief hesitation at the other end. "Maybe it would be best . . . if you didn't call me at all."

Chapter Nine

Vicky was entitled to dump him.

Justin kept reminding himself of that immutable fact while snailing home in rush hour traffic. Maybe he was getting lax in his old age, losing his touch with the opposite sex. Whatever happened to the smooth, sensitive fellow who used to buy flowers and romantic cards and tell a lady how he felt? His behavior with Vicky, thus far, had bordered on the boorish.

He was out of practice, that's what. It had been ages since a woman inspired anything but his prurient interest. Not that Vicky didn't appeal to Justin's lustier instincts, but there was so much more to her than that. For one thing, she was—

Oh, hell, give it up. Justin turned up the volume on his car stereo, drowning out his stormy thoughts with equally stormy Bach.

The sight of his small Tudor-style home eased some of the stress. With its high-pitched roof and gabled windows, it reminded him of the stone cottages in England where he sometimes spent summers with friends. He parked his Jaguar near the giant spruce at the end of the driveway and hauled his briefcase out of the front seat.

The newspaper was stuck halfway through the slot of the arched front door; it looked as though the house was sticking out its tongue. Irritated, Justin shoved the paper inside with his knee while he searched for the keys.

After dropping his briefcase inside the cool entryway, he picked up the mail from the floor and headed for the bar in the living room. A neat bourbon was most definitely in order.

Sprawled on the burgundy leather sofa, Justin took a long swallow of his drink and opened his first piece of mail. It was a souvenir copy of an invitation. Justin Coe, guest of honor at a reception honoring his promotion to full professorship and head of the faculty. Somehow seeing the news engraved made it seem more official. His grin laced with irony, Justin waved the invitation in the air. "See this, Ma? I've made it! I am now respectable."

The second envelope addressed to Justin Coe had no return label. He pulled out the single sheet of bond. Something tightened inside him as he read:

Dear Number Seven,
You already know about the chain letter, so I won't waste time with introductions. You're the one I've been interested in all along, Mr. Coe. The others were nothing more than decoys.

You see, I know who you really are, not just who you pretend to be. And I've also unearthed some fascinating new tidbits about your past, specifically about your mother. In exchange for a reasonable sum, I'll be happy to share them with you.

All you have to do is put ten thousand dollars—unmarked bills, of course—in a plastic bag and drop the bag off forty-eight hours from now at the Wagon Wheel on Butler Street. There's a low hedge at the back of the building. Leave the money behind the hedge in between the two parking signs. Within twenty-four hours of payment, you will receive your information.

In case you're tempted to go to the police, remember, Justin, I've unearthed everything about your past. Everything. If the police were to learn the truth about you, think what it could do to your future.

One final postscript. You'll find my patience tends to run out after two weeks. If you doubt it, consider what happened to the others on the list who tried my patience.

His movements methodical, Justin crumpled up the letter and tossed it across the room. But it didn't even begin to assuage the burning rage he felt inside. He downed his drink and began to pace.

After all the things that had happened lately, he should have seen it coming. He should have known that, even after twenty years, someone would finally catch up to him.

But to use such grotesque methods. A chain letter, a list of seven unrelated people. What kind of madman was he dealing with? In a perverse sort of way, the sender was brilliant. To throw the police off the scent with mail fraud and apparently unrelated homicides left the road clear for a bit of quick extortion. But, brilliant or not, Justin wasn't going to pay a damned cent to a blackmailer!

He crossed the room and retrieved the crumpled ball of paper. There was no point in destroying the evidence. All he had to do was identify the blackmailer and expose him.

Right, Coe. Brilliant. How did you propose to pull off that bit of trickery? The letter had been written on an ordinary electric typewriter. No signature, no telltale clues. He didn't have the foggiest idea of who wrote it or what to do next.

Call the cops. That was it. He strode to the phone on the rolltop desk and was halfway through dialing the number when he stopped. *Dammit, why don't you sit down and use your head before flying off half-cocked?*

He couldn't let the police get involved. Whoever sent the letter knew that as well as Justin did. What the hell would he say to them?

Yessir, I'm being blackmailed. Why? Because I'm not who I claim to be, and because there's an outstanding murder charge on my head. Check with Interpol. They'll tell you what happened to my mother and her lover. But do hurry up and find the blackmailer. I wouldn't want this to get into the papers.

Calling the police was out of the question. By the time they solved the case, he'd be serving a life sentence in Italy. And with his luck, the blackmailer would probably confess and make a fortune on the movie rights.

There had to be some way of rooting out this guy on his own. Once the blackmailer's identity was uncovered, he'd be powerless. The two of them, both alleged murderers, would be a matched pair of disarmed felons.

So think, Justin. Where and when did this scheme get its start? The chain letter was obviously the first step. From there, it was a matter of determining what changes had come into his life as a result of the chain letter.

There was Vicky, of course. But he'd already discounted her in his conversation with Maeve. If Vicky was a black-mailer, he was a six-foot rabbit.

Was there anyone else? One of her friends, perhaps. Rick Paterson? Possible, but not likely. Maybe Rick didn't like him, but from what Justin knew of the young man, he couldn't see him having the wits to pull off a scheme like this. Mr. Rubinoff? Could be. In fact, he could very well be the person who'd managed to dig up Justin's past.

It would go a long way toward explaining the man's be-havior the first night at the Cheese 'n' Deli. The questions, the pensive looks, the more than obvious eavesdropping. Then showing up at the pier last Sunday, again asking too many pertinent questions.

A second realization came to light in Justin's mind, one that refused to go away, despite his feelings. Admittedly, Vicky was the one who called about the chain letter, but Vicky was also the one who suggested they meet at the Cheese 'n' Deli, her friend's restaurant.

There was no reason it couldn't be a team effort, with Vicky handling the correspondence, and Mr. Rubinoff in charge of the dirtier deeds. Though neither case had been proven, Theo Dalta had probably been thrown down the stairs, and Eve Lomorth murdered by a man posing as a telephone repairman. The Gypsy, despite his advanced age, was certainly robust enough to handle either job.

Supposing—and it was still sheer supposition—that Vicky Green was responsible. This put her cancellation of tonight's date in a whole different light. Was her call prompted by an attack of conscience or one of fear? Was this a cue for Mr. Rubinoff to take over, or would Vicky still play a part, luring unsuspecting victims as a Siren lured sailors to the rocky shore?

He had no idea. But there was one thing he was fairly certain of. The blackmailer—he, she or they—was not going to be satisfied with a mere ten thousand bucks. No one ever got away from a blackmail scheme that easily. Unless he took action quickly, this would be only the beginning of a long-drawn-out squeeze for cash.

Justin had not survived this many years without learning a few things about subterfuge. After careful consideration, he decided that he would, at the beginning, appear to cooperate. The blackmailer was obviously smart enough not to walk into an immediate trap. But if Justin was to bait him with a few dollars at the start, the blackmailer would probably get greedy, and then maybe careless. Justin would also get a clearer picture of the "tidbits" the blackmailer had for sale.

The first thing he did was start a file. Pulling a folder from his desk, he placed the letter inside along with notations regarding the time and place it arrived. Then he put the file away and locked the drawer.

There was nothing to do but wait until morning when the bank was open. His "instant teller" card would not take kindly to a large cash withdrawal.

The evening loomed endlessly ahead of him. He was too tired to go sailing, and it was too early for bed. Although he was tempted to drown himself in bourbon, he couldn't afford not to be clearheaded.

An aching sense of loss hung over him as he watched TV, and for a while, Justin couldn't place the source of the pain. Then, sadly, he understood. A few hours ago, he'd been looking forward to the sight of Vicky's smile, the glimmer of her hazel eyes with those long dark lashes. He'd been looking forward to kissing her, touching her pale and delicate skin. Now, suddenly, before it had even begun, the relationship was over.

No. It didn't have to be over. He could still see Vicky if he wanted to. His masculine charm, his powers of persuasion weren't totally out of commission. In fact, it might even be better if they did keep seeing each other, if only to keep Vicky emotionally off balance. With a renewed sense of purpose, he drove to the three-story condominium at Gorham and Livingston.

"VICKY, PLEASE OPEN the door." Justin had been pounding on it for several minutes. "I promise I'm not going to hurt you."

"I know that." She sounded as though she'd been crying for hours. "Can't you understand, Justin? I don't want to see you anymore."

"If you'd tell me why, I'd understand."

"Be...because...th-there's someone else."

He rolled his eyes upward. He'd never heard a less-convincing lie. Was this a woman capable of extortion? "But we're friends, Vicky. At least, we were about to be. Come on, Vicky. It's okay."

For a while, he couldn't hear anything. Then finally he heard the floorboards squeak, the locks unlatch, one by one. For some absurd reason, his heart began to race in anticipation. An instant later, the door opened, and there she was, looking like absolute hell.

He didn't mean to smile, but there was something incredibly waiflike about Vicky as she stood there looking up at him. Her red-rimmed eyes were enormous, and she looked as fragile as a china figurine.

"You really shouldn't cry," he teased. "It doesn't do a thing for you."

To his delight, she laughed through her sniffles as she wiped tears away with the back of her hand. "I know," she said. "When I was a kid, I used to practice crying gracefully in front of the mirror, but it didn't do any good. Come in."

Studying Vicky's expression, Justin hesitated. She didn't seem frightened or guilty, just upset. Surely his suspicions were wrong; surely she wasn't involved in these hideous crimes. She couldn't be. At last, he stepped inside and brought a bouquet of flowers from behind his back. "These are for you."

Through the splotches on her cheeks and the mascara stains, Vicky's face lit up at the sight of the white lilies. She looked for a moment like a child on Easter Sunday. "Oh, Justin, they're beautiful."

"I didn't grow them from seed. Are they still allowed?"

Her laugh was light and inviting, like the sound of the bell she hung over the door of her shop. "I'm sure the plants won't mind. Make yourself at home while I put these in water."

She emerged from the kitchen a short time later carrying the bouquet in a white vase. Her face looked fresh and clear, as though she'd splashed cool water on it.

He'd never seen her in slacks before. She looked terrific. Her thighs were slender, her hips softly curving; her T-shirt outlined small firm breasts. She was wearing a bra, but somehow that didn't surprise him.

Brusquely Justin came to his senses. What in the hell was he doing, daydreaming about Vicky's underwear when there were plenty of other more important things to think about?

She placed the flowers on an end table, their graceful white blossoms beautiful against the soft pink of the walls. The room was very much a reflection of Vicky, he thought, with the same aching sense of loss he'd felt earlier. Pushing the feeling to the back of his mind, he patted an empty spot beside him on the sofa.

"Why don't you sit here and tell me the real reason you canceled our date?" Vicky opened her mouth to speak, but Justin raised his hand in warning. "The truth this time, okay?"

Her expression relaxed slightly. "I'll tell the truth, but first, you tell me why you didn't take that note to the police station."

He sat up, momentarily confused. "What note?"

"The one from Eve Lomorth's bedroom."

"Oh—Mother, love. I did take it to the police."

Tension hardened her face once again. "I talked to Lieutenant Simmons this afternoon, Justin. He didn't know anything about it."

"What time was that?"

"I don't know. Around two, I guess."

"That explains it. I went to the station on my way home from work. It was nearly five by then." When Vicky didn't answer, Justin gestured toward the phone in the hall. "Go ahead and check if you like. I gave the envelope to the lieutenant personally."

She regarded him for a minute or so, then shook her head. "It's okay, I believe you."

"Was that all that was bothering you, Vicky? You could've asked me about it right away."

"I realize that now, but there was something else."

She lowered her gaze to her lap where her fingers were laced together tightly. Justin had an urge to loosen and caress each finger, one by one; and then do whatever he could to relax the rest of her. Which, of course, was totally irrelevant to why he had come.

"What is it, Vicky? What could be so terrible that you don't want to see me anymore?"

"I received another letter today."

Vicky's words and the look of quiet anguish on her face jolted him. "What kind of letter?" Justin didn't realize he'd reached out and touched her leg until she flinched. He pulled his hand away.

"A follow-up to the chain letter. That's why I had to talk to Lieutenant Simmons." She related what she could remember of the letter's contents. "You see, I only have seven days and then...then I don't know what's going to happen."

A visible shudder ran through her body. Risking rejection, Justin drew her into his arms—and seeing Vicky like this was more than enough proof of her innocence. "It's okay, darling. Nothing's going to happen to you."

She buried her head in his shoulder. "H-how can you be so sure?"

"Because I won't let anything happen." He stroked her fluffy, shoulder-length hair. She was wearing it loose. He marveled at the gossamer softness of it. The lamp beside the sofa caught the gold and copper highlights. Vicky's hair was natural and healthy. To Justin, everything about Vicky was natural and healthy.

She wasn't crying anymore; that pleased him. And she seemed content in his arms, as though she'd found refuge. Justin nearly recoiled from the pang of emotion that speared through him. Maybe it was still best that he leave, before he lost what little remained of his objectivity.

"Justin," Vicky said, her voice tiny.

"Yes?"

"The police have this theory...well, that maybe you went to Eve's funeral so that you could get ahold of the note before they did."

Justin tensed, startling Vicky. "Why on earth would I do that?"

"To cover up what you'd done?" She phrased the statement like a question, one whose answer she couldn't quite believe.

"That's crazy. The police could have found the note when they first investigated her death. And if I was going to retrieve something from Eve's house, I wouldn't be so obvious as to go to the police, ask about the investigation, and then chat with everyone at the funeral. I'd be more likely to crawl in through a window after dark, wouldn't I?''

"I see your point. And if you didn't want them to see the note, you wouldn't have brought it to Lieutenant Simmons this afternoon, right?"

"Right."

Vicky sat back and crossed her legs. "Boy, I wish you could've been there when the lieutenant was doing his snow job on me. Everything he said was true, but the way he worded it had me totally convinced you were the killer."

"So that's why you wanted to call things off between us."

"Wouldn't you? I mean, if you suspected me of doing these things?"

He hoped there was enough of his mother's talent in him to pull off a convincing look of innocence. "If you were the killer, I'm sure I'd be tempted to call things off. So, shall I expect to be arrested this evening?"

Vicky shook her head. "No, the lieutenant didn't have any proof, and I don't think you're his only suspect. He's just looking out for my safety. I haven't known you very long, and he has a theory that someone on the list may be the sender."

The lieutenant's reasoning, Justin supposed, was not totally illogical. He knew nothing about the other three people on the chain letter list. But what mattered most was that his faith in Vicky had been restored. And hers in him. He still had a major problem to deal with, but for tonight at least, he intended to use his time to help Vicky.

"Let me stay here," he said.

Her eyes with their flecks of gold and green widened. "Here? With me?"

"I'll sleep on the couch. Just to make sure you're all right."

"But why would you...? No, I don't think...." Vicky pressed her hands to the side of her head, as if the decision caused her intense pain. "Justin, it's really generous of you to make the offer, but it wouldn't do any good. There's still tomorrow night to get through and the night after. You can't very well move in with me, and at some point, I have to resume living alone.''

"Which you will. I'm not offering to move in, and I'm not saying we have to negotiate a new arrangement every night. I'm only talking about now, this evening. A great deal has happened to you today. You've been under a lot of stress. If you hope to get any rest at all, this is not a good night to be alone.''

She looked so small, so vulnerable, looking up at him and trying to be brave. "You will sleep on the couch?" she asked.

"You can even slide your bedroom furniture against the door if you're afraid I might attack.''

Vicky tried to grin, but couldn't quite manage it with a quivering chin. "You wouldn't be offended?''

"I'll learn to live with it.''

Justin brought her to her feet, and Vicky, perhaps sensing what he craved, lifted her head. Crushing her fine hair between his fingers, he claimed her mouth, knowing at once that the kiss was too brutal, too demanding. But Vicky didn't pull away.

Her lips parted. She allowed him the silent invasion, drawing him into her until something primeval inside exploded. He shifted his body and felt only momentary resistance in her before she relaxed completely in his embrace. That was when he realized enough was enough, and released her.

Vicky staggered back half a step, feeling as though she'd just survived a tornado. But the house was as still as glass. Not a sound, not a stir, nothing except her own wildly pounding heart.

And Justin. Blond, beautiful Justin, looking at her as though she'd done something quite stupendous. All she'd done was kiss him. Or, to be more accurate, she'd allowed herself to be kissed. And, heaven help her, if only one kiss could do that, bedroom furniture against the door wasn't going to do any good. Not unless it was stacked on *his* side.

"Would...would you care for some tea?" Her voice came out in a barely audible squeak.

She was relieved to see that Justin had to clear his own throat before any sounds came out. "You, uh, wouldn't have anything stronger, would you?"

Vicky turned her head toward the kitchen and felt the brush of cool air against her cheek. Goodness, she was burning up. It had obviously been too long since her last real kiss. "I think I might have a bottle of sherry. Will that do?"

"Sherry's fine." Justin sat down heavily on the sofa, then moved as though he were about to get up again. "Did you want me to help you get it?"

"No!" She gestured frantically for him to stay where he was. "I mean, no thank you, I can manage."

Danger and lust, Vicky decided on her way to the kitchen, was a lethal combination. If someone could package the ingredients in a beverage, they'd make millions. She rummaged noisily through the cupboards for the sherry.

Vicky had always acknowledged that Justin was gorgeous, and she wasn't unaware of the twittery feelings she got whenever he was around, but this was rapidly becoming something more.

She wasn't the type to release her passion at the drop of a kiss. And this was much too soon to be love. It was more of an intense physical and emotional...like. That was it. She *liked* Justin Coe, and the fact that he was devastatingly attractive made it hard to resist liking him even more.

Finally Vicky found the bottle, but she was less successful at coming up with two sherry glasses. The owner of a gift shop with no glasses, she thought wryly; like the cobbler's children with no shoes. Settling for one sherry glass and one juice glass, she set them on a tray with the bottle and carried her achievement quite steadily into the living room.

They talked and drank until sometime after midnight. Vicky sat on an armchair while Justin stretched out on the couch. Neither of them referred to the earlier moment of intimacy; neither of them had to. It was there in the room, as real and tangible as the vase full of lilies. But it was also new. Too new to discuss, too fragile to explore, until they'd both had time to think.

When Justin started yawning, Vicky went to the linen closet and brought out sheets and a pillow. Together, they made up the sofa, then stood up and stared at each other for a long, awkward moment.

"Good night, Justin."

"Good night, Vicky."

He leaned over and kissed her cheek lightly, chastely. It felt quite unremarkable, really. With an immense sigh of relief, Vicky turned and went to her room.

There were wheels on the legs of the heavy oak dresser, but they were too small to do anything except snag on the bedroom carpet. Vicky pushed and shoved, sweated and swore, telling herself she was going through this idiotic motion for Lieutenant Simmons. If there was the tiniest grain of truth to his theory about Justin, she would have one heck of a time explaining why she'd allowed him to spend the night.

There. The dresser was now in place in front of her bedroom door. Six knights with a battering ram couldn't have broken through the barricade.

Truth be told, Vicky was having trouble rationalizing to herself why Justin was here. She slipped a cotton nightgown over her head and crawled under the covers. One reason was obvious: she was afraid of being alone. The second letter had rattled her more than she cared to admit. If the sender could so easily walk into her apartment building to deliver a letter, how much more could he get away with unnoticed? Refusing to consider the possibilities, she snuggled deeper into the sheets.

As for the lieutenant's theory about Justin's involvement, Vicky was no longer convinced. As Justin himself had pointed out, if he had gone to such elaborate lengths to commit murder, he certainly wouldn't bungle it by talking to the police and skulking around his victim's bedroom after the fact.

So, if she was so convinced of Justin's innocence, why were there two hundred pounds of solid oak blocking the door between them? Did she actually think he would come in here and strangle her? Or was it in case the real murderer showed up? He might come in and murder Justin, and then where would she be?

Vicky rolled over and gave the pillow a resounding punch. No, of course not, you stupid idiot! The dresser was only there because of the way Justin had kissed her tonight. They'd known each other for little more than a week. Never mind that they'd already experienced more traumas together than most people suffer in a year. Never mind that the sight of him made her knees turn to water. It was too soon for Justin to stay the night, too soon to even consider making love. But she was considering it, all right. She most definitely was, and *that* was why the dresser was there.

It was no wonder she couldn't fall asleep. A mature, sensible woman defending her chastity with a lump of furniture. Justin was no rapist, and she was no child. If there were going to be barricades between them, better that they be the invisible kind.

There were no sounds coming from the living room except for Justin's rhythmic breathing, while Vicky pushed and shoved, sweated and swore, and returned the dresser to its proper place. Then she unlocked the bedroom door and left it a few inches ajar before crawling into bed.

She fell asleep and dreamed of a secluded campground, woods on three sides, the lake crystal clear and blue. Justin was with her, and they had pitched a tent. Inside were two sleeping bags zipped together. They were sitting by the campfire, snuggled close. The flames leaped and crackled, and the smell of smoke...

The smell of smoke? Vicky opened her eyes and wondered why the room looked hazy. She sat up in bed. The room wasn't hazy; it was full of smoke. Dear God, Justin had set the apartment on fire!

Chapter Ten

Vicky stumbled out of bed and flung open the door, expecting to find the whole place ablaze. But the smoke curling out of the kitchen wasn't nearly as thick as she'd first imagined. And come to think of it, it didn't smell much like a building on fire.

Cautiously she crept down the hall and peered into the kitchen. There was Justin standing at the stove, trying to drain grease from a huge cast-iron pan into a tiny tomato paste can. Judging from the smoldering element, most of the grease had missed its mark.

Vicky covered her mouth to contain what threatened to be hysterical laughter. To think she had actually believed Justin was an arsonist, when he was merely a well-meaning, half-naked man botching breakfast.

She continued to watch, fascinated, as the shirtless Justin did battle with the errant bacon fat. Finally, slamming the pan down in disgust, he rummaged through the cupboards for paper toweling. As he wiped the stove top clean, the muscles across his back and shoulders worked in furious rhythm. Vicky's eyes followed the furrow of his spine to where slacks clung to lean hips. Until now, she'd found Justin's physical perfection intimidating. Here, in the clear light of morning and in her own kitchen, she was simply mesmerized.

Justin must have sensed her presence. He turned and gave her a sheepish grin. "Good morning. I was hoping to surprise you."

"Oh, you managed to surprise me all right. I woke up thinking you'd set the place on fire."

He looked hurt. "Why did you think that?"

Vicky went to the stove and switched on the overhead fan. "The smoke was my first clue."

Justin glanced around. "Oh, yeah, I guess it is a bit thick. The problem was I couldn't find anything except this one dinky can to drain the bacon. Don't you save empty pickle jars?"

"Not if I can help it." Vicky spied the small mountain of bacon on a plate. "No wonder you had a grease flood. You cooked the whole pound of bacon at once."

"I had to. It expires today. I don't know about the eggs—you threw away the carton—but I thought I'd take a chance."

"Oh, so you're one of those types, huh?" She glanced at the pile of mangled eggshells on the counter. Two slightly squashed, overripe tomatoes sat on the cutting board, a knife lying in defeat beside them.

"One of what types?"

"The compulsive type who schedules his life around expiry dates."

"I wouldn't word it quite so strongly, but at least I don't have cheese turning into penicillin in my fridge." He picked up the knife and tried to saw through the skin of one of the tomatoes. "When was the last time you sharpened this thing?"

"The knife? Uh, well, I don't think I have, actually."

"Then I'll to have to buy a knife sharpener as well as a battery for your smoke detector."

"Gosh, I hardly know what to say. Last night, flowers. This morning, batteries." Vicky crossed the kitchen to the coffee maker.

Justin laughed. "History's swiftest descent from romance to domesticity. Does that bother you?"

She thought about it a moment, then smiled. "No, it doesn't bother me at all."

Justin couldn't have known, of course, as he scrambled the eggs, but, for Vicky, the loneliest place in her apartment had always been the kitchen—not, as one might have expected, the bedroom. Her bedroom was a refuge, a special place for relaxation and solitude. As for other associated pastimes, finding a partner, if one was so inclined, was no challenge. Men were always eager to share the pleasures of a double bed, weren't they? But a double sink? Never.

There were times when Vicky found it almost unbearably lonely to stand over a hot stove for no one but herself, to set the table for one, to open a bottle of wine only to have the rest turn to vinegar. This morning, the absence of loneliness was almost overwhelming.

She heard Justin come up behind her, as if he were responding to her thoughts. His arms came around her waist; his lips brushed her neck. Desire spiraled through Vicky's body as the coffee urn overflowed in the sink.

"Thank you for moving the furniture away from the door last night," he murmured.

A bloom rose in her cheeks as she turned to face him. His hands glided along the thin cotton of her nightgown. "I should never have blocked the door in the first place. It was silly of me."

"No, you were only being cautious, but I hope this means you're really not afraid of me anymore."

"I don't think I ever was." She meant what she said, but Vicky wondered whether she was being entirely honest. In Justin's company, she no longer feared for her life, but fear for her emotions was something else entirely.

"YOU'RE SEEING quite a bit of Justin these days, aren't you?" Maeve Wilson said as she poked through a display of clay kitchen magnets. They were shaped like miniature pies, complete with lattice work, and were one of the best-selling items in the store.

Vicky wondered whether she imagined the resentment in Maeve's voice. Some women, she'd learned over the years, confused friendship with exclusivity, especially when it came to men. She found it hard to believe Maeve had come all the way to the Nick Nack Nook to browse. "I enjoy his company, and he's a nice man," was Vicky's noncommittal reply.

Maeve's throaty laughter filled the room. "Justin Coe, my dear, is gorgeous, teeming with ambition and terribly sure of himself. Nice doesn't even begin to describe him."

"I suppose you're right." Vicky winced as she watched the woman paw through the merchandise. "The magnets are made of clay, Maeve. They'll break easily."

Maeve looked up in surprise, as though no one had ever dared speak to her that way. Abandoning the pies, she moved to a display of scented candles. "Has he told you anything about his past?"

"Not much." Vicky busied herself rearranging novelty items near the cash. "I gather his past wasn't happy, so I don't like to ask questions."

"It wouldn't matter if you did. He doesn't discuss it with anyone. He's very much a private person."

"But he's discussed his past with you."

"That's different. He trusts me."

"Why are you telling me this, Maeve?"

"To save you needless grief. You're a sweet girl, Vicky. But if you think something special is developing between you and Justin, you're deluding yourself. I've seen it happen dozens of times. Women are drawn to Justin for obvious reasons. Foolishly they overlook the fact that they know virtually nothing about him and, before they know it, they've fallen headlong in love with the man."

Vicky looked away, hoping Maeve didn't realize how shaken she was. "What happens then?"

"Let's just say that, despite outward appearances, Justin Coe lacks the—what shall I call it—emotional stamina required for a serious relationship."

"When it comes to relationships, none of us has emotional stamina."

"Yes, but with Justin, it's much worse. You see, there are certain events in his life he hasn't adjusted to. And until he's willing to undergo professional treatment, I don't see how he can ever—"

"Maeve, I don't think I care to hear anymore."

"But I'm only trying to—"

"Please, I've heard enough."

Maeve's skin was too thick to take offense. "Have it your way, my dear. But never let it be said I didn't warn you." She picked up a mulberry candle and placed it on the counter. "I'd like this one. It should look quite lovely in my office."

Vicky struggled to keep her hands from shaking as she rang up Maeve's purchase. "I'm sure it will." She wrapped the candle in monogrammed Nick Nack Nook paper and tied the package with lavender ribbon.

"Such a lovely parcel," Maeve remarked, as though the conversation had never taken place. "A refreshing change from plastic bags."

After Maeve had gone, Vicky realized that her innuendoes alone didn't bother her. What did bother her was that Maeve was only one among a growing list of people who'd warned Vicky to be wary of Justin Coe.

THE MAN WALKED along State Street, glancing occasionally at his reflection in the shop windows. The sun was high in the sky. There was the undeniable feeling of summer in the air, a sweet smell of success right around the corner.

No one would have guessed that Mama was with him. He would have preferred to be alone, but he'd never tell Mama that. She'd be hurt and angry, and what was the point? Let her window-shop and gossip with him for a while. She wouldn't be around much longer.

Trouble was, she was getting bossier by the day. Asking too many questions, pushing him too hard, the way she used to do. He could feel the pressure mounting, like a balloon blowing up inside him, ready to burst. He should have been feeling quite the opposite, now that things were coming to an end.

"How much money do we have so far?" Mama asked.

"Thirty dollars." He checked in the reflection of a window to be sure his lips didn't move when he spoke.

"Thirty dollars? Is that all? What happened to the thousands we were supposed to be raking in?"

"You've got to be patient. It's only been a few weeks." He prided himself on his discretion. Mama didn't know there *was* more than thirty dollars, and she didn't have to, as long as she got her little place in the sun....

"You're right," she said, much to his surprise. "When I first came up with the chain letter idea, I told you it would take time, didn't I?"

"You did, Mama."

"And it's working out brilliantly, isn't it?"

"Sure is," he said, feeling anything but sure.

"And don't worry about the ones we had to punish. People will start taking us seriously as soon as they realize what happens when they don't."

"I imagine so."

"That V.E. Green is next, isn't she?"

He tried to remain expressionless as he muttered some reply.

"Do you think she'll break the chain?" Mama asked.

"I don't know. I hope not."

The anger that always simmered just below the surface threatened to boil over at the possibility of a third betrayal. It wasn't supposed to happen this way. They'd been hand-picked, every one; they were supposed to be on his side. But two of the chosen, so far, had made a fool out of him. That's why two, so far, had died.

RICK PATERSON CAME into the Nick Nack Nook with two paper bags from the Cheese 'n' Deli. "I couldn't remember what kind of sandwich you wanted. Was it chicken or tuna salad?"

Vicky drew an Exacto knife across the oilcloth she was using to line shelves. "What kind did you get?"

"Tuna."

Wouldn't you know it? She'd been craving chicken. "Tuna's fine, Rick."

They ate lunch in the stockroom at the rear of the store. Rich was in a terrific mood, having sold thirty-six ceramic chicks while Vicky was out.

"I'm proud of you," she said. "Did you ask the customer why she wanted so many?"

"They're for her wedding. It's the day before Easter. She's going to put one at every plate for people to take home with them."

"What a lovely idea." Vicky leaned back and stretched her legs. "Nice time of year for a wedding, too."

She could almost picture it. The bridal party in buttercup yellow taffeta with bouquets of white lilies; herself in white lace and yellow ribbons in her hair. The men would wear midnight blue tuxedos, and Justin's boutonniere would match her— Good grief, listen to her!

Three days ago, Justin fixed breakfast at her place, and as Maeve so succinctly remarked this morning, they'd been seeing each other ever since. But a movie, a dinner and a stroll through the UW arboretum hardly constituted commitment, let alone the right to make wedding plans.

Rick rolled waxed paper into a ball between his palms. "I almost forgot. *He* called again."

"He?" Vicky repeated, pretending not to understand.

With an excess of force, he tossed the ball into the trash can. "You know...Justin."

She drank the last of her tea and tried not to smile. Rick was probably not aware of his jealousy, but he reminded Vicky of herself at eight years of age, when her oldest brother brought his fiancée home for the first time. Vicky had quite simply refused to acknowledge the woman's existence. Eventually she got over it. Rick would, too.

"Did he leave a message?" she asked.

The young man scowled. "Nah, he just wants you to call him."

Just then, the front doorbell announced the arrival of a customer. Vicky got up. "You relax, Rick. I'll take care of this one."

A man in a green sports coat stood in the front room. "Hi, lieutenant," Vicky said.

"Miss Green, how ya doing?"

"Fine, thank you."

He poked through the store for a minute or so. Because he was a policeman, Vicky got the impression he was conducting a search rather than browsing like an ordinary customer. But she had no doubt it was all in her head.

"Is there something I can do for you?" she asked pointedly, not in the mood for another well-meaning acquaintance telling her how to run her life.

"I thought you might like to know that I've talked to everyone on the list."

Vicky's nerves tensed. "Have you? What did you find out?"

"Not much." He pulled out his notepad. "Let's see, number two is still waiting for her windfall after stuffing money in the tree and sending letters to her friends. Sean Filipi's wife pitched the letter the day it arrived, and Curtis Donet gave it to his secretary who gave it to her uncle who collects chain letters or something like that. Justin Coe claims he never got one." The lieutenant squinted at her, as though daring her to make something of his findings.

Vicky picked up a feather duster, the closest thing at hand, and began dusting knickknacks that had been cleaned an hour ago. "Has... Has anyone been threatened?"

"Nope, not a one. How about you? Had any problems since the last letter?"

Vicky shook her head.

"Good. Maybe the killer's finally given up, now that he knows we're on his trail."

"Maybe." She could only hope the lieutenant was right.

He hitched up his pants. "'Course we're not gonna relax until the guy's safely behind bars."

"Yes, well, that's certainly encouraging." It was ungracious of her, she knew, but Vicky wished the lieutenant would go away. Now that Justin was part of her life, she'd felt herself grow calmer, her fears recede with each passing day. She knew the officer meant well, keeping an eye on her, but his presence always resurrected unsettling emotions.

"There is one thing about this case that puzzles me," he said, scratching his chin.

Vicky sighed and put down the duster. "What's that?"

"It's about the seven of you—the five who are left, that is. We can't seem to come up with a common link. Let's say, if you were all doctors and nurses, we'd look for someone who was out to avenge a bad operation. Or you might have been from the same hometown where this guy was considered a loser. So far we can't find anything that would explain why the seven of you are his target."

"Couldn't it just be a random selection?"

"We thought so, at first, but the guy's too methodical. From what we can gather, the letters were sent out about five days apart—probably so he'd have time to deal with each person individually. There's a pattern in there somewhere. I'm sure of it. Just a matter of figuring out what it is."

Vicky had never heard the lieutenant speak with such enthusiasm. The thrill of the hunt, she supposed, must be part of the allure in police work. Still, she'd feel much better not knowing how baffled they were over the case.

In no apparent hurry to leave, the lieutenant picked up an apple head doll. "Are you looking for a gift, lieutenant?" Vicky asked. "Something for your wife or daughter, perhaps?" Maybe if he bought something, Vicky reasoned, she'd feel more kindly disposed toward the man.

The doll he was examining wore a full-length calico dress. She stood by a tiny blackboard, a wooden pointer in her hand. She'd been crafted by a dear little woman in a nursing home who was always delighted to hear that another of her dolls had found a home.

"Never married," he said. "It's hard to find a lady who'll put up with a cop's life. But once in a while, I kinda wish I had someone to buy things for. Know what I mean?"

Vicky felt a quiver of sympathy for him. Here she was, trying to wish the man out of her store, and he was probably quite lonely. "I know what you mean," she said in a gentler tone.

He turned the doll over in his hands. "Aw, what the heck. I'm gonna buy her anyhow. Never know when you'll need a present for somebody's kid at the station."

Vicky wrapped the doll carefully in tissue paper and packed it in a box. "Whoever gets this will love her, I'm sure. She'd probably even look good decorating a bachelor's place," she added with a grin.

He did his best to smile back. "You could be right, Miss Green." Tucking the parcel under his arm, he gave her a mock salute. "Take care of yourself."

With a mixture of relief and tension, Vicky watched the officer leave. He really wasn't such a bad sort, even if he did come across as grumpy. Maybe if he tried harder to smile…

JUSTIN HAD STUFFED ten one-hundred dollar bills into an envelope, then put this into a plastic bag, which he rolled and sealed tightly with heavy-duty packing tape. Let the creep struggle for his money, he thought bitterly, glancing at the parcel on the passenger seat.

Two days had passed since he'd gotten the letter, and tonight was the deadline for making the payment. The sky had been overcast all day, and now rain was falling in a light drizzle, just enough to render the streets slick and the windshield wipers useless.

The Wagon Wheel tavern on Butler Street was a sand-colored brick building that had seen better days. It was only two blocks from the Cheese 'n' Deli, though Justin couldn't be sure that was relevant. He parked at the rear of the building, tucked the parcel into an inner pocket and stepped out of the car.

The rain was coming down more steadily now, and Justin turned up the collar of his Windbreaker against the chill. Perfect weather for a crime, he thought, scouting the dimly lit alley.

Just as the letter had said, there was a meager privet hedge against the building that did nothing to adorn its bleak surroundings. Two parking signs flanked the wall, allowing a space of six feet or so where the parcel could be dropped.

He looked around. There were two other cars parked near his, but no sign of the owners. They were probably inside the tavern. He wondered if the blackmailer was already watching. Probably. There were low-rise office towers on either side. Any of the darkened windows would provide an ideal vantage.

So let him wait. Justin stuffed both hands in his pockets, lingered deliberately near the hedge for a minute or so, then went inside the awninged entrance to the bar.

The place was smoky, poorly lit and smelled of stale beer, indistinguishable from thousands of middle American counterparts. From the inquisitive looks he was given by the customers, Justin determined they were regular patrons.

He went up to the bar and ordered a Bud from a lanky young bartender. The kid looked familiar; he was probably a UW student. Justin lowered himself to a barstool and casually looked around the room.

By now, most everyone had lost interest in him, except for a pair of middle-aged ladies in the corner who looked like part of the decor. A pear-shaped man in cowboy boots sauntered past him toward the jukebox and dropped in a few coins. When the machine didn't cooperate, he kicked it, shook it and swore. Nobody seemed to notice.

Whoever the blackmailer was, Justin doubted that he was one of the Wagon Wheel's imbibers. The atmosphere was sullen, almost surly, but no one appeared ambitious enough to conduct such a complicated intrigue. He forced himself to drink slowly, even counting to sixty several times to make the minutes pass. It was no fault of the brewers or the tavern, but it was the worst beer he'd ever drunk in his life.

Finally he decided enough time had passed. By now the blackmailer, presuming that he lay somewhere in waiting, would be getting antsy. Justin left a tip and got up. No one in the Wagon Wheel noticed him leave.

As he rounded the building to the back, he reached into his jacket for the parcel. Rain was still falling, but there was no danger of the money, wrapped as it was in layers of plastic, getting wet. He looked around again, intending to be more than obvious and dropped the package behind the hedge, halfway between the two signs. Then he climbed into the Jaguar and, as he pulled away, glanced at the narrow gap between the hedge and the building. He caught a glimpse of the white plastic. Perfect. To anyone else who might have noticed, it looked only like a bit of normal city litter dropped behind a bush.

He took the obvious route home, down Washington Avenue toward the river, but after he turned left onto Dickinson, he pulled over to the curb, shut off the lights and waited. A few cars went by during the next few minutes, but no one seemed to be following him.

Once he was satisfied that the blackmailer was not following him, he turned the headlights on once again and made a U-turn, being careful not to make the tires squeal as he might have normally.

Justin took a slightly different route back to Butler Street, crossing the tracks and following the streets along Madison's second-largest lake, Lake Monona. He parked a few blocks past the marshaling yards, not the safest place to leave a Jaguar, but he didn't want to risk getting any closer to Butler Street. As it was, he might already be too late.

He walked quickly, but the soles of his deck shoes squelched against the pavement, making his approach noisier than he would have liked. Trees and darkness, for the most part, kept him hidden as he cautiously approached the tavern from the alley. The cars that had parked beside him earlier were gone, replaced by two nondescript sedans. His space, too, was taken by a third car, but from this angle, he couldn't see any of the license plates.

Hidden by a large tree, Justin crouched down to take a look at the hedge. He couldn't be sure, but it looked as though the parcel was still there. He wiped his eyes with a wet sleeve and peered harder. If only he could get a little bit closer...

Something rustled behind him, but before Justin could react, he felt a sharp thwack on the back of his head. "Damn!" was all he said before he fell.

Chapter Eleven

Justin woke up several feet from where he'd fallen, behind a garbage bin, in the middle of a puddle. From the way he felt and looked, it was obvious he'd been dragged bodily to his present venue.

The rain had stopped. It was daylight, just; a gloomy, bone-numbing kind of daylight. Justin tried to glance at his watch, but lowering his eyes was sheer agony. He touched the back of his head instead. There was a lump the size of an egg, and it felt crusty to the touch with dried blood. He was, it seemed, lucky to be alive, if one could call this present state of affairs lucky.

Moaning, he forced himself to his feet. His entire body felt stiff and out of commission, like a burned-out engine left in the rain. There was no one on the street. Finally managing to glance at his watch, he saw that it was a little after six.

He staggered across the alley to the Wagon Wheel. The strip of privet hedge looked even more bedraggled in the light of day. This time, Justin didn't care who saw him. Even a second bout of unconsciousness seemed preferable to the pain of his mega-headache. He pushed the shrubbery to one side and peered over. There was a plastic bag, but it was not the one he'd left.

"Stupid idiot," he muttered to himself. He might as well have gotten a good night's sleep at home, as try to catch the blackmailer in the act.

Justin reached down and retrieved the bag. At first, he thought it was empty, but there was a stiff piece of paper in the corner. He pulled it out; it was a photograph. Alone, in the middle of the empty lot, he stood and stared until his entire body went numb.

Taken with a Polaroid, the photo was that of a woman in a wheelchair, her hair faded to a yellowish gray. Her pale blue eyes looked directly at the camera, but there was a vacant quality to them, as though she was unaware of the photograph being taken. On her lap had been propped an Italian newspaper with last month's date clearly visible. The woman, who'd once been young and ravishing, had withered almost beyond recognition. But still, Justin recognized her immediately. *She was his mother.*

Stumbling across the alley in the direction of his car, he turned the picture over. Glued on the back was a typed message: "Fifty thousand dollars in five days, same place, and you'll find out where she is." Scrawled almost indecipherably at the bottom was a postscript. "Nine thousand still outstanding for development of photo. Make sure you don't mess up next time."

Justin's breathing was shallow. His head felt as though it would crumble at any moment. He'd never felt so helpless in his life.

The feeling of impotence was followed just as quickly by rage. A white-hot, blinding fury Justin hadn't felt in years. He managed to get to the car and practically collapsed into the front seat.

Then he wept.

"I'D LIKE TO SEE YOUR BOSS." Several hours later, cleaned up and presentable, Justin was leaning across the front counter of the Cheese 'n' Deli, his face inches from the plump little woman on the other side.

He must have looked depraved. Sophie's eyes were wide with fear as she motioned toward the back. "He's in the kitchen. Do you want me to get him?"

"No, I'll go to the kitchen." The woman didn't try to stop him, and in his current state of emotion, he didn't take the time he normally would have to calm her fears.

When he stepped through the swinging doors, he found Mr. Rubinoff holding a cleaver high in the air with both hands. The broad blade whistled through the air, slicing a brisket of beef in half as though it were made of butter. Mr. Rubinoff turned to face the visitor. The blade dripped with blood.

"Mr. Coe." His weathered features registered no surprise as he set down the knife and regarded the visitor.

"Mr. Rubinoff." Justin took a step forward, a hand pressed against the photograph in his pocket. Every word he spoke clanged painfully in his head, reminding him of the serious blows he'd been dealt, both physical and emotional. "How did you find out who I was?"

"I have no idea what you are talking about."

"Don't play games with me." He kept his eyes averted from the red meat to keep from throwing up. "I should've known from the start that you were up to something."

The Gypsy picked up a rag and wiped the blood from his hands. "If it is true that I am up to something, then that makes two of us. Is that a gun you have in your pocket, Mr. Coe?"

"Hardly." Justin tossed the photograph onto the stainless-steel counter. "This was . . . delivered this morning."

Mr. Rubinoff walked over and looked at the picture. "You look very much alike, you and your mother."

"Then you do know who she is."

He handed it back with a shrug. "It was a guess, nothing more. No one could fail to notice the resemblance."

Damn. Justin had been so sure, so utterly convinced that Mr. Rubinoff would do something to give himself away. All it had to be was a twitch of the eyebrow, a flicker of the eye, some insignificant gesture that would prove Justin was on the right track.

But Mr. Rubinoff's expression remained as impassive as the slabs of raw meat on the counter. No, impassive was not the word to describe the way he looked. Sympathetic was more accurate; hardly the look one might expect from a murderer.

"What is it, Mr. Coe?" the man asked. "What is so terrible about your past that you must live your life as a constant lie, even with the people who care about you?"

Justin suspected that Mr. Rubinoff was talking about Vicky. She did care, probably too much for her own good. But she wasn't the reason for his being here. He'd come to see the Gypsy for a confrontation, a fistfight, whatever it took. He had to stop this hideous scheme before anyone else got hurt or killed. So why was he feeling like a bank robber who has suddenly discovered the bank has no money?

"I'm wrong, aren't I? You aren't the blackmailer," Justin said, his voice hoarse with defeat.

The Gypsy raised an eyebrow, then shook his head. "Blackmailer? No, Justin. Whoever it is, I am afraid, is still at large." He waved toward the photograph. "This picture, she looks...unwell. Her condition must have come as a shock to you, no?"

He dropped his gaze. "For twenty years, I thought she was dead."

"Then you must fall on your knees and thank God for returning her to you."

"I'm having trouble feeling thankful right now."

"Why do you say that? Because someone is using your mother to get to you?"

"That's part of it, and also because two people have already been murdered and the lives of four others are in danger. That's too high a price to have my mother back."

"You feel responsible for the chain letter?"

"I have reason to, believe me." Justin was surprised to find himself confiding in Mr. Rubinoff so effortlessly.

"Was it the blackmailer who struck you?"

Justin shoved both hands into his pockets. "How did you know?"

"You keep touching the back of your head and wincing. Let me take a look."

Justin had decided not to see a doctor about the injury. He'd have to lie about what happened, and that might be risky. But he turned and allowed Mr. Rubinoff to examine the lump. It was only a guess, but as a Gypsy, the man was probably well versed in the art of healing.

"It is nasty, but fortunately the blow does not appear serious." Mr. Rubinoff gestured toward a set of stairs at the rear of the kitchen. "Come into my apartment. I will clean the cut, we will have a drink, and I will tell you of my past. Then you will realize that you are not alone in your feelings of guilt."

EXCEPT FOR WEDDINGS, Vicky had never attended a formal reception. This one promised to be doubly impressive because it was hosted by the dean of the university, and Justin was the guest of honor. He'd phoned the shop the other day to invite Vicky as his date. He'd apologized for the short notice, but she hadn't minded. It meant she'd had less time to panic.

Even so, the butterflies in Vicky's stomach were outdoing themselves as she and Justin ascended the elevator in the Humanities Building at UW. She shouldn't have been surprised when Maeve Wilson was the first to notice them enter the faculty lounge. "Ah, look everyone! Our man of the hour and his lady have arrived."

Daunting in black crepe and a huge silver brooch, the large woman elbowed her way through the guests to greet them, her ever-present cigarette leaving a ribbon of smoke behind her. Vicky fought an irrational urge to duck behind Justin and hide.

"Hello, Maeve," he said, his smile tight.

"Hello, dear boy." Maeve hugged Justin and kissed the air near Vicky's cheek. "You look splendid, Vicky. Doesn't she look splendid?"

Justin's gaze swept briefly over Vicky's drop-waist dress of pale turquoise. "She's breathtaking."

Vicky was worried about Justin. Granted, she didn't know him very well, but she never would have expected him to act so strangely—quiet, distracted—at a reception in his honor. She didn't know if he was suffering from stage fright or an aversion to being the center of attention. Neither possibility seemed the least bit like him.

When Justin had arrived to pick her up, he'd kissed her and told her how lovely she looked. He'd admired her hair, pulled up with pearl combs in a Gibson-style bun. Yet Vicky had the distinct impression that, if pressed, he wouldn't have recalled the color of her dress.

Whatever the reason, Vicky knew she had no choice but to cope. This evening was an important milestone for Justin, celebrating his attainment of full professorship and his becoming head of the English faculty. It wouldn't do for him to have a shrinking violet by his side, no matter how tempted she was to shrink.

Vicky tucked her arm around her escort's and issued a dazzling smile to Maeve. "Actually, I think Justin is the one who looks splendid." It was true. Not a strand of hair was out of place, his blond beard was trimmed to a fault, and his dark blue suit was the image of tailored elegance.

"I couldn't agree more," Maeve pronounced, then clapped her hands loudly. "Attention, everyone!"

"Oh God, no," Vicky heard Justin mutter, an instant before Maeve tossed back her head and led the crowd in an overpowering contralto.

"For he's a jolly good fellow..."

It didn't take long for the names, faces and titles to blur beyond recognition. Vicky had some idea now how it felt to be a politician's wife on the hustings—shaking hands, making small talk, laughing and, at times, pretending to.

If Justin was the man of the hour, then clearly Maeve Wilson would qualify as campaign manager. She worked the crowd as if she were a veteran politician. Gesturing, posturing, she drew out her anecdotes for maximum effect. By the time the reception was half over, there was no one in the room who didn't know the story of how Maeve met Justin and got him hired.

"Let's get out of here," Justin whispered to Vicky.

A more welcome invitation she had never heard. "Aren't you supposed to make a speech or something?"

"Eventually, but I've got to escape the noise and smoke for a while." He swept her through the din and into the corridor to the elevators. A minute or so later, they were alone in his immaculate, book-filled office.

Vicky had hoped the change of scenery would help him relax, but now Justin seemed more tightly coiled than ever. He went to the large picture window, jerked the blinds open and stared out at the starry sky. In the reflection from the glass, Vicky could see him scowling.

"What is it, Justin? What's wrong?"

He shook his head. "Nothing."

"I've never seen you this way."

His hand was clenched and leaning on the glass as if he intended to smash through it. "That's not so surprising, is it?" he said. "We hardly know each other."

Warnings echoed through her mind, but Vicky deliberately ignored them as she walked up to Justin. Taking his fist in her hands, she loosened each finger, one by one. He neither resisted nor reacted. But when she released his hand, he turned and stared at her for a long while.

"Would it help to talk?" she asked.

"About what?"

"Whatever you like."

He sat down at his desk and leaned back. "I don't suppose you've ever heard of Drysdale?"

"No. Is he here tonight?"

To her chagrin, Justin chuckled. "I sincerely hope not. He's been dead for three hundred years."

"Oh," she said, her cheeks coloring.

"I didn't mean to make fun. There's no reason for you to have heard of him. Sir Thomas Drysdale was to Shakespeare what Salieri was to Mozart."

Vicky sat down and gave Justin a withering look. "Sometimes, Mr. Coe, you come dangerously close to talking like a snob. Or is that how full professors express themselves?"

He looked at Vicky as though she was the one who was being obscure. "Is that how I came across? Sorry, I didn't mean to. Anyway, Drysdale was a half-baked writer who never really amounted to anything. Only his last book enjoyed moderate success. It was about a knight who fought in the Crusades and he had a bizarre love/hate relationship with his mother, and—"

Suddenly he stopped. His face paled and he took a sharp intake of breath. "Let me think. How did it start? 'Mother, love a son's honor. Life is pain...something, something...death to all.' That's all I can remember, but I'm sure I've got it here somewhere." He rolled his chair to the wall lined floor-to-ceiling with books.

Vicky didn't understand right away why she had goose bumps, until certain words from the quotation resurfaced in her mind. They were the notes that were left behind with Theo Dalta and Eve Lomorth.

Justin pulled out a thick, black anthology. He checked the index, then leafed through the pages. "Here we are. Drysdale, Sir Thomas. Born 1580, died 1612. Produced eight volumes of stories, a book of sonnets and several plays. A contemporary of Shakespeare, his work was mediocre, notable only for its macabre preoccupation with death. Shortly after receiving a knighthood, Drysdale murdered his mother and her lover in a rage brought on by hereditary insanity. While in prison, he wrote a final book of prose that brought him marginal success. His mental state, however, deteriorated rapidly and on the night of April 13, 1612, he hanged himself.''

Vicky shivered. "How tragic. Do you suppose his writing somehow inspired the chain letter murders?"

"Could be. I think his last story is in here. I haven't looked at this book in years." Justin turned the page, and his expression turned to one of abject horror. "Good Lord...."

Vicky got up and peered over Justin's shoulder. Drysdale's story was there, and the opening lines were the same ones Justin had tried to recite.

Mother, love a son's honor. Life is pain, no justice.
Revenge, destruction, death to all.

Yanking her hands off Justin's shoulders, Vicky staggered back half a step. The quote had been underlined in black. Squiggly red lines crossed out the words, "Mother, love" and "death to all."

"I thought you said you hadn't looked at the book in years," Vicky murmured, staring at the page.

"I haven't."

"Well, somebody obviously has."

"I know." He lifted his head and looked around the office, as though the surroundings might offer some clue.

"Do you keep your office locked when you're not here?"

"Always."

"Then someone must have gotten hold of the key and—"

"That much I can figure out, Vicky!" Justin shouted, then touched the back of his head as though the increase in decibels had caused him anguish. "It's not difficult to scrounge up an office key and deface a book. What I can't figure out is why."

Vicky was suddenly reminded of Maeve's warning, and a shiver ran through her. There were only two likely explanations: either Justin was being framed . . . or he really was the chain letter killer. What prevented her from running out in terror was Justin's light, and somehow reassuring, touch on her arm.

"Let's get out of here," he said. "I've got a speech to make."

SOMEHOW THEY MANAGED to bluff their way through the rest of the evening. Justin, whose mood had been leaden to begin with, was even more morose after the incident in the office. Vicky could no longer summon her earlier display of enthusiasm. What little there had been of festive feelings was gone.

The drive to her place was strained and silent. Perhaps it would have been wiser to have taken a cab home, but she was reluctant to let Justin think that she again had suspicions about him. She felt incredibly torn; for, there was a kind and rational side to him that was hurting badly at the moment, the side she cared very much about.

Justin didn't turn into the visitors' parking lot, but drew up to the curb and left the engine running.

"You're not coming in?" Vicky asked.

"I wasn't exactly expecting an invitation." He was staring straight ahead and not looking at her.

"I think we should talk," she said. Maybe she was being crazy. The lieutenant, Mr. Rubinoff and Maeve had all tried to dissuade her from spending time with Justin. Even Rick, in his simple way, was less than impressed with her newfound friendship. But Vicky, herself, had yet to discover any reason for their misgivings about Justin. She ought to have sensed something by now, some indefinable quality that would make her skin prickle in his presence, make her wary.

She had strong positive feelings for Rick Paterson three years ago and was yet to be proven wrong about him. She felt the same unshakable certainty about Justin, though admittedly her emotions ran much deeper this time. Maybe even to the extent of clouding her perception.

"I think we should resume your earlier plan, Vicky, when you decided not to see me anymore."

"No!" Her fingers curled tightly around his arm. Even she was surprised by the intensity of her response. "Maybe that's a decision we'll both come to eventually, but first I need to know the facts."

"What facts are those?" he asked tiredly.

"Who Justin Coe really is, where he comes from."

"You saw what someone did to my book tonight," he said. "Doesn't it worry you that I might have done it?"

Her fingers relaxed their grip. "If you'd done it, you wouldn't have shown me the page. It was your reaction that worried me."

"What if I didn't remember doing it?" he said, his voice heavy with challenge.

Vicky shuddered, choosing not to accept that theory yet. "I have some brandy in the apartment. I think we could both use some."

"Didn't you hear what I said, Vicky? I might have known about that quote weeks ago! I might have—"

"No! Her anguished shout filled the car. I don't know the first thing about those kinds of problems, Justin, but you are not insane. You are not a reincarnated Drysdale. You're a brilliant, wonderful, well-adjusted man."

He had covered his face with both hands. Now he looked up. "How can you make that claim, Vicky? You don't know the first thing about me."

"I may not know the details, but I know how I feel." She curled her hand around his neck, but he pulled away sharply. Not soon enough, however. Vicky had felt the goose egg. "What happened to your head?"

"Nothing."

"Nothing! How can you say that?" She got to her knees in the cramped car and looked closer. His blond hair barely covered the wound.

"Ouch, don't touch!"

"Who did this?" she asked, no longer probing the injury, but probing her own bruised thoughts. Justin couldn't be insane; he couldn't have underlined that quote. Madmen did not whack themselves on the back of the head, no matter how disturbed they were. "Let's go inside, Justin, please, where we can talk."

"All right, I'll come in, but only if you promise not to ask about my head. I can't tell you what happened because I don't know what happened. I was hit from behind and out cold for hours."

"Can't you even tell me where it happened?"

"In a back alley outside a bar." He gave her a fiendish grin. "Would you believe I got drunk and picked a fight with two rednecks?".

Vicky laughed. "Not for a minute, but if you'll come inside, I'll try to keep my promise."

Issuing a grateful look, Justin turned the car into the parking lot, feeling as though Vicky was his one and only link to sanity.

She sat at the end of the sofa with her legs folded beneath her, while he poured the drinks. She looked like a watercolor. Dressed in pale turquoise, her fawn-colored hair coming loose at the nape, she seemed so fragile and delicate. But he was beginning to realize that, like a watercolor, her apparent simplicity was deceiving. She was a strong woman, in some ways stronger than he'd ever been.

He handed her a snifter and noticed the coconut palm beside her. "Is it my imagination or are the plants looking healthier?"

She smiled as he took a seat beside her. "It's not your imagination."

"What have you done to them?" He wasn't usually the type to engage in small talk, but tonight he needed the momentary diversion.

"Nothing," she said. "I'm happier these days, that's all, and the plants are responding to the change in environment."

"In spite of everything that's happened to you, you're happier?"

Her eyes sparkled over the rim of the glass. "I do have my reasons."

False confidence. That's what he was in grave danger of attaining with Vicky in his life. She had that effect on him. So at ease with her femininity, she made him feel invincible, fearless, the ultimate strutting male. When he was with Vicky, he felt as if he could march right out and conquer the world. Which, considering the mess his world was in, was utterly laughable.

"You wanted to talk," he said. "Where should we start?"

"You could start by telling me who you really are."

Vicky's thigh, he realized, was much too close to his. He could never communicate seriously as long as they were within touching distance. He picked up his glass and relocated to an armchair across the room. Vicky looked hurt, but said nothing.

"I'm the only son of an actress who was well-known a few decades ago. After she died..." He stopped and tried again. "After she died, I changed my name... because I found it easier to live my life as someone other than her son."

"Does anyone know your real identity?"

"Only Maeve." *And the blackmailer,* he felt like adding, but decided this was not the time to discuss it.

"How can you be sure she hasn't let it slip?"

"I know Maeve. She comes across as a gossip, but she's actually very protective of my privacy. You saw how she hovered around us all night like a great mother sheep. It drives me crazy, but she means well."

"What about the book?" Vicky had yet to take a sip of her drink. "Wouldn't it be easy for Maeve to sneak into your office and underline the passage?"

"I thought of that, but it doesn't seem possible."

"Why not?"

Again, Justin felt compelled to tell a half-truth. The whole truth was that if Maeve *had* underscored the Drysdale passage, then she was not only framing him, but had also committed murder and blackmail. That was too much for him to swallow, and too much to burden Vicky with.

"I just don't think she would do it," was all he said.

"Then who did?"

He swallowed the last of his brandy and set the glass aside. "I don't know."

"Would you like another drink?" Vicky said, a bit too quickly.

Justin stood up. "No, thanks. I'd like to stay, but I...I'm tired." Another half-truth.

Vicky's eyes dimmed for a moment, but she forced herself to smile. "I understand."

He hated what he was doing—talking to Vicky without saying a thing; wanting her so badly, yet keeping the maximum distance between them. The sooner he left, the sooner he could put an end to this miserable situation.

She walked him to the door, and so help him, he'd only meant to say good-night. But when he touched her face, Vicky's hand reached up to cover his. She stood on tiptoe, and he couldn't bring himself to refuse the plea in her eyes. Her kiss at first was tremulous, uncertain, as though she was testing him. Then the hesitation passed, and her mouth on his became incisive.

Justin didn't know why this kiss should be a turning point. Holding Vicky in his arms was heaven, but no more so than other embraces they had shared. Their conversation leading up to it had nothing to do with passion or love, yet suddenly both were uppermost in his mind.

He released her as quickly as he could, comforted in the knowledge that tomorrow he would be alone on his boat. "Thanks for coming to the reception with me, Vicky. You were terrific."

"Thanks, but if it's all the same to you, next time..."

He laughed. "I know. I can attend by myself." The invitation jumped out of his mouth before he could stop it. "I'm sailing tomorrow. Would you like to come along?"

She looked as surprised as he felt. "Will I be introduced to any more faculty members?"

"No, it'll be just you and me."

"In that case, I'd love to."

"You're not afraid?"

Vicky shook her head and grinned. "Of the water, a little. Of you, no."

He considered kissing her again, but decided not to. "We could meet for breakfast first. Where would you like to go?"

"I was planning on seeing Mr. Rubinoff in the morning," Vicky said. "Why don't we meet there?"

His growing paranoia made him wonder why she wanted to see the Gypsy on her day off, but he pushed the question to the back of his mind. Everyone, after all, was entitled to their friends and their privacy. "Is eight o'clock too early?"

"I'll see you at eight." Vicky stood on tiptoe and kissed his cheek.

He was being blackmailed and framed as a psychotic killer. His mother, who'd been dead for more than twenty years, had suddenly turned up alive. There was no reason for Justin to feel as though things were finally looking up. But when he drove home and thought about his upcoming day with Vicky, that was precisely how he felt.

Chapter Twelve

"What kind of puzzle is that?" Vicky asked Mr. Rubinoff, pointing to a square grid into which he appeared to be entering words at random.

He lifted his head from the newspaper. "It is a diagramless crossword. Wonderful mental therapy. You should try it sometime."

"No, thank you. Balancing books at the shop is enough mental therapy for me." It was only seven-thirty, half an hour before Justin was due to arrive, but Vicky wanted a few minutes alone with her friend.

"I thought you would be going home to your parents for Easter weekend," he said, refilling her coffee cup at the counter.

"I've made other plans this year. I'm staying in Madison."

She'd called her parents to let them know she was attending a reception at the university on Good Friday evening. Her mother had been absolutely delighted to learn there was a professor in Vicky's life and had immediately forgiven her absence for the entire weekend. Vicky had hung up feeling guilty; there was much more to her relationship with Justin than her mother could ever know. If one could even call it a relationship.

"And tomorrow?" Mr. Rubinoff asked. "You have somewhere to go on Easter Sunday?"

"Uh . . . actually, I'm staying at home and cooking for a friend." At least, she hoped to cook for him, if Justin accepted the invitation today. She would have preferred to have invited him days ago, but she hadn't felt comfortable in presuming too much.

In her experience, dates were planned weeks in advance or, at least, with a minimum of seven day's notice. This allowed for languorous anticipation of the event; the purchase of something new, if required; or, if the invitation had been accepted more out of obligation than desire, allowed time to think up polite ways to get out of it.

She'd never known a man like Justin who literally took each day as it came. In a way, his life-style was exciting, but Vicky doubted that her system could tolerate the tension level for long.

"I am pleased that you will not be alone," the proprietor said. "I am preparing Easter dinner at the Ridgeway nursing home, a feast of roast suckling pig. If your plans change, do feel free to come join us."

"Thank you, I will," she replied without enthusiasm, preferring not to dwell on the possibility that Justin might refuse. "Mr. Rubinoff, have you ever heard of the English writer, Thomas Drysdale?"

The old man thought for a while. "I have heard the name, but I cannot say that I am familiar with his work. Why do you ask?"

"Drysdale's writing has something to do with the chain letter. Justin discovered it last night," she hedged. There was no reason for Rubinoff to know the full extent of the discovery.

Her friend poured himself a coffee and pulled out a battered portfolio from underneath the cash register. "Come, let us sit where it is quieter, and you can tell me what you have learned." He motioned for Sophie to watch the till.

"I'm not sure I can remember the entire quote, but it's the first few lines from his last story. 'Mother, love a son's honor. Life is pain..."'" Sitting at the table, she tried to continue, but her mind drew a total blank.

"'No justice. Revenge, destruction, death to all.'" Justin's voice finished the quotation.

Startled, Vicky whirled around in her seat. "I didn't hear you come in."

He looked at her curiously. "It's no wonder. Good morning, Mr. Rubinoff."

The Gypsy, to Vicky's amazement, grinned heartily. "Good morning, Justin. Lovely day, no?"

"Yes, it's not too windy. Perfect for sailing." He sat down between them, dapper in dark slacks, a blue shirt and a pair of leather topsiders.

There was no reason for Vicky to feel guilty that she'd been reciting Drysdale to Mr. Rubinoff. She hadn't divulged the underscoring nor had she intended to. But she did feel like a gossip, not to mention confused that the two men were now chatting like long-lost friends.

"You are going sailing with Justin?" Mr. Rubinoff asked. "Why did you not tell me?"

She could feel her face flood with color. "Because I didn't think—"

"He must be the one for whom you are cooking Easter dinner, no?" he pressed on, with a wink and a nudge in Justin's direction.

Vicky cast a quick glance at the blond man beside her; he was grinning like the proverbial Cheshire cat. "I hadn't actually mentioned it yet, Mr. Rubinoff."

"Were you going to invite me for Easter dinner?" Justin asked, his voice inordinately cheery.

"Well, uh, I was considering it. If you weren't busy, that is...but I'm sure you must have made other plans."

"Not really. I usually spend Easter weekend on the boat with a store of corned beef hash and cookies. But Easter dinner at your place sounds much better."

His enthusiasm set Vicky's senses soaring and nudged her self-confidence a few notches higher. "That's wonderful," she said.

Mr. Rubinoff sat back and folded his hands across an ample stomach. "It certainly is," the Gypsy agreed.

STANDING ON THE DECK of the *Che Sera*, Justin took Vicky's hand and helped her aboard. The boat bobbed gently in the slip as he pointed out the location of the life preservers and other emergency equipment. "Not that we're going to need them," he added, in deference to her increasing pallor.

She smiled bravely. "I know that."

Justin took a seat in the stern and turned on the motor, easing the craft slowly out of Spring Harbor.

Vicky listened to the purring engine and looked up at the high bare mast. "Don't sailboats use sails anymore?"

He laughed. "Don't worry. Once we're out of the harbor, I'll set the sails."

As Justin calmly steered the boat, it seemed to Vicky that he was an integral part of the craft, a streamlined, muscled extension of the hull and the rigging. White-blond hair ruffled in the breeze, his eyes protected from the dazzling sun by gold-rimmed dark glasses.

When they reached the open waters of Lake Mendota, Justin turned off the motor. The sudden silence and the lapping of waves against the boat caused Vicky to check once more for her life jacket.

Her nervousness was soon forgotten, however, as she watched Justin hoist the mainsail and set the jib. Justin was good about explaining what he was doing and why, even though most of the nautical terminology was lost on Vicky.

As the wind filled the sails and the boat began to move, Vicky's heart tripped with excitement and anticipation. Even to the untrained eye, the *Che Sera* was a magnificent boat, the lines of her freshly painted hull sleek, her blue-and-white sails dazzling.

"This is fabulous," Vicky exclaimed, lifting her head to the sky and letting the breeze catch her hair.

Justin smiled, his eyes carefully scanning the rigging. Then he sat back, his forearm firmly on the tiller. "This is a good time and place for us to talk, Vicky. The wind isn't too strong and it's smooth sailing. And we won't have to worry about being disturbed."

"We talked last night," she said, her fingers tapping the hull. So far, nearly every occasion they'd been together had been marred by some incident of reference to the chain letter. Feeling more secure in Justin's company with each passing hour, she was loath to tamper with the feeling.

"Last night, I told you nothing but a few sketchy details. I didn't want to alarm you and then leave you alone for the night."

Vicky stretched her arm out across the frigid water. "You don't think I'll be alarmed out here?" she teased. "If I decide I've heard enough, my only way home is to swim."

"I'm serious, Vicky."

"All right. Tell me whatever it is you have to say."

First he checked the sails, then moved the tiller slightly. "Last night I told you my mother was an actress. Have you ever heard of Maija Justason?"

"Sure, she was popular in the fifties. I remember Mom used to love her movies."

"I was her only child. Friends say there's quite a strong family resemblance."

Vicky tried to see the resemblance for herself, but compared to the vibrant presence of the man across from her, her mental picture of Maija Justason was vague. Granted, they were both light blond, both good-looking, but more than that, she couldn't be sure of. "Wasn't there some tragedy or scandal associated with your mother's death?" she asked.

"Not as much as there could have been. The official press release reported that my mother died of an accidental overdose of sleeping pills."

"You're saying it wasn't suicide?"

"It wasn't suicide, and the drugs were definitely not sleeping pills. Her adoring public wouldn't have liked knowing their idol was a junkie."

"So you've wanted to protect her image all these years. I think that's admirable."

"There's more to it than that, Vicky. When the body of her Italian lover washed up on the beach the next day, some romantics were calling it a star-crossed suicide pact. What it really was, was murder."

Vicky felt as if someone had kicked her below the rib cage. Justin's mother, her lover—both dead, exactly what had happened to Sir Thomas Drysdale. "Did you kill them?" she asked, trying to quell a sudden onslaught of motion sickness.

"No, I didn't kill anyone, but I did disappear, and the Italian police took that to mean I was guilty of murdering Mom's boyfriend. There is still an outstanding warrant for my arrest."

"Even after all these years?"

"There's no statute of limitations on murder."

"Why didn't you turn yourself in right away?"

"I should have, but I was only fifteen at the time and terrified. I hoped the press would ease off so I could clear my name. But the rumors kept growing about my disappearance, and there never seemed to be a right time to come forward. Eventually, it was easier to continue living a life as Justin Coe."

As the boat angled into the wind, Justin pushed the tiller sharply to one side, warning Vicky to watch her head and deftly ducking as the boom swung to the other side. Once they were safely on the starboard tack, Justin calmly reached behind and brought out a can of soda for each of them.

Vicky had watched the sailing maneuver with awe. She felt as though she could learn as much about Justin watching him sail as she could by listening. Handling a thirty-foot sloop on one's own, she imagined, would require a fierce streak of self-reliance. If the sailor didn't assess the winds correctly and took the wrong course of action, he could blame nobody but himself. Vicky sensed this same attitude in the way Justin lived his life. She admired him for it.

"What's your real name?" she asked.

"Michael. Michael Justason."

She repeated the name aloud, trying the feel of it on her tongue. But although Michael was a nice name, it bore no relevance to the man she was getting to know. "I can understand now why you're so uncomfortable with the police."

He stretched out his long lean legs. "It's a habit I've never been able to break after years of looking over my shoulder."

"And now, after all this time, someone's trying to frame you," Vicky observed sadly.

Justin stiffened for an instant. "Oh, you mean the Drysdale quote. If that's what someone's trying to do, it's a stupid way to go about it. I intend to hand the book over to Lieutenant Simmons as soon as I get a chance."

"You're not worried he'll discover who you are?"

"Not especially. I've covered my tracks, so there's no reason for the past to come up. Unless of course, I end up being arrested for the chain letter killings." There was irony in his remark, but very little humor. Vicky sensed that while there was much more to his story, details as yet not filled in, enough had been said for now. Justin was opening up to her bit by fascinating bit. She could wait. Would wait till he was ready....

LATE THAT AFTERNOON, after they'd returned the *Che Sara* to her mooring in Spring Harbor, Justin and Vicky went out to buy groceries for Easter dinner. As they pushed the shopping cart through crowded aisles, Vicky babbled excitedly about their day on the boat. The wind had picked up around noon, but by then Vicky felt confident enough to try holding the tiller—with Justin sitting close by. He was a wonderful instructor—kind, patient and well seasoned. Vicky's only regret was that the day had come to an end so quickly.

The shopping done, Justin dropped Vicky off at her apartment with a kiss and a promise that he would be there the next day. Then he drove to his office in the Humanities Building where he called Lieutenant Simmons.

The policeman wasted no time in coming to the office. Justin felt the same knot in his gut whenever he was in the presence of the law, but was slowly growing accustomed to the feeling.

"Let's take a look at this book of yours," the rumpled lieutenant said.

Justin lifted the heavy anthology from the shelf and placed it on the desk. After checking the index, he leafed through the book until he came to the appropriate section. At first, he thought there must be some mistake. He flipped through the pages, but there were no underlined passages. In fact, the pages weren't there at all.

"Something wrong, Mr. Coe?"

"They've been cut out with a razor."

"Where? Lemme see." The lieutenant turned the gooseneck lamp around to give them better light. "Are you sure it's the same book?"

Justin checked. "It's mine, all right. There's my name scrawled across the inside cover."

"Any idea who could have done it?"

There were a few obvious possibilities but, without proof, Justin was reluctant to name them. "No idea at all," he said.

The lieutenant brought out his notepad. "Oh, well, I'll write down the quotation anyway—if you remember the words." He paused and added, "Looks like the killer must know a thing or two about literature."

"Yes." Justin's reply was hollow. He recited the quotation as the officer wrote it down.

"Tell me again how it was marked."

"The entire quote was underscored in black. 'Mother, love' and 'death to all' were crossed out in red."

"Someone was using your book to keep score, huh?" Lieutenant Simmons put away the notepad and began rummaging through Justin's trash can.

"It would appear so." There was nothing in the trash can. Justin didn't expect there would be.

"Did anyone else see the underlined passages?"

"Yes, Vicky saw them. She was here last night when I first thought of looking up Drysdale."

"By Vicky, I assume you mean Miss Green?"

"That's right."

The officer sighed with the sound of someone who's just had his time wasted. "And I suppose she'd verify your statement that the pages were really there."

"I'm sure she would."

"Okay, Mr. Coe, thanks for getting in touch. Someone's either pulling a nasty prank or setting you up. You ought to remember to keep your office locked when you're not in it."

Justin swallowed the rising bile in his throat. If this was a prank, then so was the photograph of his aging mother. And so was Theo Dalta's death . . . and Eve's. But since he'd succeeded only in making a total ass of himself in front of the lieutenant, there was very little he could say.

"I am curious about one thing, Mr. Coe."

"What's that?"

"What made you think of looking up this writer anyhow?"

Justin shrugged. "The phrases sounded familiar. After a while, I remembered the source, that's all."

Lieutenant Simmons regarded him a moment, then headed for the door. "I figured it must be something like that. Okay, Mr. Coe. I'll be in touch. Incidentally, if I were you, I wouldn't think about leaving town for a while."

VICKY TURNED THE RADIO to a country station while she made the stuffing and prepared Cornish game hens for the next day's meal. Ever since she'd gotten the chain letter, Vicky had found total silence discomfiting and preferred the reassurance of background music.

Country music suited her mood—heartrending, tear-jerking, obsessed with the perils of falling in love. And to-night, Vicky was convinced that, in spite of everything, she was falling in love.

If not for Justin, she would never have made it through these past few weeks. He was her island. He'd kept her from drowning in helpless, irrational fear. He'd kept her from abandoning her responsibilities. He'd kept her sane. Justin had even helped her forget that her fourteen days were up.

And it wasn't as though they had to be together every minute. That was what pleased Vicky most. Justin, by his very nature, inspired and encouraged her independence. Knowing that he was a phone call away, or that they would see each other soon, was enough to keep her feeling secure and protected.

That night, she calmly went to bed after ensuring the door and the windows were locked. The only additional security measure was the spare pillow, and she only clung to it because she wished the pillow were Justin.

The next morning a loud and insistent knocking on her door jolted her out of a sound sleep. Vicky sat up, annoyed with herself for oversleeping. She'd intended to have a lei-surely morning bath, wear something appealing and take time to fix her hair. Now Justin would have to make do with the natural Vicky Green.

She opened the door, but Justin wasn't there; nobody was. Looking down, she saw a parcel on the floor, wrapped in white tissue paper and tied with a big pink bow.

"Isn't that lovely," Vicky exclaimed and brought the package inside.

A preprinted card attached to the package read, "With lots of love from the Easter Bunny." It couldn't have come from her parents. They hadn't given her anything for Easter in years. It had to be from Justin. Due to arrive soon, he was probably waiting just outside until she opened the gift. He was really such a thoughtful man.

Vicky knew the polite thing to do would be to wait until Justin arrived before opening the gift. But he had delivered it as a surprise, so why wait?

She tore open the paper. Chocolates! And not just any chocolates, but two pounds of the expensive Finnish variety from the Cheese 'n' Deli. Maybe they were from Mr. Rubinoff, she decided instead. Either way, it was a lovely gesture.

Vicky glanced at the clock on the kitchen wall and realized she hadn't really overslept. It was barely eight-thirty. No one ate chocolates this early in the day. But it was Easter, and even her parents used to make an exception about candy on Easter morning.

She lifted the lid. Her eyes widened as she stared delightedly at the mouth-watering variety. The dark round chocolate with the swirl on top looked like a kirsch cherry, her absolute favorite. But even if it wasn't, she could always try another.

Vicky popped the entire confection into her mouth at once, moaning with ecstasy at the texture and flavor. It *was* a kirsch cherry. Never had she tasted one so decadently rich and sweet and . . .

Suddenly, Vicky clutched at her throat, confused by the pain searing through her body. As she fell to the floor, she tried to scream. No sounds came out. An instant later, everything was black.

Chapter Thirteen

"I've already told you! I got there early because I couldn't wait to see her! Haven't you ever felt that way about anyone?" a man's exasperated voice said.

"Not for some time," muttered a second man. "What about when you— Hey, look she's coming to."

Vicky opened her eyes. Everything was white. The walls, the ceiling and the man whose face was floating over hers. Then Vicky realized his skin wasn't exactly white, but ashen. His hair wasn't white, but a fine snow-blond; his neatly trimmed beard, a shade or two darker. His eyes were the color of blue mist, misty because... because why?

Her muddled mind cleared briefly. It was Justin looking down at her, and his eyes were misty because he was upset.

She tried to touch him, but something—a strap—held her arm captive. She tried to speak, but plastic tubes gagged her. Vicky's throat hurt abominably; her stomach was on fire. *What in the love of God had happened?*

"Shh, it's all right, darling." Justin's head hovered over hers; his voice was a hoarse whisper. "You're going to be fine. All you need is rest."

Rest? From what? What was wrong with her?

A second apparition in white appeared on the other side of the bed. "Hello, Vicky. I'm Dr. Hayes. You're at Bradley Hospital. Justin brought you here this morning."

Moving her eyes from one side to another was like crawling across broken glass. She turned to Justin, trying to understand.

"They pumped your stomach, Vicky. That's why you're feeling so awful." His tone of voice made her feel uneasy, as if he were purposely evading some horrible truth.

"We're quite certain no permanent damage was done, but we're going to keep you here overnight just to be on the safe side." This was the doctor talking. She wanted to scream at them to stop playing verbal Ping-Pong. Her head hurt as she tried to keep up with them. The doctor motioned to someone across the room. "You can talk to her now, but only for five minutes. I don't want you to tire her out. Nurse Johnston will be keeping an eye on you."

"Not to worry, Doc." The voice materialized in the form of a plaid shirt and green sports coat. Dr. Hayes faded into the white background. "How ya doing, Miss Green? I was sorry to hear about your accident."

Why did the lieutenant have to be here? Couldn't he just stay out of her life once in a while? Vicky checked to be sure Justin was still there; he was. He looked haggard and weary, but at least he was there.

"How about leaving the two of us alone to talk?" the lieutenant said to Justin.

"I'm not leaving. Besides, she can't talk."

"This is official police business."

Justin looked down at Vicky. "Do you want me to stay?"

A simple nod was all she could manage. But at least Justin understood.

"She wants me to stay," he said, "so I'm staying."

The officer rolled his basset hound eyes and leaned against the bedrails. "Okay, we've only got five minutes, so better get to it. First of all, Miss Green, the lab has confirmed the presence of a toxic substance in those chocolates. Lucky for you Justin came along when he did. He found you on the kitchen floor and rushed you here to emergency. Do you remember getting the candy?"

Toxic substance? Justin found her? She tried to answer, but all she managed was a painful little squeak.

"Would you stop trying to make her talk, for God's sake?" Justin snapped. "She can't!"

"Okay, okay!" The lieutenant held up his hands. "How about I ask yes or no questions? Just nod for yes, shake for no. If you get too tired, shut your eyes, and I'll come back later."

Vicky nodded.

"Good. Now, did the chocolates arrive today?"

She nodded.

"Did someone hand them to you?"

A shake.

"They were left at the door?" When she responded in the affirmative, he wrote something down. "Okay, now I'd like to know what time they arrived. Show me on your fingers what hour it was."

Concentrating hard, Vicky opened all the fingers of her right hand and three on her left with the fourth finger bent at the knuckle.

"Good for you, Vicky." Justin gave her shoulder a reassuring squeeze. "She's saying it was eight and a half. Eight-thirty."

The lieutenant nodded. "Eight-thirty. Must have been a.m., since it's only four p.m. now." When he'd finished scribbling, he looked up again. "Do you have any idea where the chocolates might have come from?"

Vicky stared a moment, then shook her head.

"What an idiotic question, lieutenant!" Justin cut in, echoing Vicky's own sentiments. "People don't have a list of enemies they can refer to when someone tries to poison them."

"I wasn't talking about who. I meant *where* did they come from? They were not your run-of-the-mill bonbons."

The two men glared at each other across the bed, totally unalike in appearance except for the matching set of their stubborn jaws.

Justin looked at Vicky. "Do you have any idea where they came from?"

Heaven knew, she wanted to lie. She wanted to tell the lieutenant she'd never seen candies like that before; but the truth was, she'd seen them in only one place in Madison. A place that prided itself on carrying unique imported foods.

"Please tell us, Miss Green. Someone tried to kill you. You shouldn't feel obligated to protect anyone."

"He's right," Justin said with a sigh. "You have to tell him what you know."

There was no way to convey her answer by a head movement, so she tried to form the word with her mouth. Her lips were parched and swollen; her brain took a long time to relay the message. "Ru . . . bin . . . off's."

Lieutenant Simmons cocked his ear in her direction. "What was that again?"

Justin came to her assistance. "She said Rubinoff's. That's the Cheese 'n' Deli on Hamilton Street."

"Oh, yeah, I know the place."

Nurse Johnston stood up, starched and proper. "Your five minutes are up, lieutenant."

He looked as though he was about to argue, and then thought better of it. She did not look like the kind of nurse one argued with.

"Okay, I'll let you get some rest. Listen, I've assigned two uniformed officers to the hall outside. They'll be here until you're discharged. The FBI is treating this case as attempted murder, so we've got a lot of heavy brass behind us. If you need me for anything, Miss Green, just shout." Then he rearranged his jowls in an expression of sympathy. "On second thought, don't shout. Ring for the nurse. You coming, Coe?"

Ignoring the lieutenant's invitation, Justin turned appealing blue eyes to Nurse Johnston. "Could I spend two minutes alone with Vicky, please?"

Vicky did her best to look awake and alert even though she was dying to shut her eyes. She didn't want Justin to leave.

The nurse tapped her foot and ruminated. "We-ell, all right, but only two minutes!"

Lieutenant Simmons scowled at Justin. "And I'll see you at the station in one hour."

"I'll be there." Justin said, mimicking his officious tone.

When he was alone with Vicky, Justin folded his hands around hers. "Darling, you can't imagine how relieved I was when I saw those beautiful hazel eyes looking up at me."

She nodded.

"We'll talk more when you get home, but I just want you to know that I...care for you very much. And I'm not going to let anything happen to you...ever."

Like bits of debris in a rain-swollen river, things started coming back to her. The chain letter; somebody's funeral; the way Justin's hair ruffled on the sailboat. And something else. He was in—she had to force her brain to work—some kind of trouble. Or had she merely dreamed the argument between Justin and the lieutenant in the hospital room?

She honestly didn't know. But later, when her mind cleared, she might be able to make sense of it. Now, all she wanted was sleep.

"I'll come and visit this evening," was the last thing Vicky heard Justin say before she drifted off.

WITH A CURSORY NOD to the two policemen, Justin strode through the corridors in search of a public telephone. He couldn't keep up this pretense any longer, not after what had happened to Vicky. It was time he came clean about his past—to hell with the consequences—and he wasn't going to wait for Lieutenant Simmons to haul him in.

What was the worst that could happen if he confessed? A sleazy front-page trial? A life sentence spent in some grimy Italian prison? At least it would put an end to the murder and the blackmail going on now. At least it would keep Vicky from being hurt any more than she already had been.

He phoned the operator and requested the number for the FBI. The Bureau had the connections and the jurisdiction; he might as well start there.

THE NEXT DAY, Monday, Vicky was packing the overnight bag Justin had brought over from her apartment when the lieutenant came in. "Good morning, Miss Green. I'm here to take you home."

"That's very kind of you, but Justin's coming to pick me up."

The lieutenant ran a finger across his nostrils. "Well, actually, I talked to him this morning. There's been a slight change of plans."

Vicky's heart stopped. "What happened? Is something wrong?"

"Nope, nothing's wrong, but I wanted an opportunity to discuss a few things with you and figured this was as good a time as any." Vicky hadn't noticed that the lieutenant's other hand was behind his back until he brought out a bunch of slightly wilted carnations. "These are for you."

She couldn't have been more surprised if he'd pulled out a cane and begun to tap dance. "How sweet of you. I've never gotten flowers from a policeman before."

His complexion turned ruddy, and he almost smiled. "First time for everything, huh? There's a wheelchair out in the hall. Are you ready to go?"

"Yes, I'll carry the flowers in my lap, and those over by the window, too."

Vicky had considered abandoning the ones by the window, but decided it wouldn't be very considerate of the next patient. Maeve Wilson had sent a huge, gaudy arrangement of gladioli that were more appropriate to a gangster funeral than a hospital room. On the card she'd written, "Get well soon, my dear, and do try to be more careful next time."

Vicky felt weak, but much better than she had the day before. The rawness in her throat was easing, and her stomach felt only a little bit nauseated. The doctor had ordered several days of bed rest and was optimistic that she would make a full recovery.

"I talked to the powers that be about getting you full-time protection," the lieutenant told her in the squad car. "But unfortunately our budget won't allow it."

Vicky had deliberately postponed reflecting on what life would be like when she was at home. Nor had she thought much about the attempt on her life. It was simply too horrifying to acknowledge that someone wanted to kill her. But she also knew that someone—and it might as well be the lieutenant—had to open her eyes to reality. She had to go on living a normal life. She couldn't hide in her apartment indefinitely; she couldn't ignore her business—the Nick Nack Nook.

"What should I do, lieutenant?" she asked in a quavering voice.

"Do you have any friends you could stay with for a while?"

She had friends—girlfriends from college days, business acquaintances, neighbors—but they had their own obligations, their own problems. She couldn't go into their homes and subject them to the danger she was facing.

"I'd prefer to continue living on my own," she answered.

Lieutenant Simmons glanced at her with concern as he wheeled the car around the corner. "It's up to you. I've talked to the officers who patrol your area, and they'll be keeping an eye open for any unusual activity around your building."

"Thank you."

The lieutenant pulled up to her apartment and helped her out of the car. "I'll get you settled inside, and then I'm going to make a few inquiries about the security in your building. I might be able to come up with a suggestion or two—such as other occupants in your building making a point of locking the main doors.''

Vicky nodded. That was, she supposed, better than nothing.

Lieutenant Simmons fixed her some tea while she rested on the sofa, then he went out to talk to the building manager, returning a few minutes later. ''The super knows you're home. He says he'll try to see that the front doors stay locked—he'll tell the other tenants. He'll also be dropping around now and then to make sure you're okay. Mind if I take a look around?''

She waved a tired hand through the air. ''Be my guest.'' Her head was throbbing, and she hoped all these part-time bodyguards would be considerate enough to let her get some rest during the next few days.

Lieutenant Simmons came out of the bedroom and went to the door to her apartment. ''The lock's okay out here, but you could use some extra precautions with your windows. You're only one floor up, and the way your windows are set up now, a person could lift them right out of the track and crawl in.''

Fear coiled in Vicky's stomach. ''What do you suggest?''

''There are special nails you can insert into the window track so no one can budge the windows from the outside.''

''Where do I find them?''

''Don't worry, I'll take care of it. I'll get a peephole for your front door while I'm at it. The important thing is never to open your door to strangers. Got that?''

She pressed her fingers to throbbing temples. ''Got it.''

''And if anything happens, day or night, call the station. I've got a beeper. They'll page me.''

''Okay, thanks, lieutenant.''

He went to the door. ''One more thing, Miss Green.''

''Yes?''

''Take care of yourself.''

Neither of them had noticed the dark brown sedan following Lieutenant Simmons from the hospital. It was now parked in a driveway half a block from Vicky's apartment building, and near enough that both passengers could clearly see the lieutenant drive away.

AFTER HER NAP, Vicky felt much better. She watered her plants and wandered through the apartment, testing the mettle of her emotions. Would she be able to live with the solitude? Would the silence eventually overwhelm her? So far, it seemed she was able to cope.

It wasn't like a robbery in which the sanctity of her apartment had been violated. There were no reminders of the incident, no rifled drawers, no muddy footprints. Despite what had happened, the place still felt like a refuge; it still felt like home.

The next question was whether or not she could face the outside world. Taking buses, buying groceries, chatting with salesclerks and tellers. Suddenly, daily life seemed so intimidating and complex. Vicky had never realized how tightly a person was bound to the rest of society. And to think, one of the members of that society had tried to...

But *that* was something she was not ready to think about. One step at a time was the only way to handle it. First, she would concentrate on conquering the neighborhood. Thank heaven she didn't have to worry about the shop. It was closed on Easter Monday as a rule, and Rick could handle things for the week.

Vicky inched open the draperies on the living-room window and peered out. People were strolling and cycling along the lakeshore. Cars drove by with the windows rolled down. Everyone was enjoying the tranquillity of a spring afternoon.

Vicky ignored the knot of apprehension in her stomach. She stepped into a pair of loafers, threw on a light jacket and quietly let herself out of the apartment. The hall was deserted, as was the stairwell. It took less than a minute to reach the double glass doors in front. Vicky remembered to lock them behind her.

The air was cooler outside than in. Vicky was glad she'd thought to take a jacket. The ordeal had probably lowered her resistance, and the last thing she needed was a head cold.

She stood for a moment at the corner of Gorham and Livingston, trying to decide how far she should walk. The doctor had warned her against overexertion, and she was already beginning to feel fatigued. But a couple of blocks would do her good. It shouldn't be difficult to walk only as far as Blair Street and back.

At first, every time Vicky heard footsteps behind her, she froze. She would stop and she would wait, feeling like a fool when a pedestrian walked past her without a second glance. But by the time she reached the first corner, she could feel her courage begin to take hold again.

Traffic posed a similar problem. Whenever vehicles slowed for an amber light, she got the feeling they were watching her. Several drivers made eye contact, and it was all she could do not to dive into the shrubbery. But then she remembered that men in cars often looked at women they passed. No matter that Vicky was certain she appeared less than spectacular, especially today, she thought with a self-deprecating chuckle.

The corner of Blair and Gorham was only two blocks away, but by the time Vicky reached it, she felt as if she'd completed a lifelong pilgrimage. After what she'd been through, it was probably to be expected. Tomorrow would be easier, she told herself, and the day after that, easier still.

Halfway home, Vicky heard another car slow down behind her. This time she didn't bother to look over her shoulder. Then she heard a voice call out, "What are you doing out here? Shouldn't you be in bed?"

Her body went rigid. She couldn't have run if she'd wanted to. But then her rational mind nudged away the panic, and she turned to find Justin grinning at her through the windshield of his Jaguar.

He looked different. Vicky pushed the hair away from her eyes to see better. "I needed fresh air," she replied.

"But you ought to be resting," he said, craning his head out the driver's window.

"I've been resting all day. I couldn't stand it anymore."

He drove a few feet closer and leaned across to the passenger side. "Sorry I couldn't pick you up from the hospital. The lieutenant insisted on doing it himself."

It was the beard. Justin had shaved it off! He looked marvelous. Younger, handsomer than ever. "What happened to your face?" she teased.

He stroked his smooth chin. "Like it? This is my new image."

"I love it." Careful, Vicky thought. Love was not a word to be bandied about in the presence of this man. Not yet, anyway. "I mean, it's very nice."

"I'd like to come around and see you this evening, if you think you'll be up to company."

Vicky wasn't sure. After only a short walk, her legs were wobbly and her head ached abominably. She leaned against a mailbox and shoved both hands into her pockets so Justin wouldn't notice they were trembling. But all she really needed was a bit more rest. Surely, by this evening, she'd be feeling better.

"I'd be delighted to see you," she said. "Come over anytime."

Justin looked at her quizzically as if he wasn't totally convinced by her blithe display of good health. "Okay, I'll see you around seven. Do you want a lift the rest of the way?"

By now, her forehead was sweating profusely. Vicky tried to estimate the distance between her and Justin's car. It wasn't far, but she honestly wasn't certain she could make it without him knowing she was feeling awful.

"Don't be silly," Vicky insisted. "I'm less than a block from home." If Justin didn't leave soon, she was going to throw up on the sidewalk. Somehow she managed a meager wave. "See you later."

He lingered at first, still uncertain, then returned her wave. "Call me if you need anything."

As Justin sped off, Vicky saw him watching her through the rearview mirror. When he was finally out of sight, she pushed herself from the mailbox and staggered the short distance home.

THE MAN SAT at the kitchen table, papers spread out before him. On one side was a chart with the seven names and the dates they were first contacted. On the other side of the table were carbon copies of the letters he'd sent.

People were not cooperating the way they were supposed to. He couldn't understand it; he'd been so meticulous about choosing them. Maybe he'd been wrong to list their names in random order. He should have followed the order dictated by quote, despite the greater risk of being found out.

It wasn't as though he'd asked too much of these people. A few dollars, a few minutes of their time—all for a good cause. But most of them had ignored him, despite the fact that he'd proven three times how serious he was.

Although, to be perfectly accurate, the third time didn't count. He'd miscalculated with V. E. Green, not putting enough poison into each candy. He should have realized she wouldn't get a chance to eat a second chocolate.

Mama had accused him of going soft. Maybe she was right as usual. He would have preferred not to hurt Vicky. He would have preferred not to have her on the list at all, but he had no choice. She was the only one who fit. And, as Mama used to say, if you are going to do something, do it right, or not at all.

The man smiled to himself. What would Mama say, he wondered, if she realized how thoroughly he was following her advice? In the center of the table was a pile of letters cut from magazines. He worked quickly, hoping to be finished before Mama came back. He didn't know where she was, but lately she'd been disappearing for hours at a time. That was probably a good sign.

He checked the list once more to be sure. Yes, it was definitely number five's turn; his fourteen days were up. No more reminders. From the pile, he picked out letters that would spell Sean Filipi.

Then he reread the quotation, to make sure there were no mistakes. But he needn't have worried. He'd been over the quote a thousand times, not to mention the thousand times he'd gone through the phone book.

Onto a clean sheet of white bond, he applied a strip of glue. Then, rearranging the letters from Sean Filipi's name, he composed the note: Life is pain.

Chapter Fourteen

A few minutes before seven, Vicky dragged herself out of bed, groggily exchanging her nightgown for a cotton caftan. She would have preferred to be properly dressed, but it seemed extravagant to waste what little energy she had battling buttons and zippers.

The bathroom mirror was brutal in its honesty. Vicky's complexion, pale at the best of times, was a startling yellowish gray. Cavernous circles ringed her eyes, and her hair, though clean, hung drab and lifeless to her shoulders.

The doorbell rang just as Vicky was trying to decide whether to call Justin and cancel the visit. She pinched her cheeks to bring some color to them and practiced a smile in the mirror. Maybe she didn't look all that bad, as long as she kept the lights low. She did, however, still have to negotiate the stairs to let him in the main door. Safety precautions had their price, she thought ruefully.

To her surprise, there were two people at the door—Justin, clean shaven, and Mr. Rubinoff with a saucepan in his arms, both wearing equally anxious expressions.

Vicky stared at them in amazement. "Did you two bump into each other outside?"

"We came together," Justin replied.

"He drove," Mr. Rubinoff added, "like a maniac."

A pleasurable warmth bubbled through her at the sight of them. "I could've told you that. Come in."

"You look like a ghost," Mr. Rubinoff observed bluntly when they were inside her apartment. "Have you had dinner?"

"I boiled an egg for lunch," she admitted, "but by the time it was ready, I'd lost my appetite."

"Then you must eat now. Where is the kitchen? This way?"

Justin winked at Vicky as they followed the Gypsy. "He brought homemade chicken soup. I had some at the deli. It's great."

Though she wasn't feeling up to it, Vicky made an effort to help Mr. Rubinoff. But he steered her firmly by the shoulders and sat her down. "You rest. I cook." Then he gestured autocratically to Justin. "You set the table."

With an obedient nod, Justin set about finding a bowl and spoon. He looked over his shoulder at Vicky. "Would you like milk or tea?"

"She will have only soup for now," Mr. Rubinoff answered on her behalf. "She may have weak tea later, perhaps."

Vicky enjoyed the steaming chicken broth with tiny egg noodles. Mr. Rubinoff sat across from her and watched her eat, lest she be tempted to leave some. But she was ravenous and finished it off without being prompted.

The soup worked wonders. By the time they gathered in the living room, Vicky was feeling much stronger. And since her color had improved so markedly, Mr. Rubinoff brewed a pot of weak tea and brought it in on a tray. Justin poured a cup for each of them, took one sip and grimaced, leaving the rest of his untouched.

"I'm so pleased to see both of you here," Vicky said, curled up at one end of the sofa with Justin beside her. Mr. Rubinoff was in an armchair, which threatened to be overtaken by Maeve's gladiola arrangement.

"It is entirely my fault, Victoria, that Justin and I did not become friends sooner. I can be a stubborn, suspicious old man, at times."

Vicky grinned. "Now where did you ever get an idea like that?"

He spread out his hands. "It's true, I'm afraid."

"I went to see Mr. Rubinoff last night after leaving the hospital," Justin said. "It occurred to me that maybe no one had told him what happened, and I felt he should know."

Vicky swallowed the rising lump in her throat. "That was thoughtful of you, Justin."

"It was," Mr. Rubinoff agreed, leaning forward with elbows on his knees. "I had actually heard the news earlier, but from the FBI. Less than ideal circumstances."

Recalling the admission she'd been obliged to make in the hospital bed, Vicky covered her face. "I'm sorry. It's all my fault."

"No, no. Do not apologize, Victoria. I am as anxious as you for this case to be solved. The police were right to come and talk to me because, you see, I am the one who sold that box of chocolates."

Floundering with guilt and relief, Vicky glanced at Justin. Devoid of whiskers, he conveyed strength in the square cut of his jaw. He looked at Vicky, reached for her hand, and somehow she felt she could draw from his strength.

"Do you feel well enough to hear about it?" Justin asked.

"I think so," she said, turning to Mr. Rubinoff. "When did this happen?"

"A few days ago. A man with filthy clothes, reeking of cheap wine, came into the deli."

"Did you recognize him?"

"No, I had never seen him before, but I assumed he came from the Square, where the unfortunates congregate. I was about to pour him some coffee—it's what they always ask for—when he placed a fifty-dollar bill on the counter and asked for a box of my finest chocolates."

"Weren't you suspicious at the sight of that much money?" Justin asked.

"Certainly. I checked to be sure the bill was not counterfeit, and then casually asked the man what he intended to do with the chocolates. Of course, there was no reason for me to connect the incident with Victoria."

"Wh-what did he say when you asked him?" Vicky barely managed to get the words out. The idea that a stranger—some nameless down-and-out—would want to kill her was almost beyond her comprehension.

"He said a woman approached him on the Square, asked him to buy the chocolates for her and told him to keep the change. It did not occur to me, until it was too late, to request a description of the lady who hired him."

"As soon as I called Mr. Rubinoff," Justin said, "he went out on the Square to look for the man, but couldn't find him."

"That is so," the Gypsy agreed sadly. "No one I spoke to could recall seeing him or the woman, and later when I accompanied the FBI agents, there was still no sign of him. He seems to have vanished into thin air."

Justin slammed his fist down on the armrest of the sofa. "Damned convenient, isn't it? The only link we had to the person who poisoned Vicky, and it's as though he never existed."

A woman? There was no reason for Vicky to make the association. In fact, she would have been the first to admit she was unduly prejudiced. But as soon as Mr. Rubinoff said a woman had approached the man on the Square, Vicky's gaze had moved inexorably to the large gaudy arrangement.

It couldn't be Maeve who'd killed Theo and Eve and tried to do the same to Vicky, could it? Everyone assumed the killer was a man, but couldn't everyone be wrong? She glanced from Justin to Mr. Rubinoff and back again. Neither one seemed to be struggling with the possibility. She was probably alone on this one.

The doorbell rang, and Vicky let out a small shriek. Justin was by her side at once. "It's okay, darling. Stay here, I'll go down and answer it."

She snatched a cushion from the sofa and held it tightly to her chest. The trivial things, she realized, were going to be the hardest. The doorbell, the telephone—never mind that it might be the paperboy or a wrong number—these would be the things that tinkered with her sanity. Tonight, with Mr. Rubinoff and Justin here, she was barely coping. How much worse would it be when she was alone?

Even when Rick Paterson walked into the room with Justin, Vicky was still trembling. She had been so convinced it would be Maeve.

Rick was carrying a bundle of magazines, which he placed by Vicky's feet. "These are from my sister," he said. "They're ladies' magazines with novels in them. Diane thought you might like reading them while you're stuck in the house."

Vicky began to calm down, and no wonder. Feelings of concern and generosity flowed through the room like pure oxygen. If only a few lungfuls were all one needed to recover. "That was sweet of you to bring them over, Rick. And I'll be sure to call your sister and thank her. She even knows my taste in reading." Vicky winked at Justin who responded with an appreciative laugh.

"Would you care for weak tea?" Justin offered, pointing at the pot.

Rick, unaware that Justin was joking about the unpalatable brew, looked at him quizzically. "No, thank you, I don't like weak tea." He sat cross-legged on the floor beside Vicky, with a loyalty that called to mind a family pet. "Why weren't you more careful about the chocolates?"

Vicky didn't know how to respond until Mr. Rubinoff explained. "I phoned Rick this morning and told him you had eaten old, tainted candy and were now suffering the effects."

"Is it true, Vicky? Were the chocolates moldy?" Rick's manner of speaking resembled that of a child, but, tonight his eyes looked as bright and lucid as anyone's in the room. Vicky wondered whether it was fair to mislead him, but then decided in this case, it probably was. If Rick knew that someone had tried to kill her, he might be tempted to retaliate. Obviously, Mr. Rubinoff had come to the same conclusion.

"Yes, it's true." Vicky wondered whether the sudden flush in her cheeks was a recurring fever or an attack of conscience for telling a white lie. It was probably a combination of both. "I wasn't careful enough, so I'm going to have to rest at home for a few days. I was thinking we should close the shop, and you could have a week off."

His solemn expression grew even more so. "Why should you close the shop?"

"Well, because it's hard for one person to—"

"You can't afford to close for a week. I know. I made the last bank deposit."

With an apologetic grin to the others, Vicky leaned closer. "Yes, I realize that, but sometimes we have to weather difficult situations." Then, lowering her voice even further, she added, "Do you need the money? Is that it, Rick?"

"No!" His eyebrows came together in an expression of supreme affront. "I don't need the money. I get disability every month. But I gotta have something to do, Vicky. I'll go crazy without something to do."

"Why don't you spend the time enjoying yourself?" Justin suggested. "Get out and shoot some baskets, play pool—"

"I wasn't talking to you!" Rick tossed back. "This is between Vicky and me."

"That is no reason to be rude to Victoria's guest," Mr. Rubinoff chided sharply.

Rick glared at the older man, and then fell silent.

Vicky laid a hand gently on Rick's arm. "Would you really like to keep the shop open?"

He nodded. "I can handle it. I'm not dumb."

"I know you're not. But it's hard to manage a store alone all day, so I'm going to call once in a while to make sure you're okay." She held up an index finger. "An employer's prerogative, you know."

He picked at a frayed thread on his jeans. "Yeah, I know."

"I shall send one of my waitresses over after lunch every day to give you a break," Mr. Rubinoff offered.

"And I'll..." Justin began, then apparently thought better of it. "I'll, uh, make sure Vicky doesn't pester you too much. How's that?"

Rick didn't want to smile—that much was obvious—but Justin's infectious grin finally won him over. "Okay," he mumbled. "You do that."

Vicky's gaze followed Rick as he stood up. Being with him daily in the shop and seeing his gentle mannerisms, she no longer thought of him as a bull in a china shop. But here in her living room, he seemed gigantic, and clearly ill at ease.

"Are you sure you won't stay and have something to eat or drink?" she asked, suddenly wishing everyone would leave. Underneath the caftan, she was soaking wet, and her eyeballs felt as if they were full of gravel. The room was getting a little blurry, too.

"No, thanks. I gotta go." Shoving a pair of ham-hock hands into his pockets, Rick loped toward the door.

Mr. Rubinoff also got up. "Are you taking the bus back to town? I'll join you."

"I can give one of you a lift, at least, if you like," Justin offered. Vicky hoped he'd be taken up on the offer. Perhaps it was delayed shock or a reaction to the things Mr. Rubinoff had told her, but she was feeling nauseated again and had an overwhelming urge to be alone.

The Gypsy waved Justin magnanimously back to his seat. "Stay where you are. I am certain Victoria will appreciate your company. Rick and I will do just fine on the bus." He draped an affectionate arm over the shoulders of the former football star. "Isn't that so, Richard?"

"Come on, Mr. R, you know I hate being called Richard. I get the feeling you're gonna tell me to clean my room next."

Mr. Rubinoff's laughter boomed through Vicky's throbbing head even after she had closed the door. She turned, and for the second time that evening, shrieked.

Justin had followed her, silent as a cat, from the living room. Before Vicky could move away, he'd planted an arm at either side and pinned her against the door.

"Alone at last," he murmured.

She didn't understand how or why it happened, but it was like a photograph reverting suddenly to a negative. An embrace that turned to imminent capture; words of seduction, a threat. She tried to push him away. "Let me by, Justin."

But his head came down to the side of her neck, and he moved his body closer. "It's been too long. I've missed you, darling."

Her breasts prickled. All at once, she felt hot and cold. "Please, Justin, you're...you're in my way!"

He moved back half a step, but still left her no room to escape. "Pardon me. I didn't realize I was crowding you."

Her eyes glazed, her mind fevered, Vicky tried desperately to focus on the situation. Justin was her friend; he'd saved her life. But what did she really know about him?

You're acting crazy, Vicky. Five minutes ago, he could do nothing wrong. Then why had Mr. Rubinoff mistrusted him from the start? And why were they friends all of a sudden? Someone had tried to kill her. A woman had bought the chocolates. Was it Maeve? Justin's best friend?

What had Lieutenant Simmons said? He wouldn't be surprised if someone on the list had written the letter. Someone who'd murdered twice. Who'd tried to kill Vicky and failed...

"Why are you staring at me like that?" Justin's arms slid low on her waist. She ignored the pleasing sensations they evoked.

"I think you'd better leave right now," she said.

"Not until I know what's bothering you."

"Nothing's bothering me!" The words came out sounding shrill and forced.

"You don't look well. How are you feeling?" Justin's hand moved up toward her face, but she slapped it away before he could touch her.

"How do you expect me to feel?" Blood thrummed loudly in her ears. Even the lights felt like jagged glass. "Someone poisoned me yesterday. Someone wants me dead, and now here I am, alone with you. I must be crazy!"

Using her head and arms, Vicky tried to break through the barrier of Justin's body. For a moment, he was taken off guard, but then he grabbed her shoulders and held her at arm's length. She continued to flail, but it was hopeless. Her strength was rapidly depleting.

"Stop it, darling, stop it! You're going to exhaust yourself."

Darling? Was that supposed to impress her? "That's what you want, isn't it? For me to be too exhausted to fight?" Vicky hurled every word like a savage, but ineffectual, blow. "What's it going to be this time, Justin? Strangulation? A whack on the head?"

"You're delirious," he said, wrapping her in his arms so tightly she could scarcely breathe.

With no strength left to struggle, Vicky collapsed, sobbing, in his arms. All she'd ever wanted was to live a quiet, decent life. Why, after only twenty-eight years, did it have to end like this?

Justin's forearm around her neck was like a vise. With a twist and a small amount of pressure, he could have killed her instantly. But instead he was murmuring endearments into her ear, telling her not to worry, telling her he would take care of her.

So he had other plans first, did he? If she wasn't careful, her defenses might crumble. The contrast between his embrace and his real intentions was almost too much to withstand. Vicky drew in a deep, erratic breath and lifted her hand, not quite certain whether to stroke him or rake her nails across his cheek.

For an instant, she had the sensation of stepping away and watching her irrational self, but then the fever took hold of her again.

Justin was quicker than she was. Before she could lash out, he'd captured both wrists and twisted her forearms so she couldn't help but follow as he led her down the hall. Oh God, she prayed, stumbling, let this be over quickly.

Justin didn't throw her down onto the bed; he didn't need to. Her wrists were still captive, the dull ache of his grip threatening at the slightest misstep to turn into agony.

Slowly, he lowered her onto the sheets, taking inordinate care not to catch her hair beneath his hands. But Vicky wasn't fooled by the display of compassion. Her eyes, glittering with sickness and fear, bored into his. She lay poised and rigid, waiting for the moment when Justin let down his guard. Surely there would be at least one such moment.

With one hand, he let go and slid an arm beneath her lower back. Then, effortlessly he shifted her body so that her head was near the pillow. He placed his right knee on the bed and, lifting his other leg, straddled her.

Vicky squeezed her eyes shut and held her breath, knowing she was too weak to fight. She could only pray that she wasn't too weak to survive.

Justin's body now covered the full length of hers, but his elbows took most of the weight. "Lie still. I'm not going to hurt you, but you're shivering. I only want to warm you for a minute."

The words didn't compute, but the sensations, one by one, seeped through Vicky's conscious mind. The incredible, penetrating warmth of him; the sound of his heart hammering in counterpoint to hers; the musky smell of his sweat; and finally his desire.

While it seemed logical that arousal was a precursor to assault as well as making love, Vicky was totally unprepared for her own reaction to it. She tried to shift her thighs to escape the blatant contact, but the rasp of fabric against shivering flesh ignited something deep and low inside her. She moved again, and the flame shot higher. A third time, and she was appalled to discover her fingers digging into the hard muscle of his buttocks.

At first he flinched. She could feel the tension quiver through him. Then, he relaxed and seemed to surrender himself to her. Reason must have fled them both, for suddenly Vicky was no longer captive, but captor. Justin no longer aggressor, but victim. Her hands, her legs, her mouth were everywhere. She murmured his name and heard him groan. She touched him, and his flesh seared.

They rolled across the mattress, over and over, each dip and sway a new and vivid sensation. Vicky had never felt such craving, such heat, such madness. When her hand slid down boldly, she'd expected Justin's assent. This was, after all, what he'd been leading up to.

Instead he froze. Every inch of his body became as rigid as the part her fingertips now touched. "Vicky, don't." His whisper was both harsh and plaintive.

Her hand fell away. "Why... why not?" Her own voice was raspy, hardly there at all.

"Because. This isn't how it's supposed to be." Gently he peeled her arms from his body, and slowly he got out of bed. Reaching down, he stroked her tear-ravaged cheeks with the back of his hand.

His face in the light from the window looked haggard, almost wounded. Vicky longed to reach out to touch him, but she was too tired now for even such a simple gesture.

"How is it supposed to be?" she whispered.

Justin didn't answer. He covered her with a sheet, a blanket and the quilt that was folded at the foot of the bed.

"Where are you going?" she asked, the prospect of Justin leaving her alone suddenly more terrifying than anything that had happened tonight.

"I'm going to sleep on the sofa. If you need anything, you'll know where to find me."

VICKY SLEPT HARD. Motionless, dreamless, her body used the time to replenish itself, to purge itself of lingering shock. When she awoke shortly before dawn, she felt rested. The fever was gone; so were the dizzy spells. All that remained was a humiliating recollection of her behavior the night before.

It must have been caused by lingering symptoms of the poison. She would never have believed herself capable of such violent, conflicting emotions toward Justin. This morning, rational and refreshed, she felt none of those things—except desire. Not last night's grasping, clawing variety, but a profound, bittersweet longing to be in her lover's arms.

Vicky got up, washed and brushed her teeth, then walked quietly into the living room. Justin lay on the sofa with his back to her, an arm tossed over his head. She bent down and touched him on the shoulder. He rolled over and looked at her; he must have been awake.

Knowing instinctively that Justin was naked under the sheet, Vicky lifted the cotton caftan over her head. This time, there would be no mistaking her intentions. She stood before him, shivering slightly in the morning chill. Justin rose, smiling, and offered her the warmth of where he'd been sleeping.

Vicky felt the nubble of the sofa beneath smooth cotton sheets. The room was awash with night hues, cool blue shadows warmed by the flush of Justin's nearness.

He reached; she invited. He kissed; she responded. He spoke words of love, and she echoed them softly. His eyes requested, and hers replied.

He filled her deeply with himself, and gladly she accepted. For a moment, they paused, awestruck, trembling. Then they surrendered to the rhythm of their passion. Romping, playing, laughing, crying. Time had no meaning; the moment was all.

Finally, he thrust and she arched once more. She matched his last shudder. He melted inside.

Chapter Fifteen

"You know something, darling? I'm only beginning to realize how little I know about you."

"Hmm?" Vicky had heard him, but preferred to wriggle deeper into the crook of his body. She had never felt like this before. Satisfied, certainly; but never so attuned to the infinite subtleties of lovemaking. The glide of his tongue at the back of her knee; the warmth of a whisper against her thigh...

"I thought you'd be reserved," he continued.

Now she peered up at him, expending the absolute minimum of energy. "I am reserved," she insisted.

Tousling her already tousled hair, Justin grinned. "As a citizen, perhaps. As a lover, hardly."

"You liked it?" she asked, suddenly shy.

He moaned softly and drew her closer. "Oh, yes, I liked it very much."

Sometime during the morning, they had relocated from the sofa to the more favorable dimensions of the bed. Sinuously, Vicky stretched. Her toes reached Justin's ankles under the quilt. "Me, too."

How eloquent, she thought with a groan. Why was it that people were recaptured by their inhibitions almost immediately after making love? Being with Justin had been earthshaking, bell ringing—he was spectacular! So why couldn't she reply with something more appropriate than *me, too*?

Justin kissed the tip of her nose. "I hate to say this, but I have to go to work."

Vicky buried her face in the pillow, preferring not to watch while Justin climbed out of bed. "I know," she mumbled, disconsolate.

"Would you like company again this evening?"

She looked up, feeling better already. "You know I'd love company."

"Then I'll see you around six. I'll take care of dinner." Justin brought the covers up to her chin. "Get plenty of rest today. Beneath that sated flush of yours, you're still a bit pale. By the way..." he murmured, bending down to nuzzle her ear.

"Yes?" she said, wrapping her arms around his neck.

"Did I happen to mention that you were spectacular?"

BY THE END of the day, he should have been a physical and emotional wreck. Justin had hardly slept a wink on Vicky's sofa the night before. There were appointments with grad students all morning, exams to prepare, faculty reports to write. Then there was the grinding realization that some lowlife was expecting fifty thousand dollars to tell him where his mother was.

Yet, despite everything, Justin felt as buoyant as a kid out of school. He pushed the buggy through the grocery store, selected sole and fresh vegetables for dinner; but uppermost in his mind was how wonderful Vicky had felt in his arms that morning.

Thank God he'd had the rare good sense to restrain himself the night before. It wasn't an easy thing to do. Rolling across the bed, with Vicky wrapped deliciously around him, he'd very nearly given in. But the timing was wrong. She'd been terrified of him only minutes before, and terror had no place in the bedroom. Even if she'd have forgiven him later, Justin could never have forgiven himself.

The shades were drawn, so when he stepped inside the house late that afternoon it was cool. A single white envelope lay on the floor below the mail slot, but he stepped over it to deposit the grocery bags in the kitchen. Then he came back to pick it up, knowing instinctively who it was from and bracing himself.

Justin brought the letter into the living room, disgusted with his complacency. Falling in love was not a good enough reason for ignoring the mess he was in. Ignoring it subjected not only himself to danger, but Vicky, the others on the list and—if she was actually alive—his mother.

He poured a measure of bourbon into a glass and sat down in his favorite chair. Self-control and a semblance of routine were crucial in dealing with the unknown. He'd survived for years in Europe because he had known that.

Justin tore open the envelope and began to read. It didn't take him long to realize that nothing in his younger years had prepared him for this.

Dear Justin, or should I say Michael?
I was disappointed to discover no parcel waiting for me at the Wagon Wheel last night. I thought you would show some interest in your poor mother's well-being. Obviously, I was mistaken.

Nevertheless, you must realize by now that I am deadly serious about my demands. I've killed twice to prove my point. As for Vicky, I never actually intended for her to die. Not yet, anyway. She's turning out to be quite cooperative, you see.

Because I'm a reasonable person, I will give you another forty-eight hours to come up with the money. My asking price now, however, is seventy-five thousand, method of payment, same as before. Remember, there is also an outstanding balance of nine thousand from your first payment.

Your mother remembers you. I spoke to her on the phone just the other day. She doesn't know about the outstanding warrant in Italy, or your suspected involvement in the chain letter killings. I'd prefer not to tell her. But then, again, I'd prefer not to put a pillow over your poor mother's face either.

Think about it, Justin.

"No! For God's sake, stop!" Justin shouted the plea to an empty house and cringed at the sound of his echo. The bourbon went down like liquid fire. Craving the sensation again, Justin stood up and poured himself another one. Now his mother's life was at stake, in addition to all the others. But where was she? How was she? Maybe he should've paid after all. But it could still be some kind of hoax.

What did the letter mean when it said that Vicky was turning out to be cooperative? She was part of the list. She couldn't be involved.

He'd been through this argument in his head so many times before and come up with nothing, except the same insignificant details: Vicky was the one who'd first called him, who'd suggested they meet at the Cheese 'n' Deli. But he no longer believed Mr. Rubinoff was part of the scheme, not after the long talk they'd had.

And there was still Rick Paterson. Big, hulking Rick who'd taken an instant, and irrational, dislike to Justin. His loyalty to Vicky seemed genuine enough, but who could say what twists and turns his damaged brain might take?

If Rick was the killer, then it was not inconceivable that he was also terrorizing Vicky, swearing her to secrecy on pain of death—or on the possibility of the death of others. Vicky had always trusted Rick; Justin knew it would be devastating for her to realize she was wrong about him.

At that moment, a memory surfaced in Justin's thoughts. He might have dismissed it as insignificant except that it had lodged so indelibly in his mind.

Yesterday, he'd been driving along Gorham Street, worried about Vicky, anxious to see her. Suddenly, there she was on the street corner, almost staggering, obviously weak from the aftereffects of the poison. He'd wondered at the time why she wasn't at home in bed.

When he called her name, she jumped as though she'd heard a ghost. Her face at first was ashen, then gradually grew damp and florid as they talked. She adamantly refused his offer of a ride home, as if reluctant to move from her spot. Both hands were in her pockets, and she had been, most definitely, leaning against a mailbox. The impression he'd gotten was that she'd wanted him to leave at once.

At the time, he didn't interpret her reaction as one of fear or guilt. But it could have been, he supposed. She could have been forced to run an errand for Rick, or whomever.

The supposition was easy enough to discount. If this letter had been mailed any time before yesterday, then Vicky couldn't have sent it. She'd been in the hospital on Sunday, and they'd been together on the boat all day Saturday.

He picked up the envelope, hoping he'd be able to put this latest quandary to rest. But the local postmark, in fact, was stamped with yesterday's date. Vicky could have been the one who had mailed it.

SHE'D BEEN WAITING at the living-room window ever since Justin had phoned to say he was on his way. When Vicky saw his car turn into the visitors' parking lot, she rushed down to the front door. One look at Justin's face confirmed her fears. "What's wrong?" she asked at once.

"Let's have some tea, and we'll talk." They went upstairs, and he carried the groceries into the kitchen and set them on the counter. Then he led her to a chair and sat her down, reminding himself to stay calm. None of this was really Vicky's fault. "Did you, by any chance, mail a letter to me yesterday?"

She looked at him strangely. "Why would I do that? I've seen you practically every day."

Justin pulled the latest letter from his pocket and dropped it on the table. "Read this."

She read the letter and became more confused with each line, confused and devastated. "Who wrote this?" she asked, her voice barely above a whisper.

"I suspect it was Rick." He turned to fill the kettle with water. "What I'd like to know is how he's forcing you to cooperate with him."

"Me? I'm not cooperating with anyone. Good grief, Justin, I was almost killed, remember? Why on earth would I want to cooperate with a murderer?"

"That's not so hard to understand," he replied quietly, his gaze probing.

Her hands trembling, Vicky brought down two mugs from the cupboard. "I don't have a clue who could have written this letter or what it means. But I do know that Rick Paterson would never do anything like this."

"How can you be sure?"

"Because I've known him for three years. He wouldn't knowingly hurt a flea."

Justin took Vicky lightly by the shoulders. "Who said anything about 'knowingly'?"

She drew in a sharp breath. Justin was right. The person who was doing this was not rational; he might not even be aware of his actions. But it couldn't be Rick. He was no blackmailer. And since when had this turned into blackmail? she wondered. Then she remembered the bump on the back of his head.

"I thought you hadn't gotten the chain letter," Vicky said.

"Not the same kind you received, but that's because he's been after me all along."

"Are you sure about that?"

"He admitted as much in the first letter I got."

"But for him to kill Theo and Eve..." Vicky shuddered, and Justin pulled her to his chest.

"I know, darling, I know. The person is absolutely without conscience. But listen to me. If you have any idea who this person is, don't be afraid to share it with me. We'll work something out together, so you don't have to fear for your life."

She pushed away and looked up into his face. "I'm not afraid, Justin, at least, not in the way you think. If I knew who this person was, believe me, I'd be the first one to run to the police."

He stared at her long and hard. "I do believe you. I guess I've been grasping at straws."

Vicky prepared the tea and brought the two mugs into the living room. Justin followed silently behind.

She understood how he felt, grasping at straws. She couldn't comprehend it herself—how her life had suddenly become so jumbled. Nightmares turned into daydreams and back again, before she could even turn around. What she wouldn't give for the return of her old quiet life, before Theo Dalta showed up at her door with a chain letter.

They sat down on the sofa. Vicky handed Justin his tea. Her heart twisted to see the worry lines on his face. They were etched too deep for a man his age. "What's this about your mother? I thought she was dead."

"So did I." He took a sip of tea and set the cup down.

"What are you going to do?"

"Try to set another trap. I can't be certain the blackmailer will ever provide more details about my mother, no matter how much I pay. I don't want to risk her life any longer than I have to."

Vicky reached out and touched the back of Justin's head. "Is that what you were trying to do when you got this?"

He looked embarrassed. "My survival skills apparently aren't what they used to be."

"Then it would be foolish to set up the blackmailer again, Justin. He's probably expecting a second trap."

"What do you suggest—that I pay him the seventy-five thousand?"

"According to the letter, you already have paid."

"Only enough to bait him, but it backfired." Justin raked his hands through already rumpled hair. "I've got to go home and do some thinking, Vicky. I'm sorry. I never should have thought for a second you could be involved."

She caught his arm, suddenly fearful at the thought of being alone. "But what about dinner?"

"Put it all in the freezer. I'll cook it another time."

She hurried behind him to the door. "You're not going to take on this person by yourself, Justin. He obviously doesn't care who he kills."

"I've got nothing to lose, Vicky. If I don't find out who this person is, and quickly, I'll be charged with two counts of homicide and one of attempted."

"What?"

Justin smiled bitterly. "Haven't you heard? I'm Lieutenant Simmons's prime suspect in the chain letter killings. He's already warned me not to leave town."

"When did this happen? Why didn't you tell me?"

"The conversation first came up in the hospital room while you were under sedation."

Vaguely Vicky recalled the argument, one she'd thought was a dream. "But you brought me to the hospital. You're the one who saved my life!"

His laugh was harsh. "Apparently, that's not enough to convince the lieutenant. His theory is that I got cold feet at the last minute when I realized I might not get away with poisoning you."

"Be he has no proof."

"Not yet, but believe me, he's working on it."

Pushing aside fears for her own safety, Vicky forced herself to concentrate on Justin's dilemma. "So if you succeed in catching the blackmailer red-handed, you'll be off the hook."

"Precisely, not to mention the added satisfaction of finding out what he knows about my mother, without throwing away eighty grand."

"But you could still end up being extradited for the murder charge in Italy."

"That doesn't matter to me anymore, Vicky. I'm tired of looking over my shoulder, and there's always a chance that I'll be acquitted of that charge."

The seconds ticked away as they stood by the door. The longer she could keep Justin talking, Vicky reasoned, the longer he would stay. The thought of letting him walk away was terrifying. She had the feeling he might never come back.

"Do you have a plan worked out for catching the blackmailer?"

He shook his head. "My first hurdle was to come over here and make sure you weren't being threatened."

"You didn't really suspect me of anything, did you?"

"Oh, maybe . . ." he admitted, with a sad, loving smile. "But deep down, I think I've always known better. You're a strong, passionate lady. I can't imagine anyone ever swaying you from your convictions."

"Then let me help." She curved her fingers around his forearm.

"Don't be ridiculous. I could never let you get involved."

"I'm not being ridiculous. You know what they say about two heads, and besides, I have a vested interest in the outcome, too, you know."

"Why do you say that?"

"This person has already set me up as a decoy. How do I know what else I'll be implicated in?"

Justin folded him arms. "It's too dangerous."

Vicky folded hers. "But not too dangerous for you, I suppose?"

"That's different. I've gotten used to living with danger."

"And I've survived an attempt on my life, Justin, so I'm getting used to it, too! I don't intend to sit around and wait for this creep to try again."

Justin's expression softened, and he slipped his arms around her waist. "I don't blame you for feeling frustrated, darling, but what I intend to do is a lot different from attending funerals and poking through people's bedrooms in broad daylight. You could get yourself killed."

Dammit anyway. Here she was, trying to convince Justin of her burgeoning invincibility, and tears were starting to leak from the corners of her eyes. "But y-you could get killed, too. And if something happens to you, Justin, I'll be all alone."

Her sudden change of mood caught him off guard. "I won't get killed," he said gently. "And anyway, you wouldn't be alone. You have your family, your friends—Mr. Rubinoff, Rick—"

"But they weren't on the chain letter list! I don't know anyone except you who's gone through this nightmare, and if you died while this . . . beast was still at large, I wouldn't know what to do."

He considered this a moment. "I see your point. We can't be certain the police are going to crack this case as soon as we'd like them to. But why don't you come to my place, and I'll introduce you to my past? Once you have the full story, then maybe you'll understand why I don't want you to get involved."

Vicky's eyes widened. "You're asking me to come to your house? Now?"

"Yes. Are you afraid?"

She was, but not for the obvious reasons. There was a certain false security in keeping the details of Justin's past at arm's length. Yet, considering everything that had happened so far, false security was worse than no security at all.

"I'm not afraid," she said, grabbing her purse and locking the door behind them.

VICKY WAS IMPRESSED by Justin's home. It was small, cozy, and of course, neat as a pin. Careful thought was apparent in the decor. The living room resembled a study, with hardwood floors and shelves of leather-bound books. There was an interesting collection of pewter, but not too many pieces to distract the observer. Huge trees outside the front window gave one the feeling of woodsy seclusion.

"We left our dinner at your place," Justin said. "Are you hungry? I can go back for it."

She shook her head. "Not at all."

"Would you like a drink?"

"No, thanks." Though she felt well enough, Vicky knew her stomach would not take kindly to alcohol. And now, especially, she needed her wits about her.

He crouched down in front of an oak cabinet in search of a video cassette. "The first blackmail notes I received are in the right-hand drawer of the desk. Why don't you take a look at them while you're waiting?"

Vicky read the letters and stared at the photograph. A chill ran through her at their threatening tone; anger ran through her at the shabby display of the woman in the wheelchair. "Did you recognize her right away?"

"Yes. She looks a lot older than her age, but I guess that's to be expected." Justin found the tape and slid it into the machine.

As soon as Maija's face filled the screen, Vicky was struck by the resemblance. Except for the difference in gender, mother and son were identical. The same silky blond hair; the same wholesome features, from the long straight nose to the crystal blue eyes.

"Did you wear a beard to keep people from recognizing you?" she asked.

Justin was glued to the screen. "Yes."

"Then why did you shave it off?"

"As I told you, I don't intend to hide anymore."

Though Vicky was restless, she forced herself to concentrate on the plot. The story was a light romantic romp in the tradition of Gable and Lombard, with comic twists and tender love scenes. It soon became apparent to Vicky that Maija Justason's talents were underrated. Like Monroe and so many others, her beauty had gotten in the way of her considerable ability.

Halfway through the film, Justin got up and turned off the machine.

"Why did you do that? I was enjoying it." Vicky was curled up in a corner of the burgundy sofa, trying to ignore a craving for popcorn.

"That's not the reason I put it on, although I do appreciate your praise. Mom was a good actress." From a bookshelf, he pulled out a thick leather photo album and opened it on the coffee table. "I wanted you to be convinced of who I am, once and for all."

"The film is pretty convincing. If you weren't her son, you'd pass for her double any day." She moved closer to Justin so she could see the album. There were glossy publicity photos of a teenage Maija, her voluptuous figure exaggerated by the lifts and stays of fifties'-style swimwear. Then came the wedding shots: Maija with a dark, handsome man, radiant as she came down the aisle in yards of tulle.

"Who was your father, Justin?"

"You wouldn't have heard of him. He was a two-bit New York agent who left Mom soon after I was born. He died of cirrhosis a few years later. I never knew him."

Justin's baby pictures could melt a statue. Big eyed and dimply, he was a perfect little cherub. "Your mother must have been nuts about you," Vicky gushed, as she pored over each photo.

"All mothers are nuts about their kids," was his disillusioned reply.

There were yellowed press clippings of Maija in amongst the photographs. Maija at a benefit screening, Maija with Brando, Maija with everyone and anyone.

"Where were you during all these events?"

"Usually at boarding school in England. Summers, I spent at my grandparents' farm in Minnesota. This was their scrapbook." Turning the page, he smiled. "Here's my favorite picture of the two of us. She had it written into her contract that she would have four weeks off every Christmas. That's when the two of us would go to the Italian Riviera.''

Vicky studied the photo of a ten-year-old with his mother, standing ankle deep in the Mediterranean. "You must have enjoyed that."

"I lived for it."

Justin would have turned the page, but Vicky stopped him so that she could look at a snapshot of the two of them. He and his mother were on the deck of a large yacht, but it was taken a few years later. Justin must have been a teenager at the time. What caught Vicky's eye was a deeply tanned man whose arm was looped around Maija's neck. He was grinning, but there was something unpleasant, almost nasty about his visage.

Vicky pointed at the arm. "Who was that?"

"The man I was accused of murdering."

She sat back. She'd seen enough pictures for now. "Tell me what happened."

He not only seemed resigned to talk about it; he seemed almost anxious. "As I told you before, I turned fifteen that year. Mom and I weren't getting along as well as we once had. Part of the reason was my age, I suppose, but Mom was also having severe emotional problems."

"Because of her career?"

"That, and her age. She was thirty-six and getting dangerously close to over the hill in Hollywood. She was depressed by the lack of good scripts and started popping pills to wake up, and to sleep, and to do just about everything."

"You knew she was taking pills?"

"Sure, I read the tabloids at school. And being a somewhat fanatical athlete, I could see the effect the drugs were having and hated her for it."

"Did you and your mother ever discuss how you felt?"

"We didn't discuss. We fought, constantly, especially the last time we were in Italy together. That's when she started seeing Renaldo, the local Casanova and pusher."

"I can imagine how you two got along."

Justin nodded. "It was pretty bad. He was always trying to get rid of me so he and Mom could be alone. I had no objection to her sleeping with him. Men had been coming and going through her life for years. But I knew Renaldo was supplying her with drugs—not just barbiturates, but the hard stuff."

"Did the police know what he did for a living?"

"Of course they did. The whole village knew, but when Renaldo strutted down the main street, women swooned and men took their hats off to him. For him to have an American movie star like Maija Justason on his arm earned him even more notoriety."

Justin fell silent. "I need another drink. Are you sure you won't have one?"

"I'm sure."

He got up, then sat down again. "Guess I won't have one either. Anyway, late one afternoon I came in to the hotel from the beach and found my mother lying naked and unconscious on the bed. I tried to revive her and couldn't. So I ran from the room to get help and saw Renaldo turn a corner on his way out of the hotel."

Justin's hand curled into a fist, and his breathing grew shallow. "That's when I made the biggest mistake of my life. Instead of getting a doctor, I took off after Renaldo. I went crazy. I wanted to smash his skull in for what he'd done to Mom. If I'd caught him, I honestly think I would have killed him."

"But you didn't catch him?"

"No. Last thing I saw, he took off on a motorboat. I tried to hire someone at the pier to take me out, but no matter how much I offered, they wouldn't get involved. People were terrified of that guy. I waited until nightfall, hoping to steal a boat, but fell asleep on a pile of rocks." He laughed mirthlessly. "Would you believe I actually dreamed that I'd gone back to the hotel and saved my mother's life?"

The anguish in his words stirred Vicky's emotions. She took Justin's hand; it felt like ice. "What happened then?"

"Sometime after noon, I finally crawled out from under the pier. I stumbled around, trying to get my bearings, and then saw the headlines at a newspaper kiosk. I was fluent enough in Italian to understand. American Film Star Dies in Hospital of Overdose. That's when I realized what a jackass I was. I could've saved her, but I was too damned busy with revenge."

"Did you go back to the hotel?"

"I was going to, until I'd read a few papers and saw the other headlines: Body of Local Gangster Washes up on Beach; Maija Justason's Son Disappears. There was a picture of Renaldo's body, his face mangled, and underneath that, my latest school picture."

"My God, they really thought you'd killed him."

"I'm not so sure that they did, but it sure as hell was convenient to make it look like I had. Renaldo was a top gun in organized crime, and the Mob virtually ran that town. I ducked through back streets to the hotel, and found the place swarming with cops, every one of them probably on the take."

"But you were only fifteen and an American citizen. Surely they wouldn't have arrested you, if you'd come forward right away."

"Are you kidding? Those guys would have loved the opportunity to rough up an American. Besides, embassies aren't terribly keen on handling murder raps. I managed to put a call through to Mom's press agent in New York. He'd heard the news by then, of course, and his advice to me was, 'Lay low, kid, you're in big trouble.'"

"Nice guy."

"A real pal."

"What did you do then?"

"I thought about phoning my grandparents in Minnesota, but considering Renaldo's international connections, I decided against it. I left the Riviera and hid for a while in the poorer sections of the country where people didn't pay much attention to American film stars. I dyed my hair, changed my name and learned how to live by my wits."

He strode across the living room and looked out at the spruce trees. "I was fluent in five languages and looked older than fifteen, so people didn't ask many questions when I applied for work. I hung around Europe for a few years, worked odd jobs, saved money and learned a few things I shouldn't have."

Vicky felt herself drawn into his story as if she herself were living through it. "What kinds of things?"

"How to pick pockets, how to ride the trains for free, how to forge a passport." He opened a drawer in his rolltop desk and pulled out a small dog-eared passport. "This was printed for me by a one-eyed Indonesian sailor in Amsterdam, the first official document ever issued to Justin Coe."

"May I see it?" Vicky handled the passport almost reverently. Strange how a perfect forgery inspired greater awe than the real thing. "You've never had problems renewing it?"

He shrugged. "There are ways around almost any problem."

"When did you come back to the United States?"

"About twelve years ago. I worked my way up to England first, got in touch with a few school chums and managed to pass the exams for Oxford."

"So your degree is legitimate?"

Justin chuckled. "One of the few things that is. After a few years in England, I got homesick. There was still the possibility that someone in the Mob might catch up to me, but I decided to risk it. My grandparents were still alive, and they were delighted to have me stay with them until I got my life back in order. They died within a few months of each other and left me a substantial amount of cash from Mom's royalties. I took off again, and the rest is pretty uneventful, until the day I met Maeve Wilson at the vegetable stand and was hired at UW."

Vicky let out a long breath. "Are you sure the murder warrant is still outstanding?"

"No. It was a few years ago."

For the first time in days, Vicky felt a sense of purpose taking hold. Justin was in trouble; he needed her. "Do you think the blackmailer is someone from your past, someone who was in Italy when your mother died?" Catching herself, Vicky amended the remark. "Or when you thought she died?"

"It wouldn't surprise me."

"But to have found you in Madison of all places, and after more than twenty years. There must be dozens of people you've met who know about your past."

"There are people who know, yes, but they're friends."

"Like Maeve," Vicky muttered.

"Yes, like Maeve. I know how you feel about her, but she's not a murderer, Vicky. She's as loyal and discreet a friend as I've ever had."

Oh, Justin, if only you knew what she says about you. But this was not the place to discuss Maeve's lesser qualities. Time, Vicky hoped, would prove her right.

"There's not much point in speculating, is there?" she said. "We might as well start putting a plan together."

"No." Justin shook his head. "The purpose of my bringing you here was to dissuade you from your offer. We're talking about a twenty-year vendetta, Vicky. We're talking about someone who doesn't give a damn who he murders, as long as he gets to me and my money, and not necessarily in that order. You can be sure he won't let a pretty face stop him."

"For crying out loud, Justin. Don't go getting chauvinistic on me, all of a sudden. Who said anything about using a pretty face to stop him . . . or her? I intend to use brains— yours and mine. And I think I've come up with a plan."

Chapter Sixteen

"It'll never work," was what Justin said after hearing Vicky's plan. He was right. Though the premise was sound enough, the plan itself was full of holes, sketched vaguely in her subconscious while Justin had been filling in the details of his past for her.

But after several hours of discussion, argument, and sometimes outright confrontation, they were both reasonably satisfied with the trap they planned to lay. By the time they were finished, it was well after two in the morning.

Justin, who was not a nocturnal creature, sat at the kitchen with his head propped between his hands. "I'll drive you . . . home, Vicky." The pause was a huge yawn, his fifth in as many minutes.

Vicky matched it with one of her own. "You don't have to. I'll call a cab. No, forget it. I wouldn't be able to stay awake long enough to wait for it. Would it be all right if I stayed here?"

He lifted one bleary eye and even managed a suggestive, if halfhearted, grin. "Of course it would be all right."

"I meant in the spare room, on the sofa, whatever is handy."

His eyelid settled back into place. "I knew that's what you meant. The spare room's this way."

Vicky would have loved to fall asleep in Justin's arms, but for what was left of tonight, rest was more important than the physical expression of their feelings. There would, with any luck, be plenty of time for making love later.

The next morning, according to plan, Justin drove Vicky to the Nick Nack Nook and, with a quick kiss, said goodbye and drove on to the campus. They wouldn't be meeting again until that night after dark.

Rick was dismantling the Easter display when Vicky walked in. At first, he seemed pleased to see her; then he looked worried. "Aren't you supposed to stay at home until you're all better?"

"I am better, almost. I just came in to see how you were doing and spend a few hours on the books. You don't mind having me back early, do you, Rick?"

"Heck, no. Running this place alone isn't so great. After a while, you start talking to yourself."

She gave him a playful punch in the arm. "I could've told you that. Why do you think I like having you around?"

Rick's ears turned pink at the praise, and he solemnly resumed gathering plastic grass. Then he stopped and looked at her curiously. "You didn't go to the Cheese 'n' Deli."

Vicky was already packing painted Ukrainian Easter eggs into a box. "Uh, no, I . . . forgot."

"You never forget your coffee and paper in the morning."

"I had coffee at Justin's," she said, avoiding Rick's eyes.

"You had breakfast with him? At his place?"

"Yes, but only because we stayed up half the night talking. It was too late for me to go home."

He guffawed. "Yeah, I get it."

This was ridiculous, Vicky told herself. Twenty-eight years old and she couldn't bring herself to admit she'd spent the night with a man. Nothing had even "happened." Yet, given Rick's feelings toward Justin and Rick's emotional immaturity, she felt uncomfortable confiding in him about her personal life. But since the subject of Justin had come up, this was as good a time as any to initiate Step One of their plan.

"Rick, there's something I want to tell you."

He sat back on his heels, hands splayed across muscular thighs. "You're getting married?"

She blushed. "No, nothing like that. I just wanted to let you know that I'll be going out of town tomorrow for a few days."

"Where are you going?"

"On a boating trip with Justin. It's exam time, so he's able to get away."

"How long will you be gone?"

"Two or three days at the most." Vicky replaced the lid on the box of painted eggs. "If you like, we could close the Nick Nack Nook while I'm away. You've been on your own quite a bit lately. You could probably use the break."

His placid face creased into a scowl. "You're always doing this to me, Vicky. First you tell me I can handle the place on my own, then you tell me I need a vacation. I had two years of vacation in the hospital and a year on the Square when people used to cross the street to avoid looking at me."

"Oh, Rick, I didn't mean—"

"Sure, that's what people always say. 'I didn't mean, I didn't mean.' But they do mean it!" He kicked an empty carton across the floor and stormed into the back room. "Do whatever you want. It's your store."

"What are you doing, Rick?"

"I'm getting money out of the vault. We've gotta make a bank deposit."

She watched him slouch out of the shop, money pouch under his arm. Rick was getting testier by the day it seemed—jumping down her throat at the slightest provocation, taking everything she said much too seriously.

Maybe it was her own fault. She'd been loading him with a tremendous amount of responsibility lately. He might be happier doing what he'd done at the start, working in the back, carting heavy inventory. But this wasn't the time to do anything about it. Later, when things were back to normal, she would give Rick's problem some serious thought.

She was changing the date on the cash register when the telephone rang. "Good morning, Nick Nack Nook."

"Is this Vicky?" a woman's voice asked.

"Yes, it is."

"Did you like the chocolates?"

Chocolates? Vicky's blood ran cold. "Wh-who are you?"

"What a silly question. Why, I'm the Easter Bunny's mother, of course. I know Easter has come and gone, but my son and I did want to wish you a pleasant recovery, seeing as how you only ate one."

Trembling, Vicky strained to recognize the voice. It was husky, quavering, like an older woman who'd been chain-smoking for years. "What do you want from me?"

"I was wondering if you'd read the little message we taped inside the candy box."

She longed to run, but fear kept her clutching the telephone receiver. "What m-message was that?"

"Oh, dear, then you did miss it. My son worked so hard to make each message personal, and people don't even appreciate it. Your message, Miss Green, said 'revenge.'"

"Revenge?" Vicki repeated.

"That's right," the woman replied with a throaty chuckle. "Now, if you hadn't been so foolish, you would have been spared a great deal of discomfort."

"I don't understand. What did I do that was so foolish?" If Vicky could only concentrate and hang on a few minutes longer, there was a chance the woman might say something to give herself away. But even a few minutes felt like eternity.

"You broke the chain. Don't you remember?" the woman said. "How many times did we specifically warn you *not to break the chain*?"

"I . . . well, I—"

"There's no use trying to make excuses. It would have been so simple. Now it's simply too late."

Before Vicky could think of a reply, the woman had hung up.

Dropping the phone, Vicky didn't stop to think. She didn't stop at all, but fled the store as fast as her legs could carry her. She pushed past pedestrians on State Street, skirted the circular flower boxes and continued to run until she came to the first place of refuge she could think of.

"Mr...Rubi...Rubinoff." She was out of breath; her knees were trembling as Vicky staggered to the nearest stool. "I've got to...got to call the...police."

Abandoning a customer, Mr. Rubinoff came to Vicky. "What is the matter, Victoria? Drink this first. Then tell me." He poured water into a glass and handed it to her. After a few gulps, she was able to breathe more easily and hurriedly related what had happened.

Mr. Rubinoff picked up the telephone at once and dialed the number of the Madison Police Department. "What was the name of the lieutenant who came here?"

"Simmons."

"Ah, yes. Lieutenant Simmons, please."

Vicky was grateful that her friend was doing the talking. She shouldn't have panicked the way she did, but the call was so unexpected. It was bad enough that she'd almost been murdered but to speak to the would-be killer in person was too hideous to bear. And admittedly, now that she and Justin were in the throes of exposing the killer, Vicky had fallen into a kind of unrealistic complacency. The killer was still out there, and still extremely dangerous.

"Yes, I will tell her. Thank you, lieutenant." Mr. Rubinoff set the receiver down. "He said he will meet you at the Nick Nack Nook in fifteen minutes."

Vicky allowed herself a deep sigh of relief. "Thank you, Mr. Rubinoff. I don't know what I'd have done without you."

He gave her a benevolent smile. "And I don't know what I'd do without you. There are not many people willing to befriend a ranting old man. Here, have some coffee before you return to the store."

Realizing how much she'd missed Mr. Rubinoff's coffee, she accepted the cup gratefully. "Thank you. This hits the spot."

"The note in the candy. It said 'revenge,' no?"

Vicky closed her eyes and took another sip. "Apparently so."

He pulled out a battered portfolio from beneath the counter. Inside were scraps of paper, scribbled notes, Mr. Rubinoff's own detailed chronicle of Vicky's ordeal. He wrote down the word 'revenge' with a stubby pencil and studied it a moment. Then he stabbed it triumphantly with his finger.

"Aha, I knew it! I knew this had to be a puzzle of some kind. It is an anagram."

"What are you talking about?"

"Look at this." He pointed to her name among the original list of seven. "V, E. Green. Rearrange the letters, and they spell 'revenge.'"

"Yes, I see what you mean, but I don't know what you're getting at."

By now, three or four customers were waiting impatiently at the counter to pay for their purchases. "Excuse me for a moment," Mr. Rubinoff said to them. "Sophie, come take the cash, please!"

The Gypsy motioned for Vicky to follow him to a quiet table at the rear. Then he spread the papers out for her to examine. "I should have noticed this sooner, but clogged arteries are taking their toll. This last word was the final clue I needed. As I told you, 'revenge' is an anagram of V.E. Green, just as Theo L. Dalta spells 'death to all.' Eve Lomorth's name translates to 'mother, love.'"

"You mean all of our names formed part of the quote from that writer?"

"Drysdale, that is correct. I have it written down here. 'Mother, love a son's honor. Life is pain, no justice. Revenge, destruction, death to all.' The other people on the list are Rosa N. Shoon, 'a son's honor.' Sean Filipi, 'life is pain.' Curtis Donet, 'destruction.' And finally, Justin Coe, 'no justice.' Do you see?"

Vicky shook her head slowly. "I see it, but I don't really understand why it was done."

"Probably no one ever will understand why, except the perpetrator himself. He is obviously quite mad, not unlike Drysdale himself."

"She," Vicky corrected.

"I beg your pardon?"

"The caller was a woman, so presumably the killer was a woman."

Shaking his head, the Gypsy pushed the papers aside. "A woman, no. I cannot believe a woman would be responsible. I read the papers. It is very seldom that women become serial killers."

Vicky thought about Maeve. She hadn't been able to match the voices, but Dr. Wilson might have been disguising hers. "There are exceptions, aren't there, Mr. Rubinoff?"

"Certainly, there are always exceptions. Listen to me, Victoria. I do not wish to frighten you, but this person—he or she—is obviously driven by some demented internal forces. I do not believe he will rest until every one on the list is either obedient to him . . . or dead."

On that score, at least, she agreed with him. Vicky went to take another sip of coffee, but the cup was empty. Her nerves jangled with the onslaught of caffeine. Whatever became of the courage and the soaring self-confidence she'd felt the night before at Justin's house? Now she was prepared to take the first bus home to northern Wisconsin. "Maybe I should just put the ten dollars into the tree," she said. "If that's all the person is after . . ."

"Perhaps you are right. I discouraged you from doing so once before, but if a small payment will buy you time and peace of mind until the police can solve the case, there is probably no harm in it."

The thought, however sensible it seemed, rankled Vicky. She and Justin had spent half the night perfecting a trap. She'd survived one attempt on her life, and one thing it had taught her was to be cautious, prepared for anything. To blithely give in now to the killer's demands seemed a travesty. She really had no choice but to follow through with the plans she'd made.

"I'll think about it, Mr. Rubinoff. Oh, by the way, Justin and I are going out on his sailboat for a few days."

He raised bushy eyebrows. "Are you now?"

"We'll be leaving first thing tomorrow morning and coming back Friday or Saturday."

"That sounds wonderful. Will Rick be looking after the shop for you?"

Vicky's mouth fell. "Oh, my gosh, I completely forgot about Rick. I've got to go! Thanks a million. Talk to you later."

Mr. Rubinoff watched Vicky race out of the door, then carefully gathered up his notes and went to the kitchen where there was a private phone. He dialed a number and waited with less than his usual patience.

"Justin, it's Rubinoff. Vicky was here. Yes, she got a phone call . . . Let them know right away . . . I had no choice but to let her go. What else could I do?" After answering a few more questions, he quietly hung up.

Mr. Rubinoff lingered in the kitchen a moment, savoring the solitude that could be broken at any moment. Opening the portfolio, he shuffled with thick fingers through the notes and bits of paper.

V. E. Green—revenge. It was ironic, he thought, how the fates worked. If Michael Justason had selected any other name but Justin Coe, he and Vicky never would have met.

Vicky's return to the Nick Nack Nook was twice as fast and nearly as frantic as her departure had been, but she was still too late. Rick was already back from the bank, and most definitely upset.

She stumbled into the shop. "I'm sorry, Rick!"

"I guess it's different when you're the boss, huh? I leave the store unlocked for five minutes and get royal hell. But you can leave for as long as you want and nothing happens."

"That's not true. I should've locked up—"

His arm swung out in a gesture of frustration, knocking over a clay wizard. The shatter made Vicky jump, but Rick hardly noticed the noise.

"I should've known you'd say one thing and do another," he continued. "My sister is like that. My mother used to be like that. 'Don't smoke, Rick. It's bad for your lungs. Don't drink, you'll be too fat to make the team,' she'd say. But it was okay for her to smoke and drink and get as fat as she wanted."

Vicky ventured a step nearer. "I know it must sound like I'm being hypocritical, but I left the store because—"

"And the way she used to bitch about my driving. 'Watch the lights; don't go so fast; you're gonna get us all killed.'" His face contorted into a pained expression. "But guess what happened after all that nagging? My mother rammed us into a truck. She's the one who messed up my brain!"

Rich pressed his palms to his head and sank to the floor with a long wail of anguish. Vicky stood there staring. She had no idea whether to run to his side or leave him alone until he calmed down.

"I know how you feel, Rick." It was Lieutenant Simmons's voice.

Vicky spun around, startled. She hadn't heard the bell when the lieutenant came in, but obviously he'd been there long enough to hear much of what Rick had said. With a reassuring glance at Vicky, he approached the younger man and knelt beside him.

"I used to have trouble at home, too. My mother was a teacher, and you can't imagine what strict is until you've had a teacher for a mother."

Rick wiped his eyes and looked up at the officer. "Why? What was so bad about that?"

"I wasn't allowed to get lousy grades. I couldn't get dirty like other kids. I had to stay home and read instead of playing baseball. Just 'cause I was Mrs. Simmons's kid, I had to be perfect." He looked up at Vicky and grinned. "That's why I like to go around wrinkled. Mom's not around to tell me any different."

With a quick glance at his rumpled green sports coat and ever-present plaid shirt, Vicky laughed. "You're certainly making your point, lieutenant."

He draped an arm around Rick's shoulder. "What do you say we clean up this mess, huh?"

Rick, Vicky had learned, responded well to clear-cut instructions. Soon he stopped his sniveling and got up, even giving Vicky a look of remorse.

"I really am sorry about leaving the store unlocked," she said. "If I do it again, what would you consider suitable damages?"

Rick couldn't prevent the corner of his mouth from turning up in a grin. "A hundred bucks, cash."

"Make it fifty, and I won't dock you for the wizard you knocked off the shelf."

"Seventy-five. The wizard's only worth twenty-five bucks wholesale."

Vicky laughed. "It's a deal."

The lieutenant refrained from asking Vicky any questions while Rick was in the room. Together, the three of them cleaned up the broken figurine, then Vicky asked Rick to pick up some coffee and Danishes at the Cheese 'n' Deli.

"The kid's got a few problems, huh?" the lieutenant remarked after Rick had gone.

"He's coming along," Vicky replied.

"Tell me what happened here this morning."

Vicky related the details of the phone call, which he scribbled down in his notepad. He listened sympathetically, assuring Vicky that he and the FBI were close to breaking the case. This last bit of evidence—the fact that the killer might be a woman—could well be the clincher.

Because Justin had been given specific instructions not to leave town, Vicky didn't mention the boating trip to the lieutenant. What he didn't know, in this case, wouldn't hurt him.

Putting away his notepad, the officer rummaged through his pocket. "Oh, yeah, I nearly forgot. Here's the peephole for your door. The hardware store was out of window nails, but I can pick them up somewhere else."

"How thoughtful of you."

"When would you like me to install it?"

Vicky had to think quickly. She and Justin were supposed to disappear first thing in the morning. If she postponed the lieutenant's offer until Friday or Saturday, he might get suspicious. "How about this afternoon?" she asked. "I'm not staying at the shop. I only dropped in to see how Rick was doing."

"Sure, this afternoon's fine. I'll get the nails into your windows tomorrow."

"No!" she said, much too quickly. "I mean...there's no hurry. I'll be busy tomorrow—uh, I've got a doctor's appointment and some other urgent errands to run."

He regarded her with the discomfiting look of a seasoned cop. "Whatever you say. I'll come around later, then. About two?"

"Two is fine."

He got as far as the door and stopped. "You're absolutely sure it was a woman who called this morning?"

"I'm pretty sure. But I might be wrong. Whoever it was, I've never heard a voice quite like it."

Lieutenant Simmons scratched his head. "Strange. Oh well, see ya, Miss Green."

After he left, Vicky realized she hadn't told him about the anagram Mr. Rubinoff had discovered. No matter. She could tell him about it that afternoon when he installed the peephole.

"I ALREADY KNOW about it," was the lieutenant's response when she told him.

"You do? How?"

He aimed the electric drill at the appropriate spot on the door and switched it on. Vicky had to wait for the piercing whine to finish before the officer replied. "I saw your friend, Mr. Coe, at his office the other day. He wanted to show me the quotation you were talking about."

"And you deciphered the anagram?"

"After a while, sure, but that was only because Coe recited the quote and explained how the two phrases had been crossed out with red ink."

"Explained? Didn't you see it for yourself?"

The officer blew away sawdust and peered through the hole. "Nope, he explained it to me. The pages had been sliced out of the book, Miss Green."

Vicky paled. "They were? He...didn't tell me." What else, she couldn't help wondering, had Justin forgotten to tell?

Chapter Seventeen

The water in the bathtub gurgled down the drain as she held up a new bottle of nail polish. "Fuchsia Fury," she read aloud in a husky voice. "I do like the sound of that."

The robe she wore was of ivory satin, much more pleasant to the skin than the heavy terry cloth monstrosity she was usually forced to endure. She glanced around the room to make certain she was alone. Then, giggling to herself like a schoolgirl, she lifted up a large, hairy foot.

She'd managed to paint the first three toes before a familiar voice shouted, "Mama, what on earth are you doing?"

"What does it look like I'm doing? I'm painting my toes."

"But you can't! Those are *my*..." Not wanting to offend his mother, he stopped.

"I know what you were going to say. You were going to say they're your toes. And just where do you think your toes came from, son? They came from *me*! My womb, my body!"

"But I have to go to work, and people are going to know."

"Oh, quit your bellyaching. You sound just like your useless, good-for-nothing father. I'm only painting my toenails. You wear shoes and socks, don't you?"

"Where'd you get this robe?" The man ran his hands along the silky fabric. "I've never seen it before."

"Haven't you?" She laughed her deep, throaty laugh. "I bought it the same day I got Vicky's chocolates. Well, actually I didn't get the chocolates. I paid a wino fifty dollars to get them."

"You didn't," he said, horrified. "You actually went shopping without me?"

"Only for a little while. You must have been napping. Of course, I was obliged to wear one of my old dresses so no one would suspect. It was dreadful. I could barely get it over my shoulders." Holding her feet out in front of her, she wriggled them happily. "Not bad for a first coat."

The man sighed and shook his head.

"Now, son, you really did a poor job with Vicky. You're going to have to do better next time."

"But, Mama, you've spoken to her yourself. You know what a nice person she is."

"Since when did niceness have anything to do with it? She broke the chain. You and I agreed what had to be done when someone broke the chain."

"But the money is coming in. People are paying attention. Isn't that what you wanted?"

"The money is coming from Rosa's friends, the only ones who've had the good sense to keep the chain going. The original list is useless. I don't see why you don't get rid of all of them. It might even be sort of challenging, don't you think?"

He fell to his knees, as he'd done so many times as a child. "No, Mama, please. If we don't stop soon, we're gonna get caught."

"If we get caught, it's your own fault."

"No, it's not. I've been trying really hard . . ." Oh, what was the point? He'd never won an argument with her in his life. Ignoring his mother's protests, the man stormed out of the bathroom.

There was only one place in the house where Mama never found him, but he'd have to get there quickly. Tearing off the offensive satin robe, the man dropped to the floor and slithered on his stomach under the bed. Then he listened. All he could hear was the clock ticking on the nightstand.

He'd managed to outsmart her again.

TWO HOURS BEFORE DAWN, the sky was inky black and the streets of Madison deserted. Justin and Vicky were hurrying along Butler Street, but because of the hour they were quite certain they were not being watched. Their plans included the possibility that the blackmailer would keep a close eye on Justin during the forty-eight hours before payment was due. It was now Wednesday. Payment was due Thursday afternoon at the outside. Chances were, Vicky and Justin thought, the blackmailer would check the drop-off point tonight.

The Wagon Wheel Tavern had a deserted air, the long narrow windows stark against the sand-colored brick. Justin held the plastic-wrapped parcel under his arm, stuffed with newspaper to approximate a substantial bundle of cash. Vicky was carrying a small bag of potting tools that clanked terribly with each step she took.

"I'll do the digging," Vicky offered when they reached the hedge behind the bar. "You keep watch."

"That's fine with me." He pulled the stiff foliage of the privet hedge back and held it so that Vicky could crawl in more easily.

Justin was dressed in black and had a knitted hat over his head to hide the light brightness of his pale blond hair. But that was little more than a precaution—just in case anyone happened to be passing. Not likely, but snow blond hair might stick in someone's memory.

Vicky was grateful that she'd remembered to bring along a heavy pair of work gloves. Scraping away the grungy layer of topsoil with a trowel, she found rusty bottle caps, shards of glass, old nails. It was a wonder anything could grow in the parking lot of a tavern; she tried not to think about what must have fertilized the hedge all these years.

Still, burying the package seemed the best solution. It had to sit there, unnoticed and unharmed, for hours, maybe days, so the precaution was essential.

"Remember to leave part of the bag showing," Justin said.

"I will," replied Vicky. The sounds of the trowel were distorted and magnified in the clear night air, like the clawing of a giant raccoon.

"Someone's coming," Justin whispered and hunkered down between the hedge and a slight recess in the building.

Vicky stopped digging and waited. She could hear the approaching footsteps, the slap of leather soles on concrete. They were the fast, determined steps of someone who didn't like being out at this hour.

Vicky's hands were sweating profusely in the heavy gardening gloves. Something was tickling the back of her neck, probably a twig from the hedge, but she didn't dare relieve the irritation by moving. Her thighs ached, her feet were going to sleep; she wished whoever it was would move faster.

There was a pause in the walker's rhythm as he or she approached the Wagon Wheel, a hesitation suggesting the person suspected he was not alone. Vicky couldn't hear anything from Justin; she hoped to hell he was still there. The steps slowed, almost to a stop, then resumed twice as quickly. Less than a minute later, except for the occasional car on nearby Main Street, silence returned.

"It's okay," Justin whispered through the shrubbery. "She's gone."

"She?"

"A cook on her way to work at some breakfast place, I'd guess."

"Did she see you?"

"I think so, but she wasn't curious enough to stay and introduce herself. How much longer are you going to be?"

"A minute or two. This dirt is pretty solid."

"Do you want me to take over?"

"No, I'm nearly done... Okay, that's it for the digging." Covering the parcel with the loosened soil was much easier than digging the hole for it. She left the top edge of the bag exposed so that anyone looking for it would spot the parcel immediately. At the same time the bag was concealed well enough that no one else would be likely to notice its presence.

Justin helped Vicky crawl out of the shrubbery and took the bag of tools from her. He gave her hand a reassuring squeeze as they made their way back to his car, but neither of them spoke until they were on the road.

"Do you think the blackmailer was watching?" Vicky asked as they sped toward Spring Harbor where the sailboat was moored.

"No," Justin answered. His eyes narrowed as he watched the road. "He—or she—had better not have been or there goes our plan! And if the blackmailer is someone we know and have spoken to recently, then if anything he might be watching to make sure we actually leave town. Anyway, there'd be no reason for the blackmailer to watch the drop-off point until nearer the deadline."

Vicky groaned and slumped lower into the passenger seat. "Would you slow down, for pete's sake? All we'd need now is to get pulled over by the cops!"

Justin lifted his foot slightly off the accelerator and grinned at Vicky. "You know something? You're starting to sound like a fugitive. Should I start calling you Bonnie?"

"Very funny, Clyde. Keep your eyes on the road."

Che Sara was already on a trailer and hitched to the back of a van, lent to them by a fellow sailing friend of Justin's. It wouldn't have been convincing enough to simply sail on Lake Mendota since, though quite large, the lake was virtually contained within the city limits.

Justin parked the Jaguar in an obvious spot and locked the doors. The two of them took what little gear they had out of the small trunk and put it into the van. A hamper of food was in the front by Vicky's feet, food that would keep them going through the long day to follow.

It took a few minutes for Justin to adjust to driving a clunky van with a boat towed behind it. But at least he was forced to keep to the speed limit, Vicky thought with a modicum of relief.

They drove around the eastern shore of Lake Mendota until they came to Governor's Island, a small peninsula of land that jutted southward into the lake. They backed the van up to the launching ramp and together they lowered the boat into the water. It was nearly light by now, but Vicky and Justin were reasonably sure no one had followed them.

Their day on the boat, which Justin had powered out to the middle of the lake and anchored, was less than idyllic. Fortunately the rain held off, but the sky remained a dull lead gray. Choppy water was a novel experience for Vicky, and while she managed to refrain from throwing up, her mood was irascible.

The only consolation was that at the end of the day, they would be heading back to Governor's Island and setting in motion the most crucial aspect of the trap. In the meantime, all they had to do was kill time.

Justin did his best to keep Vicky amused belowdeck, but after a while, he gave up trying to teach her chess. Feeling guilty for being such poor company, Vicky tried to teach him backgammon and fared no better. Despite Justin's concerns, she couldn't eat a thing, let alone watch him eat. She spent a good part of the day lying in the cabin with a wet cloth over her head.

By evening, however, accustomed to the rocking movements of the anchored boat, Vicky began to improve. She sat at the edge of the bunk bed and waited for the pounding in her head to subside. Then she climbed to the deck where Justin sat watching the smudgy horizon.

He turned to her and smiled. "Feeling better?"

"A little, thanks."

"You're a lighter shade of green. That's a good sign. How would you like some tea?"

She nodded and sank to the nearest seat. "I'd love some." The wind had slowed to a cool breeze. It was dusk, with a dull matte of clouds that gave one a sense of suspended time.

Justin reached for a thermos and poured her a cup. "I don't think you should come with me tonight. You still look weak."

"I have to come with you."

"No, you don't. There'll be enough of us—"

"I don't exactly mean that you need me," she said, curling her hands around the warm metal cup, "but I want to be there. I'll go crazy sitting somewhere by myself and waiting, not knowing what's happening."

Justin stroked her cheek. "Nothing at all might happen tonight, if the blackmailer suspects a trap."

"That doesn't matter. I just...I want us to be together through all of this, okay?"

"Okay."

They sat in silence for a while, drinking tea, both absorbed in their own thoughts. Finally Vicky brought up something that had been troubling her for hours. "Why didn't you tell me you showed Lieutenant Simmons the book?"

"It didn't occur to me," he said, looking away.

"Of course it occurred to you, Justin. Don't lie."

His face, in the fading light of dusk, darkened perceptibly. "I've never lied to you, Vicky. There may be times when telling you the whole truth is inappropriate, but I'd never lie."

Though her headache was receding, Vicky's nerves felt raw. "That's hardly reassuring, but never mind. What I want to know is what happened to the pages in the book?"

"The lieutenant told you, didn't he? They were sliced out with a sharp blade of some kind. Probably a razor."

"By whom?"

"I don't know!" He slammed his cup down. "Listen, Vicky, did it ever occur to you that I might have done those things myself without being aware of it?"

She shuddered, recalling her moments of doubt concerning Justin. But she was beyond them now. It was time Justin, too, outgrew his own doubts. "Maeve must have done it," she announced bluntly.

"Maeve? Why would she do a thing like that?"

"Who knows? But she's in and out of your office all the time, isn't she?"

"So are a lot of other people." Justin checked his watch for at least the hundredth time. "Believe it or not, I have considered the possibility, but suspecting someone of a practical joke like defacing a book is a lot different from suspecting them of murder."

"I know," Vicky said quietly, pulling her hands deeper into the sleeves of her sweatshirt.

Justin went to her side and put an arm around her shoulders. "Whoever it is, we might find out tonight."

THE OWNER of the Wagon Wheel had been expecting them. It was half an hour before closing time. As he unlocked the emergency exit to let them in, he assured Justin and Vicky that no one except his regular customers had come into the bar that night. His attitude was one of a person delighted to be part of such intrigue. When Justin had spoken to him two days earlier about his role, the man had very nearly rubbed his hands with glee.

Now he led them to a small dark room overlooking the parking lot. Two chairs had been placed by the window for their use.

"Is the parcel still out there?" Justin asked.

"Last time I checked was about an hour ago, and it was still there," the owner said.

"Have the others arrived?" Justin took a seat across from Vicky.

"Yeah, they're all in their places. There's a couple of coffees behind you, miss, and a box of doughnuts. The coffee might be cold by now, though."

She smiled as she tried to adjust to the darkness. The room was hot and dusty; she hoped they wouldn't have to wait too long for something to happen. "Thank you," she said. "I'm sure the coffee will hit the spot."

A few minutes later, Justin and Vicky were alone, watching out the window as people left the bar, climbed into their cars and drove away. There were some who shouldn't have been getting into their cars at all.

The coffee was long gone, the doughnuts stale, by the time the parking lot had emptied. Vicky and Justin had driven a rental car from Governor's Island, leaving the sailboat moored and the van nearby. And even though the rented car made Vicky and Justin harder to identify, they still parked several blocks from the bar and took a taxi to the back entrance.

The blackmailer must not have seen them arrive. The two men assisting them in this trap had left a pocket-size monitor for them in the rental car. If the men *had* noticed anything unusual, they would have signaled by now.

Vicky had long since lost all track of time. Her eyes were growing heavy, her head was nodding as the minutes plodded by. It was all she could do to stay awake, let alone watch the total absence of activity through the dusty window. Justin had warned her not to disturb the dust, which might make it obvious the window was being used as a lookout.

His sharp whisper came at the same time as the buzzing of the pocket monitor. Vicky jerked up in her chair and peered through the glass. A bulky figure dressed head to toe in black was at the hedge, burrowing through the foliage like a giant rodent. It was impossible to identify the person from this angle, but Vicky could see shadows of the two FBI agents creeping in from behind, their guns aimed, ready to fire. So far, the blackmailer, too intent on the quarry, had seen nothing.

It took a minute or two for the stranger to dig up the bag. The agents stood immobile, waiting. A sense of icy revulsion crept through Vicky as she witnessed a crime being committed firsthand. An insect crawled across her hand; the dust made her feel like sneezing, but she forced herself not to move.

The figure's movements were slow and awkward backing out of the shrubbery, but Vicky could see the gleam of white plastic beneath one arm.

The FBI agents made their move. They closed in from opposite sides and shouted, "Stop!" The blackmailer tried to run, but the larger agent tackled and brought the criminal to the ground.

Vicky wasn't able to watch any longer. An agitated Justin had snatched her by the hand and was pulling her down the backstairs. As they rushed around the building, they could hear a familiar voice shrieking, "Let me go, damn you, let me go!"

Justin came upon the scene as though his legs were made of wood. His voice was taut with disbelief as he uttered, "Maeve?"

By this time the two agents had brought their quarry to her feet. "Yes, you son-of-a-bitch," she spluttered.

As Agents Carter and Darrigo greeted Vicky and Justin, Maeve continued her futile struggle. But her captors were large, burly men, and Vicky, feeling none of Justin's surprise, knew Maeve could never hope to escape.

The plastic-wrapped newsprint lay on the ground. As the sandy-haired Carter clapped handcuffs on Maeve, Agent Darrigo gingerly picked up the evidence.

"You have the right to remain silent...." Carter began.

"I know my rights!" the woman snapped, the black knitted toque slipping down over one eye. "No need to offend my intelligence with them." As if he hadn't heard her, the agent continued to intone his prisoner's rights.

"Why, Maeve?" Justin asked when Carter was through. "After all these years, why blackmail?"

"Either straighten my damned hat or take it off, would you?" she ordered one of the agents. Then she turned to Justin. "Think you're pretty clever, framing me like this? Well, it's not over yet, dear boy."

"You were the one person I thought I could trust," Justin said.

"Trust?" Maeve laughed harshly. "Do let us talk about trust, dear boy. Let's talk about the time I found a man with a guarded past and an empty future and took him under my wing. I was *Doctor* Maeve Wilson, the finest dramatic arts professor UW had ever known. And who were you? Nothing but a fugitive—albeit a handsome, clever fugitive."

Vicky watched Justin's pained expression and would gladly have throttled Maeve on the spot.

"I had plans, dear boy," the woman went on. "Not huge plans, but ones that suited me, nonetheless. Tenure, full professorship, to be head of the department. I was well on my way until a young whippersnapper named Justin Coe, a fellow I'd helped into a cushy job as an academic, left me choking in his dust. I'd never for a moment thought *that* would happen. But it did, and that's when I knew I'd have to pursue other means, other dreams."

The pain in Justin's eyes hardened to anger. "What do you know about my mother?" The FBI agents, in exchange for his cooperation, had promised Justin an opportunity to question her about his mother.

Maeve threw back her head and laughed. "Ah, yes, my *coup d' état*. It was fate, you know, recognizing the long lost Michael Justason at a vegetable stand, then miraculously running into his mother's press agent in New York a month ago."

"You met my mother's agent?"

"Yes. Somewhat older and paunchier, I presumed, and with a considerable penchant for Grand Marnier. After imbibing to a maudlin state, he commenced reminiscing about the golden years of Maija Justason. It wasn't difficult to drag the whole story out of him."

By now Maeve's captors, too, were hanging on her every word, precisely what the woman lived for. "Your mother didn't die in that hotel room where you'd left her, nor later in that Italian hospital, though she might as well have. Her brain was nothing but oatmeal—"

"That's no way to talk about someone's mother!" Vicky blurted.

Justin touched her arm. "It's all right, Vicky. Go on, Maeve."

Dr. Wilson issued Vicky a look of haughty triumph. "I really ought to have my attorney present, but it wouldn't make much difference. Your mother's in a nursing home in the Italian Alps, quite content from what I can gather. That photo I left you—her agent showed it to me, and I grabbed it when he wasn't looking—shows you that."

"Why was I never told?"

"You were nowhere to be found. Besides, her agent and her attorney thought it best that you and her fans believed she had died accidentally. Of course, it would never do to reveal the truth now, would it? I mean, the press would swarm the nursing home and take all sorts of hideous pictures."

With a moan, Justin covered his face with his hands. "I can't believe it. She's been alone all these years, and I've never known."

"How could you have known? You were busy eluding every cop in Europe." She pointed a finger at Justin and turned to the police. "You do realize, gentlemen, that this man has a murder charge hanging over him?"

Agent Darrigo remained expressionless. "His background is not in question right now, ma'am."

"You put us through all of this for seventy-five thousand dollars? That amount won't even buy a small house," Justin said.

"Oh, it would have been much more than seventy-five, I assure you. I wager I'll be out in a few years for good behavior, then I can sell the film rights to the book I'll have written in prison.''

''With two counts of murder against you?'' Justin retorted. ''I doubt it, Maeve.''

She gave him an incredulous look. ''What? You must be joking. I haven't murdered anyone.'' She turned to the FBI men. ''I thought I was being arrested for extortion. What's this nonsense about murder?''

''Theo Dalta and Eve Lomorth, ma'am,'' Agent Carter replied. ''You're also being arrested on two counts of homicide.''

''I had nothing to do with their demise. I only picked up on this chain letter business because it seemed a handy vehicle at the time.''

''But you called the other day,'' Vicky interjected, ''claiming to be the Easter Bunny's mother.''

The woman stared at her blankly. ''My dear child, you've gotten me mixed up with somebody else. I have never claimed to be anyone's mother.''

''But you did underline my book, the anthology with Drysdale's works,'' Justin said. ''And then you cut the pages out.''

Maeve tossed her head proudly. ''I assure you I did no such thing.'' Then, with an imperious smirk, she glanced from one agent to the other. ''I am feeling rather fatigued. Shall we go, gentlemen?''

Vicky was sure Maeve was lying. The trouble was, she couldn't determine where the lies began—with the denial of the book's defacement, the denial of the phone call to Vicky, or the two murders. In the car, she voiced her doubts to Justin.

''I know,'' he said. ''I was thinking the same thing.''

IT WAS NEARLY DAWN by the time Vicky and Justin finished giving their statements to the FBI. Vicky was surprised to discover that Agent Carter and Agent Darrigo were friendly and easygoing—not at all the way she'd imagined FBI operatives to be—but that didn't stop her from worrying the entire time she and Justin were in the office.

Later, when they were alone in an all-night doughnut shop, she leaned over to Justin. "Weren't you worried that they might do a computer check on you?"

"For the warrant, you mean?" He shook his head. "No, they had enough to keep them busy tonight and probably figured Maeve was fabricating the story."

"What will you do when they find out it's true?"

He took her hand, and his expression grew sad. "Nothing. I've told you I don't intend to run anymore. I'd rather take my chances with a trial. Meanwhile, I'm going to spend all my spare time with you."

She smiled. "I can't say I.mind."

"You were a real trouper last night, Vicky. You have been, ever since this whole mess began."

"But it's not over yet, is it?" Her smile faded as she recalled Maeve's adamant denial of the murders.

"I don't know. But let's not talk about that now." He leaned forward, his silver-blue gaze roaming her face.

Vicky tried to ignore the realization that her future with Justin might be coming to an end. "What do you want to talk about?"

"You. I'm worried, Vicky. I don't know how I'll be able to look after you if . . ."

"I'll be fine," she insisted, her voice shaky with emotion.

Justin laughed softly. "I know you'll be fine. You're a strong lady, and you're not afraid to stand up for what you believe in. It's one of the things I love about you."

Taking a sip of lukewarm coffee, she dropped her gaze. "That's nice of you to say."

"No. No, it's not nice," he muttered. "It's totally inadequate. What I meant to say was that . . . I love you."

He loved her. As long as that was true, Vicky told herself, what could possibly go wrong? But she knew that was a naive response based on little more than delirium from lack of sleep. Love was no shield against an uncertain future, no guarantee against pain or sorrow. But for now, at least, she was determined to enjoy the feeling.

Her face glowing with rapture, Vicky leaned closer to Justin and whispered, "I love you, too. Could we go home now?"

THEY SLEPT MOST of the following day. Vicky called the store in the morning to make sure Rick was all right, then unplugged the phone. She and Justin deserved their rest, and they'd earned their privacy.

Now that their feelings were in the open and in perfect harmony, making love was even better than before. At the far corners of Vicky's mind, she knew the police could show up at any moment and arrest Justin for murder.

But what was important was that she knew, knew in her heart, that Justin could never have killed anyone. She wasn't harboring a fugitive; she was loving an innocent man. She had to cling to that truth. And no one, nothing, was going to stop them from sharing the time they had left.

They were apart only once—briefly—during the day. Vicky had run out of milk and couldn't drink tea without it. Justin borrowed her keys so he wouldn't have to disturb her in bed and went out to the corner store.

While he was away, Vicky was a nervous wreck—not for her own safety, but for Justin's. She was terrified the FBI would be waiting on the sidewalk. Despite the fact that she'd been half asleep when Justin left, she got up and spent the entire time with her eye glued to the peephole, watching for his return.

That evening, Justin had a faculty meeting he couldn't postpone. Vicky couldn't bear the idea of staying at home alone, so she asked Justin to drop her off at the Nick Nack Nook. Her bookkeeping was more than a week behind, and she hoped that working with figures might distract her for a while. Justin promised to call when the meeting was over. Then he would come by and pick her up.

Vicky worked at a table in the back room. The front door was locked, and the door to the stockroom closed so that no one on the street would know she was there.

She felt a peace working with figures. They were logical, precise, totally unlike her life at the moment. Would it ever be logical? she wondered. Did she and Justin have any chance at all for happiness?

Vicky heard the front bell jingle. Someone had come in. At first she thought it was Justin. But he didn't have a key to the shop. Her keys were on the ring in her purse. It had to be Rick.

As she got up to check, the room was suddenly plunged into darkness. The light switch was on the other side of the door.

"Who is it? Who's there? Rick?" Vicky called out, her fingers gripping the edge of the table.

No one replied. There were no windows in the room. It was utterly black; she couldn't see a thing. Hesitantly she slid one foot ahead of her.

Then the shattering began. Pottery, glassware, ceramics—crashing and splintering. A madman, a gorilla was unleashing his fury in the shop that Vicky loved! Angered, beyond fear, she lunged, pushing all her weight against the stockroom door.

As abruptly as it began, the destruction ceased. But before Vicky could react, a pair of strong hands clamped around her neck.

Chapter Eighteen

She couldn't breathe; she couldn't see, but she could smell the intruder's noxious breath. He was panting in her face, grunting with exertion while his fingers squeezed harder.

Vicky kicked and scratched, but she didn't have the strength to loosen her attacker's grip. She managed a few ineffectual kicks, but they only served to anger him. As he wrenched her body backward, Vicky feared she had only moments to live.

Her breath was nothing more than pitiful gurgles; her lungs burned for oxygen. Blindly she reached out to one side. Blindly she groped for anything that would save her.

The tips of her fingers hit a shelf, and it was as though she'd been thrown a lifeline. She squeezed the plank of wood, concentrating with all of her might to regain some control.

Briefly she relaxed, forcing her assailant to take all her body weight. It threw him off; his grip slackened. Only for an instant, but long enough for Vicky to reach across the shelf.

Please, dear God, let it be there.

It was.

The Exacto knife she'd used to cut the liner for shelves a few days earlier. Her fingers touched it, but it slipped and moved out of reach. She lunged again, mindless of her agony. Every fiber of her being was drawn to the small object on the shelf.

The second time, her luck was better. Her fingers curled around the metal knife. She could only pray that the blade faced the right way. There was no time to test it.

Vicky raised her arm and swiftly brought it down across the strangler's cheek. His garbled scream confirmed the blade had hit its mark.

His hands fell from her neck. He hunched over, clutching his face, then turned and stumbled from the store.

The door stood ajar. A cool night breeze wafted inside.

For a long while Vicky stood motionless in the dark, her throat ravaged, her senses stripped. The glow from the streetlights cast a cruel shimmer across the shards of clay and glass on the floor. Vicky would have collapsed in tears, but her anguish was too deep, her pain too real to be eased by hysteria.

She stumbled across the room, gingerly holding her bruised neck with one hand. Every breath she took was agony, each step an endless journey. Finally, she managed to reach the telephone.

"Operator...this is an emergency. Get me...the police."

They were there within minutes. Two uniformed officers and the same FBI agents she and Justin had met the night before. Officer Carter, the older one, took her to the hospital while the others searched the store.

A doctor in emergency examined her and told her she was very lucky. She didn't feel lucky. He gave her something for the pain, and then she returned to the Nick Nack Nook with the officer.

He made her tea in the back room and asked questions. Could the attacker have been her employee, this Rick? No way, Vicky replied. Rick would never do that. Could she describe him? Not really, Vicky answered. Was he short, tall? Hard to tell; he was hunched over. No, she didn't see his face. No, he didn't say anything.

After she'd finished the tea, Vicky went out to the main room where the officers were nearly finished with their investigation. She listened to them talk among themselves.

"Any prints?"

"Plenty, but they could belong to Miss Green or her employee. They're probably customers' prints."

"Not likely he had time to take anything."

"Nope, doesn't appear to be a burglary. No sign of the lock being jimmied. He didn't go anywhere near the cash."

"Just plain old vandalism, huh?" Sighing, the uniformed veteran strode across the room to where Vicky had been attacked and made her successful counter attack. "Better ask the lab to take a look at these bloodstains," he said, studying the dark brown spots on the floor.

Heartbroken, Vicky gazed at what was left of her treasures. Most of the shelves in the center of the store had been swiped clean, their contents strewn and shattered. Porcelain animals, music boxes, ships of blown glass. Vicky stooped to pick up an apple-head doll resilient enough not to break. She hugged it to her chest, not caring what the policemen thought.

"We're going to take you home now, Miss Green," Agent Darrigo told her. "Do you have a spare key so the officers can lock up after they've finished?"

She nodded and pointed to a place under the counter.

"Thanks, guys, you've been great," the agents said to the Madison policemen. "Talk to you tomorrow."

As Vicky climbed into the sedan, she heard the phone ringing in the store. She was too weary, too despondent to wonder who it was. The ringing stopped quickly; the police must have answered it.

When they reached her apartment and went inside with her, the agents were very kind. They commended her for her courage, brewed more tea and asked if there was anything else they could do to make her comfortable.

Vicky shook her head. "I do have one question, though. Why were you involved tonight? Isn't vandalism something that's usually handled by the local police?"

"You're right, it's not our jurisdiction," the sandy-haired Carter said, "but we've been instructed to investigate any events related to the chain letter. Lieutenant Simmons would have wanted to be there just as he would have last night, but he puts in a long day shift. We'll fill him in in the morning."

"I see," she said in a small voice.

Agent Darrigo gave her a sympathetic smile. "If it's any consolation, Vicky, we think we're close to making an arrest."

Under the circumstances, it was small consolation. But she thanked them anyway, saw the agents to the door and went to bed.

THE MAN STUMBLED ALONE through the cemetery. Clouds covered the moon, making it hard for him to see. He went to a place where the ground rose slightly, where no graves had yet been laid.

This was what Mama had always wanted, her little place in the sun. The headstone would be majestic, pink marble, covered with angels and cherubs playing harps. It would be a lot better than the cheap cross and pine coffin that had rotted away years ago.

"Can't you just see it, Mama? Tall and fancy, the biggest monument in the whole place."

But Mama wasn't talking, and that made him nervous. He didn't like it when she disappeared without telling him. He'd feel much better once he got her into a fancy brass coffin with latches and locks. Mama didn't know it yet— and he sure as hell wasn't gonna tell her—but when she was laid to rest this time, in a proper tomb, there'd be no more getting out to pester him. She'd be stone cold dead. For good this time.

"The money's still coming in," he called out hopefully.

Nothing but silence.

What really worried him was that even when she wasn't around, he felt her presence. At times he was afraid to open his mouth in public, in case Mama spoke up instead of him. Once, to his horror, it had happened.

They had been in a drugstore. He had been buying lipstick and had told the cashier, as he usually did, that it was for his wife. Except that Mama had spoken up instead and had said clear as day. "The lipstick's for me. Do you like the color?"

The cashier had laughed nervously and rung the purchase through without a word. The man never wanted to go through that sort of humiliation again.

"Do you hear me, Mama?" he cried into the night air. "I don't ever want you doing that to me again!"

Bending down, he touched the damp ground where Mama would soon be locked away. Then, touching the gash on his cheek, he staggered back to the car. Wouldn't be long now, he told himself. Mama would be where she belonged.

THE NEXT DAY Vicky had to force herself out of bed. She felt hollow, lifeless. One look in the mirror was nearly enough to make her crawl under the sheets again. Her neck was a mass of purple splotches, tender to the touch.

She took a hot shower, as hot as she could stand, and let the tears flow freely with the water. For a time, she even considered phoning her parents and telling them she'd be on the next bus home. She realized that was the second time in as many weeks she'd felt that way. Oh, God.

But not only would they be horrified to learn what had happened, they wouldn't be able to help. She couldn't rely on Mommy and Daddy to kiss away the hurt anymore. She was a big girl with big responsibilities.

Vicky put on a high-necked white blouse, then with a bitter laugh, took it off. The garment covered her bruises well enough, but she wasn't going to be serving customers today, and white lace was hardly practical for the job she had ahead of her.

She put on a blue cotton turtleneck sweater and pushed the sleeves up to her elbows. She'd probably swelter, but it was better than nothing. The sturdy jeans she pulled on might offer some protection from broken glass while she worked.

It was too early to call the insurance company. That could wait until she got to the store. But she could phone Rick now and tell him not to bother coming in to work today. She realized he would be a big help in the cleanup, but she wasn't in the mood for his company today. There were some incidents one was better off handling alone.

Rick's sister answered the phone.

"Diane? It's Vicky. I'm calling to let Rick know that he doesn't have to come into work today."

His sister sounded as though she'd been crying. "Oh, Vicky, I'm so glad you called. I wanted to phone you, but I was afraid it was too early."

Vicky's hands tightened around the receiver. "Why? What's the matter? Is Rick hurt?"

"I...I don't know. Rick's missing. He didn't come home at all last night."

"Didn't come home?" Vicky stared sightlessly across the room. Why wouldn't Rick go home? Was he trying to hide something, she wondered—like a gash on his cheek?

"Are you still there, Vicky?"

"I'm still here. Have you called the police?"

"Yes, they've put out a—what do you call it—APB. They know about Rick's mental condition, so they're giving it top priority."

And what of his physical condition? Vicky struggled with the notion of telling Diane what had happened. But if it *was* Rick who'd attacked her last night, it would do no good to upset his sister now. The police were already looking for the man, and no doubt they had pieced things together by now. Vicky was assaulted, after which her simpleminded employee went missing. The conclusion one had to draw was obvious.

"I'm sorry about Rick," Vicky said. "You must be frantic. But I'm sure they'll find him. Let me know if you hear anything."

"I will," Diane replied, unsuspecting. "Thanks for calling."

Vicky took the bus to the Cheese 'n' Deli. She had no appetite for breakfast, but a cup of Mr. Rubinoff's bracing coffee would do her a world of good.

His face was dark with concern when Vicky walked into the deli. "I heard what happened, Victoria. The police were here this morning."

"So they told you about Rick, too?"

He looked at her strangely. "Rick? What about him?"

"He's missing."

Her friend drew in a sharp breath as he poured the coffee. "Dear God. They probably think he was the one who attacked you."

"I suppose so," she acknowledged, fitting a plastic lid over the cup. "They'll know, one way or another, as soon as they see him."

"Why do you say that?"

"I sliced his cheek with an Exacto knife."

"It might have been someone other than Rick, you know."

Vicky nodded. "I hope it was." She turned to go, then looked back. "You haven't seen him since yesterday afternoon, by any chance?"

"No." The Gypsy shook his head emphatically. "I have not seen Rick Paterson anywhere."

Vicky was certain that if Mr. Rubinoff wanted to tell a bold-faced lie, he would do it convincingly. But he wasn't convincing now. Some gut instinct told her Mr. Rubinoff had seen Rick. He was lying to her. The only question was why.

As soon as she had called the insurance company, Vicky phoned Justin at the office. He wasn't in; she left a message. There was no answer at his house either.

Next she tried calling Lieutenant Simmons at the station; he wasn't there. According to the switchboard dispatcher, he was scheduled for traffic court all morning. Again Vicky left a message.

So this was how her day was going to be. Rick Paterson missing, Mr. Rubinoff lying, Justin and the lieutenant incommunicado. Where were friends when you needed them?

The insurance investigator had told her not to touch anything until he got there. It was just as well. She wasn't eager to begin sweeping up last night's devastation. She could hardly stand looking at it.

Vicky sat at the front counter with her coffee and opened the front page of the paper. The photograph of a demolished car made no impression at first. Then she scanned the caption underneath. "Sean Filipi was hospitalized after his car hit an abutment on West Broadway last night."

Sean Filipi. Wasn't that one of the names on the chain letter list? Her taxed mind couldn't get a handle on it. She repeated the name to herself several times, then tried to remember the quotation. "Mother, love a something," she muttered. "Something...life is...life is what? Pain, that's it!"

Vicky picked up a pencil and wrote the words "life is pain." Then, one by one, she crossed off each letter in Sean Filipi's name. She was right. He was on the list. And he'd nearly been killed last night!

Adrenaline pumped through her. She banged around the store, feeling as though there was something she ought to do, somewhere she should go, someone she should call. But finally her arms fell to her sides, and she shambled back to the stool. There was nothing she could do. Nothing at all, except wait for the insurance man to come and assess the damages.

Lieutenant Simmons phoned later that morning. "I'm awfully sorry to hear about the trouble last night. I should have been there."

"It's okay. The police were very helpful. I guess you must have heard by now that Rick's missing."

There was silence at the other end. "No, actually, I hadn't heard. Rick, huh? Too bad. He's a nice kid."

"Lieutenant," Vicky said hesitantly, "I think Rick might have been the one who attacked me last night. I don't know for sure, of course, but he does have a key, and it seems awfully coincidental that he's disappeared now, of all times."

"It could have been him, I suppose, but I doubt it."

"Why?"

"Did you read the papers this morning?"

Vicky's heart began to hammer, dreading what she might hear. "You mean Sean Filipi's accident?"

"That's right. A witness has called in since to say he saw a silver Jaguar deliberately run Filipi's car off the road sometime after one in the morning."

"That's ridiculous, lieutenant," she countered. "Justin was...he was..." She had to think hard. So much had happened, she couldn't remember where Justin was supposed to have been. "He was at a faculty meeting. I know, because he dropped me off and went straight to campus after that."

"What time did he drop you off?"

"Around seven-fifteen. The meeting was going to start at half-past."

"I phoned the station this morning, Miss Green. The FBI have already questioned Mr. Coe. His meeting finished at ten-thirty last night. Nobody saw him after that."

"Does that mean...y-you've arrested him?"

"Not yet. We'll need more evidence. But we're close, Miss Green, damn close, if you'll pardon the language."

"It's impossible!" she cried. "Justin would never hurt anyone. I know him too well!"

"How long have you known him, Miss Green? Two weeks, three?"

Her shoulders sagged. "Nearly three weeks."

"There was also a note found on the front seat of Filipi's car, similar to the other ones."

"Don't tell me," Vicky said. "Life is pain, right?"

"Yeah, you figured it out."

She sighed. "It wasn't that hard, lieutenant. The killer's becoming predictable."

Lieutenant Simmons was silent for a moment, undoubtedly trying to extract some significance from Vicky's comment. But there wasn't any significance. She was just fed up.

"I don't suppose Justin has told you about the outstanding warrant in Italy," the officer said, changing the subject.

"Murder. Yes, I know about that, too."

The officer clicked his tongue against his teeth. "Look, Miss Green, why don't you take my advice and forget about this guy? He's a loser, a class-A loser."

Vicky had an urge to tell the lieutenant that she, too, felt like a loser at the moment. But she didn't have the energy. "I'll think about what you've told me, lieutenant. Thanks for calling."

Chapter Nineteen

"Darling, I need to see you."

"Where are you?" she said. "I called the office. They said you hadn't come in, and I've been phoning your house ever since."

Vicky had never been so glad to hear anyone's voice. To hell with what the lieutenant had told her! The witness, whoever he was, was mistaken. Mistaken—or lying.

"I've had the phone unplugged all day." Justin sounded tired. No, he sounded worse than tired. Defeated. "I figured if I'm going to be arrested any minute, I might as well enjoy privacy while I wait."

"What are the police stalling for?"

"They need a sworn statement from the witness. If I don't come up with a convincing alibi in the meantime, that will be it. I'll be arraigned as the infamous chain letter killer."

Vicky refused to acknowledge his fatalistic remark. She could hear ice cubes clinking in a glass. "You wanted to see me?" she asked.

"I've been worried sick about you. I phoned the store last night, and a cop said there'd been a break-in, and the FBI was taking you home."

"Yes, but I'm all right," she said, her fingers reaching for her bruised throat.

"I won't believe you until I see for myself. Would you consider coming over?"

She glanced at the clock on the wall. It was after seven p.m. She was tired and achy after cleaning the shop all day, but part of her misery, she was certain, could be directly attributed to her missing Justin.

He misunderstood her hesitation. "I suppose the police have warned you to stay away from me."

Her heart wrenched to hear the desperation in his voice. Perhaps the police knew more about Justin than she did, but there had to be some basis for her faith in him. She'd never been starry-eyed about men—at least, not until now.

"They've warned me," she admitted, "but it doesn't matter. I'll be there in fifteen minutes."

The walk to his house took only ten. The sun was still above the horizon, so Vicky wasn't at all afraid of walking alone. If she did have anything to be frightened of, it was what she would find at the other end.

The first hurdle was cleared as soon as Justin opened the door. His face, though pale and drawn, was unmarked. While it did not exonerate him from Sean Filipi's accident, at least Vicky knew he hadn't tried to strangle her last night.

She stepped into the cool entryway and lifted her eyes to Justin. This evening he looked more than his thirty-seven years, but to her he still looked wonderful. When he opened his arms, she buried herself in his embrace. If only this moment would last, she thought.

Justin glided his hand upward to tousle Vicky's hair. Involuntarily she flinched. He pulled his hand away and stared at her gravely, then lowered a corner of her turtleneck sweater. His face twisted with pain and rage.

"Dammit, Vicky. Why didn't you tell me?"

She turned her head away, as if she were ashamed. "I would have eventually."

"I'll kill him," he muttered.

"I think there's been enough of that lately."

He took her face tenderly in his hands. "Did he do anything else to you?"

"Apart from destroying the shop? No." She could no longer prevent the hot, silent tears from rolling down her cheeks. Justin seemed to understand. He simply held her until the worst was over.

"Have you had dinner?" he asked.

"No, I don't have much appetite tonight."

"Me neither, but I have some frozen gourmet dinners and there's a half-decent Reisling in the cellar. Why don't you join me?"

Vicky shrugged. "Why not? It'll give us something to do while we wait."

Justin poured the wine while the dinners heated in the microwave. They sat at a beautiful rosewood table in the formal dining room, a nod to gentility in a less-than-genteel situation.

"How's Maeve?" Vicky asked. "Have you heard anything about her?"

The way Justin's fingers gripped the glass told her his friend's betrayal still stung. "A cousin of hers posted bail, which I understood was considerable. Maeve's staying with her now in Milwaukee."

"It must have been quite a blow for the faculty."

"And the students. Maeve wasn't always the easiest person to like, but people couldn't help admiring her."

"What about your mother? Have you learned anything more?"

"Yes, I got in touch with her press agent. At first, the jerk tried to deny the story. I even thought for a while that Maeve had made the whole thing up, but it's true, all right."

"No one knew she was alive except him?"

"And my mother's attorney, the executor of her estate. He's been paying her upkeep all these years with interest from her royalties."

"I guess you'll want to make plans to see her."

"I'd like to, but I can't leave, remember?"

"Won't they make an exception on humanitarian grounds or something?"

"Not likely. I disappeared in Europe once before. They have no reason to believe I wouldn't do it again." His mouth twisted in a cynical grin. "Incidentally, I forgot to tell you. The FBI did look into my past."

"They came up with the warrant?"

"Yes, and guess what? The case was solved six years ago."

"You're kidding! Who did it?"

"A corrupt town official, known for his association with the underworld. The guy was forced to confess after a new local party came into power. It was in some of the papers, but the case was so old most people didn't pay any attention to it."

"So you've finally been proven innocent!" she said happily.

He made a sound of derision. "Wouldn't you know it? I finally get off the hook for one murder, and now I'm facing two counts of homicide and two of attempted. No one ever said life was fair."

Vicky got up, went behind Justin's chair and wrapped her arms around his shoulders. "Things are going to work out. I know they are." Actually she knew no such thing, but someone had to keep up the pretense of optimism.

When Justin didn't reply, she went into the kitchen where the microwave timer had sounded, and removed the dinners. Placing them on quilted mats, she carried them into the dining room. Justin took matches from the hutch and lit a pair of candles in the center of the table.

"Now, tell me exactly what happened to you last night," Justin said as he sat down across from her.

Vicky stabbed a water chestnut and stirred it around in the sauce. The deep warm tones of the room were soothing, as was the reflection of candlelight on the rosewood table. But her appetite was still nonexistent.

"I was in the back room doing the books when I heard the front door open . . ."

When Vicky had finished talking, Justin took her hand. "Do you have any idea who did it?"

"I'm afraid I do," she replied softly. "It was probably Rick. He didn't go home at all last night, and the police are looking for him now."

Justin looked unconvinced. "Why would Rick want to hurt you?"

"It's not that he wants to, but Rick has been terribly confused. Nothing's been normal the past few weeks, and he's the type of person who needs routine and stability in his life. I think I might have put too much responsibility on him, for one thing. And I know he's never really adjusted to you."

Justin gave her a tiny smile. "You don't think so? Why not?"

"I'm not sure. He either associates you with the strange things that have happened lately, or he's just plain jealous."

Justin thought about this for a moment. "Well, if it was Rick, and I'm not saying it wasn't, I don't think he realized what he was doing. He wouldn't knowingly hurt anyone."

"That's what I've always thought, but his sister told me when I first hired him that he was capable of violent tantrums. Yet in the three years I've known him, he's been a lamb." She wiped a wayward tear from her eye. "I hope they find him soon. Rick doesn't know how to cope out there."

"Don't worry too much, darling. They'll find him. I'm sure of it."

For a while, they ate their meals in silence. It probably wasn't the food's fault, but Vicky didn't taste a thing. She went through the motions of chewing and swallowing, while her mind wandered in a dull gray haze. The only bright spot in her life was Justin, and from all accounts, it looked as though he too would soon be gone.

Vicky gave up trying to eat and set down her fork. "You mentioned that you called the store last night."

"I wanted to let you know the meeting was finished and that I'd be along soon to pick you up."

"Why didn't you call me at home? I was there by eleven."

"I wanted to, but the FBI agents showed up at my door. They questioned me about where I'd been the past few hours and warned me not to disturb you. You were badly in need of rest, they said."

"You had no trouble proving that you attended a faculty meeting?"

"That part was easy. It was the rest of the night I had problems with."

Vicky nodded. "I know, the accident. Lieutenant Simmons said that it happened sometime around one in the morning."

Justin swirled the wine in his glass. "Apparently so."

"What were you doing at one o'clock?"

He looked up at her in surprise. "What any normal, warm-blooded male would be doing under the circumstances. I was lying in bed, wondering how you were."

"So you have no alibi?"

"None that will satisfy the police department."

Purposefully Vicky picked up the wine bottle and emptied it into her glass. "You have now."

"What?"

"You were with me last night."

"No, I wasn't."

"But they don't know that," Vicky pointed out. "I was in bed at one o'clock too, wide awake. Who's to say you didn't ignore the FBI agents' warning to leave me alone? I was hurting, you were worried. And we have been known to spend the night together."

Justin placed both elbows on the table and stared at her, incredulous. "Do you realize what you're saying, Vicky?"

She met his gaze head-on. "I'm saying that the man I love was in my apartment from approximately midnight last night until...what, seven o'clock this morning. He couldn't possibly have been in his Jaguar forcing cars off the road at one.''

"That's perjury, Vicky. A federal offense.''

"I know, but there have been a lot of federal offenses committed around here lately. Once the police find the real culprit, they aren't going to care that I told one lie to keep an innocent man from going to prison.''

"What makes you so certain I am innocent?" Justin asked, his voice thick with emotion.

The question threw her. Emotionally Vicky was totally convinced of his innocence. Intellectually? She was forced once again to rely on her emotions. There were, unfortunately, no intellectual arguments in Justin's favor.

Earlier she'd been relieved to find no gash on Justin's cheek, but now she realized that her optimism was premature. There was nothing to prove that last night's break-in was related to the chain letter. Sean Filipi's accident, however, clearly had been. The first might have been committed by Rick; the second by... God only knew whom.

"If you're having that much trouble rationalizing your argument, Vicky, then you'd better withdraw your offer.''

She placed her forearms on the table and leaned forward. "I won't withdraw my offer. You are innocent, Justin. And I intend to give the police that alibi, whether you want me to or not.''

"But I've already told them I don't have any proof of where I was last night.''

"Then I'll have to tell them you were lying to... to protect me.''

Their eyes met: hers hazel, lately as tough as the nut they were named for; his, crystal blue and nearly shattered.

Apparently at a loss for words, Justin got up from the table. "I'm going to get the coffee.''

While he was in the kitchen, the phone rang. He answered it there. "Hello?" Vicky heard him say. "Yes, this is the number, but there's no one by that name living here... no problem... goodbye.''

He returned a moment later with two mugs.

"You've plugged your phone back in?" Vicky remarked.

"I forgot to unplug it after I talked to you." He poured milk in her coffee and handed it to her. It was as though they'd never even mentioned the alibi.

Justin hadn't reacted the way Vicky'd hoped he would. Granted, her offer to lie on his behalf had been impulsive, but it wasn't such a terrible thing. Protecting someone you loved, someone you believed in. If she didn't stand up for him, no one would.

From what Vicky had seen, his colleagues and his students liked Justin, but they knew very little about him. He was a private man, accustomed to doing things on his own. At times like these, a life-style like Justin's was a definite liability.

"Why don't we get back to our conversation?" Vicky asked, deciding she might as well force the issue.

She felt a certain urgency to get it resolved now. Otherwise there was a very real danger that she might lose her nerve. Lying to the police would not be easy; lying before a court of law would be even harder. She was going to need all the righteous anger she could muster.

"Fine, let's get back to it," Justin said. "I don't want you to lie for me. Plain and simple."

If the message in his eyes had matched his words, Vicky might have agreed to forget the whole thing. But his eyes were pleading even as he tried to appear stern. They glistened with uncertainty, belying the false confidence of his words. There was no one else for Justin to turn to, and he damned well knew it.

"What if the situation was reversed?" Vicky asked. "Would you offer to do the same for me?"

He sighed heavily. "I wouldn't hesitate."

"Then that settles it."

She took a sip of coffee, knowing there would be no further argument. Justin would not offend her with some hackneyed line about her being a woman and him a man, honor bound to protect the so-called weaker sex. Friendship and loyalty transcended sexual boundaries, and they were both mature enough to recognize it.

Justin sullenly pushed his coffee away. "If you don't mind, Vicky, I think I'm going to turn in early tonight."

She knew better than to expect gratitude. "Should I go to the police station now to sign a statement?"

"No, you might as well wait until morning when Lieutenant Simmons is on duty."

Vicky hoped—no prayed—that soon this would all be behind them, that she and Justin could begin life again as a happy normal couple. "Thanks for dinner," she said as she walked to the door.

"I'd offer you a ride home, but I am unofficially grounded. Let me call you a cab. It's dark outside."

Hugging her arms to her sides, Vicky shook her head. "I'll walk home. It's not far." To be honest, she would have loved to have taken a cab home. But if she was going to get through this ordeal unscathed, she needed courage. Real courage. And the only way to get it, it seemed to her, was to practice on the small things, like walking for ten minutes after dark on her own.

Justin took her shoulders and drew her to him. "Be careful, Vicky, and remember that I love you."

Her vision blurred with tears of joy and sadness. "I love you, too, Justin. More than I can ever say."

He stood at the door, watching her leave. Vicky walked a short distance, then looked back and waved. To continue walking was one of the hardest things she'd ever done.

Once she'd settled into the familiarity of the street, Vicky's fear ebbed. When she came right down to it, darkness did not harbor any more danger than daylight. The people living in the small tidy bungalows were still good people; the cars driving by had legitimate reasons for being on the road. Crickets chirped; frogs croaked. Everything was fine.

As if to prove it to herself, Vicky made a concerted effort not to hurry. There was nothing waiting for her at home except the plants and, surprisingly enough, they were still thriving.

The lights from the pleasure boats on Lake Mendota cast shimmering ribbons across the water. The night air was clear, peaceful, the perfect setting for a lovers' stroll. Would there ever come a time, Vicky wondered, when she and her lover could take such a stroll?

She had just turned from Sherman onto Brearly Street, about halfway home, when she heard a slight movement in the hedge along the sidewalk. Her step slowed. She tensed, then realized it must have been a cat. Her nerves were threatening to get the better of her.

She continued to walk and heard the rustle again, louder this time. Then came the footfall of someone directly behind her.

The hair on her neck bristled. It was nothing, she argued with herself. Just someone coming out of his driveway, taking out the trash.

She quickened her pace. He kept up easily.

"What's your hurry, Vicky?"

She froze, then slowly she turned.

It was Rick.

Chapter Twenty

"Hello, Vicky."

Her feet were rooted to the sidewalk, her eyes fixed on Rick. The right side of his face was in shadow, but she didn't need to get any closer. Vicky no longer suffered any doubts that there was a slash across his cheek.

"What's the matter?" he asked. "Aren't you glad to see me?"

"I, uh, I..." It was no use. She couldn't force the words out.

He took a half step closer. "Don't you know it's not safe to walk alone after dark, Vicky? You should have friends walking with you."

Slowly she slid one foot back, then the other, hoping Rick wouldn't notice her retreat. "It *was* you, after all," she said, feeling numb.

"What do you mean?"

"Last night. You came into the Nick Nack Nook ... you destroyed it ... and you tried to—tried to..." There was no need to go on. Rick Paterson really was a big, hulking brute of a man. His shoulders were broad enough to fill the average doorway. He held his arms away from his sides—a football player's stance. Vicky shuddered.

"Are you saying I tried to kill you?" He tipped his head to one side, like a puppy whose feelings were hurt. "Vicky, how can you say that about me?"

She had to keep him talking, keep him off guard. Her only chance was to get some distance between them and make a run for it. "Where did you go last night," she asked. "after you left the store?"

"I went for a walk and did things."

"What kind of things?"

"All kinds. I took a bus to the zoo. They have animals you can pet."

"That's nice. Where else did you go?"

Vicky took another sliding step backward and kept a rigid smile pinned to her face. But so far it wasn't working. Rick was matching each of her steps with a forward slide of his own. If she didn't know better, she'd have sworn the distance between them was lessening. He was no more than ten feet away. One good lunge, and he'd have her.

"I wanted to go to the fish hatchery," he said, "but it was closed. That made me angry."

"Your sister was worried about you. You should have called her."

Only about three blocks to go, but Vicky felt far from reassured. Even if she could outrun Rick, first she had to turn around and build up enough speed from the start so he couldn't tackle her. Football players were trained to tackle. Was it something they never forgot, she wondered, like riding a bike?

"I forgot to call." Rick shrugged and shook his head. "Actually, I didn't forget. I wanted to be by myself. Diane worries too much. She thinks I'm a moron."

"Rick, don't say that..." Vicky began automatically, then stopped. It was hard, despite everything, not to think of him still as her sweet, harmless employee.

"But she does think so. I can take care of myself. You know that better than anyone." He craned his neck. "Why are you walking away from me like that, Vicky? I'm not going to hurt you." His wheedling tones were those of a child, a child who had no idea of his own strength, his own lack of perception.

"I know you won't," Vicky said. It seemed wiser to go along with his ruse of innocence. Accusing him might only fuel his rage, and he was much easier to handle in a placid state of mind. "I'm just...I'm in a hurry to get home, that's all."

"Then I'll go with you. I can walk fast." His long legs halved the distance between them in a single stride.

Vicky couldn't stall any longer. She spun on one foot and began to run. It took a few seconds to build up speed, but she could tell that Rick was taken off guard.

He didn't start chasing her right away. By the time he did, she'd passed the intersection of Gorham and Castle Place. Only a block and a half left.

His footsteps were awkward and heavy. They seemed to shake the very concrete beneath Vicky's feet. But he was catching up. Lowering her head, Vicky tried to run faster and wondered why no one driving by stopped to help.

"Wait, Vicky, wait!" Rick called out.

His pleading voice spurred her on. At last, the apartment building loomed into view. But Rick, by now, was so close she could almost feel his gasps on her neck. He could have grabbed her by the legs easily and brought her down, but obviously, he hadn't thought of it. Thank heaven for small favors.

Pivoting sharply, Vicky tore up the walkway to her building. Please, God, let the front doors be unlocked. She hadn't troubled to lock them when she'd left earlier, and maybe...

They were unlocked. She pulled the doors open and saw from the reflection of the glass that Rick was lagging. He was getting tired. But she didn't dare congratulate herself yet. He was still coming after her.

Her feet took the stairs two at a time as she rummaged through her purse for the apartment key. She stabbed it into the lock, grateful when, for once, it chose not to stick. She could hear the lobby doors swinging open just as she locked her own door behind her.

Vicky did not stop running until she was in her bedroom. She slammed the door shut, then collapsing on the mattress, she gave herself a moment to catch her breath before picking up the phone on the nightstand.

The room was illuminated only by a streetlamp outside, but Vicky did not want to risk turning on the lights. Her curtains were open, and Rick might decide to break in through a window instead. He should have been pounding on her door by now. The fact that he wasn't worried her. But at least there was a chance, with the lights off, that he wouldn't know which windows were hers.

She'd just finished dialing zero when she realized there was a strange odor in the room. A sour smell, perfume and sweat. "Operator, this is an emer—" she began.

"Mother, love a son's honor..." The quavering falsetto made Vicky's words die in her throat. She'd heard that voice before, the voice that was now coming from somewhere in her room.

"...life is pain, no justice." The silhouette of a hand with fingers outstretched reached up from under Vicky's bed. "Revenge, destruction...death to all!"

Leaping off the mattress, Vicky backed against the wall, too horror stricken to move. The husky voice belonged to a woman, the one who'd called Vicky at the shop. The hand grew into an arm, then slowly a body unfolded in front of the dimly lit window.

"So, Vicky, we meet at last."

The woman's face was in shadow, her figure obscured by the shapeless bulk of her jacket. It was a jacket she'd seen many times. *It was Lieutenant Simmons's rumpled green sports coat.*

"My, God!" Vicky moaned, pressing her hands to her face.

"I've heard a great deal about you from my son," he said in the sickening vibrato.

Now she could understand why the voice had been so hard to distinguish on the phone. He did sound remarkably like a woman.

"What...are you doing here?" Vicky formed each word slowly and carefully as she inched her way to the bedroom door.

"I came to introduce myself. My son was always so inconsiderate. I tried my best to teach him manners, but nothing ever sunk in. You'd think with my being a teacher and all . . . but no, I have to admit it. He was a failure."

Vicky felt torn by revulsion, pity and abject terror. The creature sauntered around to the foot of the bed and sat down, crossing her legs—*his* legs. Now it was going to be that much harder for Vicky to get to the door.

"Where is your...son?" Vicky stammered.

"I killed him."

Oh, my Lord. "Why did you do that?" *Dear God, keep him talking. Don't let him notice she was trying to escape.* She risked a long sideways slide toward the bedroom door. Lieutenant Simmons didn't budge.

"He killed me. Why shouldn't I repay the favor?" He examined his nails in the semidarkness, every movement grossly effeminate. "The silly boy always used to hide under his bed, thinking I didn't know where he was. So, tonight, while he was waiting for you to come home, I surprised him."

As Vicky listened to the grotesque tale, she could hear the telephone operator calling out through the receiver. "Please, ma'am, tell me your address!"

The lieutenant brought out a piece of rolled cloth from his pocket. A crumpled piece of paper was dislodged from the pocket at the same time, and it fell, unheeded, to the floor.

Unrolling the cloth, he said, "He did leave me a little present, though, something he made himself. It's a needlepoint sampler. The stitches could use a little work, but—"

"Ma'am, don't hang up the phone," the operator insisted.

Deciding she had nothing to lose, Vicky screamed her address loud enough for the operator to hear. It was a grave mistake.

Roaring like a savage, the lieutenant lunged from the bed toward her. Vicky managed to grab hold of the doorknob, but his hands were already in a stranglehold she recognized all too well.

Jerking her arm back, Vicky plunged her elbow deep into his belly. He doubled over long enough for her to wrestle from his grip and yank open the door. She fled toward the living room, but cleared only a few paces before she was tackled by the ankles. Sprawled across the floor, Vicky was certain her luck had run out.

At that instant, the front door seemed to explode. Two men leaped inside, their guns aimed. "FBI! Let her go, or we'll shoot!"

The lieutenant made a guttural sound, and was distracted long enough for Vicky to scramble out of firing range. She rolled herself up in a ball in the corner, squeezing her eyes shut and listening to the scuffles and shouts, kicks and punches.

Finally, except for the sounds of the lieutenant sobbing, it was over. "Okay, guys," she heard Agent Darrigo call out. "You can come in now."

Vicky opened one cautious eye as the hall lights came on. Lieutenant Simmons was a few feet away, handcuffed and shackled, between Agents Carter and Darrigo. He looked up at Vicky, and she recoiled at the sight. His face was smeared with heavy eye makeup and lipstick. A jagged wound festered on his right cheek.

And in his hand was the needlepoint sampler. With a floral border in garish colors, Drysdale's quotation had been stitched.

Justin and Rick appeared at the door.

"Where is she? Is she okay?" Justin asked, looking around anxiously.

Vicky waved at him from the floor. "I'm here. I'm okay."

Rick poked an elbow in Justin's ribs. "See? I told you she would be."

She was in the two mens' arms before anyone could stop her. She kissed Justin and hugged Rick. She laughed and cried and blubbered her apologies. Before going out to the FBI's brown sedan waiting at the curb, she dashed into her bedroom to get her handbag. It was then she noticed the crumpled piece of paper that had fallen from the lieutenant's pocket. She picked it up and smoothed it open.

It was the missing page from Justin's anthology.

"YOU SET ME UP? How could you?" Vicky glared at Justin who sat beside her in the nondescript office of the Federal Bureau of Investigation.

"It wasn't his idea," the sandy-haired Agent Carter said in Justin's defense. "He was dead set against it at first."

"That's right," Darrigo agreed. "But we tried to do everything humanly possible to make sure you wouldn't get hurt."

"Really? Then how did the lieutenant manage to break into my store and do this?" Vicky demanded, revealing the freshly bruised marks on her neck.

"That's what I wanted to know, too," Justin growled.

Carter's fair complexion grew pink. "We're awfully sorry about that. We were expecting Simmons to make a move on Sean Filipi last night—the guy's fourteen days were up. And we didn't think he'd try anything with you so soon after the poisoned chocolates."

"I should never have left you at the shop by yourself." Justin shook his head ruefully.

"That's right," Rick added with a scowl. "You're just as much to blame as the FBI for not looking after Vicky."

Agent Darrigo, who was nearly as large as Rick, put an arm around the younger man's shoulder. "By the way, Mr. Paterson, you did a fantastic job for us tonight."

Rick's face beamed with pride. "Thanks."

Vicky gazed at her friend in astonishment. "You were part of this, too?"

"Sure was. Last night, after I found out I couldn't get a tour of the fish hatchery, I went to the Cheese 'n' Deli for supper. Darrigo and Carter came in and talked to Mr. Rubinoff and me. They asked if we'd like to help catch the chain letter killer."

"So, of course, you said yes." Vicky folded her arms across her chest, feigning anger.

"I sure did," Rick replied. "They told me they were pretty certain it was Lieutenant Simmons, but they had to catch him in the act of commencing—no, committing a crime." He glanced at Agent Carter for approval before going on.

"In the meantime, I had to stay out of sight for two reasons." Rick held up two fingers to illustrate his point. "One, in case the lieutenant got wind that I was onto him, and two, to make it look like I was the killer and had gone into hiding."

Agent Carter interjected, "We'd concluded that Simmons didn't like to make a move unless he could convincingly point the blame at someone else. That's why he made the anonymous call claiming to have seen Justin's car run Sean Filipi off the road."

"I haven't finished telling my story yet," Rick cut in.

"Sorry." The agent invited him to continue.

"Where did you stay last night?" Vicky asked Rick.

"In Mr. Rubinoff's apartment."

"So that's why he acted so strangely this morning when I asked if he'd seen you."

"Yeah. He was harboring a suspected criminal." Rick grinned, proud of his vocabulary.

"Remember the 'wrong number' last night?" Justin asked.

Vicky glanced at him. "It wasn't a wrong number?"

"It was Agent Carter telling me they'd seen Lieutenant Simmons entering your apartment. That was my signal to tell you I was tired."

She whacked him on the hand. "Thanks a bunch. I'll remember next time you use that excuse." Turning to the agents, she asked, "How did the lieutenant get into my place anyway?"

"He had a whole arsenal of lock-breaking supplies at home," the dark-haired Darrigo replied. "He'd obviously been collecting them for years."

"My God." Vicky shuddered. "He'd seemed so concerned about the locks in my apartment when all along he must have been casing the place."

"That's right," said Carter. "Anyway, after we called Mr. Coe, Darrigo and I hid in a storage closet across the hall from your apartment. Rick's job was to look after you while you walked home from Justin's."

Vicky's mouth dropped. "But you scared me half to death, Rick."

He puffed out his chest. "Yeah, I was pretty good, huh? I was supposed to make sure you didn't change your mind and go to a movie or something. That's why I had to pretend I was following you. Course, if anyone had tried to hurt you, I'd have been the first one to punch his lights out."

Vicky managed her first genuine laugh of the evening. "That's reassuring. But what I don't understand is how anyone got the idea it was the lieutenant in the first place. He always struck me as a dedicated officer."

"He was," Darrigo said. "Why don't you tell her, Mr. Coe?"

Justin poured more coffee for himself after Vicky refused a refill. "Lieutenant Simmons bothered me from the start, probably because he dug up my traffic record the first time we met. I was worried that it was just a matter of time before he discovered my real identity. Then there were the little things—his attitude toward the so-called accidental deaths, not bothering to investigate Eve Lomorth's funeral, and the way he kept warning you to stay away from me, as though I was somehow involved. Oh yes, and the business with my Drysdale book. He knew I'd probably have a copy, being an English professor and all. He'd seemed so unsurprised by the pages being cut out... Anyway, I knew I was being framed, and he began to look like the most logical one."

Vicky gave him a sheepish grin. "I hate to admit there were times I believed him."

"The chocolates were the last straw. I knew I was going to be the prime suspect for that one, since I was the one who had found you that morning. So I decided to call the FBI and tell them who I was before they found out through Interpol."

"You can imagine our surprise," Carter said, "when Mr. Coe talked about the chain letter murders and we didn't have a clue what he meant."

Vicky's eyes widened. "You hadn't been working on the case?"

"Lieutenant Simmons had conveniently not bothered to inform them," Justin said. "As far as the rest of the police department knew, he was working hand in hand with the FBI, but all he'd really done was bury the file."

"If Mr. Coe hadn't been up-front about the warrant in Italy, we might have considered him a suspect. But the computer check confirmed that Michael Justason, alias

Justin Coe, was in the clear. So we started focusing on Lieutenant Simmons, his background, that sort of thing.''

"What was his background?" Vicky asked.

"He was an only child," Agent Carter answered. "His mother was a high-school teacher. His dad deserted them when Simmons was three. For years, people thought the kid was retarded, but he was eventually diagnosed as having emotional problems brought on by an abusive and repressive mother.''

Vicky remembered the lieutenant's comments about his mother, the day he'd helped to calm Rick down. She felt a sharp stab of sympathy for the man.

"He did poorly in school," the agent went on to say, "until grade twelve. That was the year his mother died accidentally. Almost overnight, he was a changed man. Graduated at the top of his class and went straight into the police academy.''

Vicky recalled the chilling statement made by Lieutenant Simmons's alter ego. "How exactly did his mother die?"

"She fell down a set of basement stairs.''

Her heart stopped. The mother side of him had clearly said, *He killed me.* "Do you think it's possible she was pushed?'' Vicky asked.

Agent Carter did not seem surprised by her remark. "It's possible. We'll never know for sure, but that would explain the emergence of a second personality. I'm no psychiatrist, but maybe he needed some way to cope with his guilt.''

"What do you think will happen to him?" Vicky tried to think only about the nice man who'd bought an apple-head doll in case he needed a gift for someone at the station. The sooner she forgot the rest, the better.

"After the trial, he'll likely be committed someplace where they can give him the best of care.''

"I'm glad," she said, suddenly fighting back tears.

Linking his fingers with Vicky's, Justin stood up, "If you gentlemen have finished with us for now, I'd like to take this lady home."

"Sure thing," said Carter. "Get some rest. You're gonna need it."

Justin winked at Vicky. "Don't worry, Carter. We will."

Epilogue

The Madison Police Department, an exemplary force, took the news about Lieutenant Simmons hard. He'd been a fine policeman, an excellent career officer. Now he spent his days in a state-run institution, and it was as if the lieutenant had never existed. And from what they heard he still didn't. He had become his mother.

VICKY AND JUSTIN were married in a chapel near her parents' home in northern Wisconsin. Her father gave her away, and Rick Paterson was best man. Mr. Rubinoff played a Gypsy violin for the bride's first dance.

Instead of flowers to decorate the church and hall, Vicky brought her best trees—Calliope, Arthur, Desiree. Her attendants wore buttercup yellow, and Justin was dashing in midnight blue. It was, all in all, a perfect wedding.

They spent the first day of their month-long honeymoon driving back to Madison. The following day, they were to board a plane for Italy. The first stop would be a visit to his mother's nursing home, a reconnection to the past he'd left behind so long ago. After much discussion, he and Vicky decided that he would retain the name Justin Coe, since it was the name that, fatefully, had brought them together.

Justin turned the car onto Sherman Avenue.

"I thought we were going straight to the hotel," Vicky said to her husband.

"We will, but I want to check my mail first."

Vicky returned her attention to the travel brochures of Rome, Milan and Venice. "Go ahead," she said. "I'll wait in the car."

A few minutes later, Justin came out of the house with a strange look on his face. He held up an envelope plastered with postmarks. "You'll never guess what this is."

Vicky swallowed hard. "It can't be. It's been nearly a year."

"It's the chain letter, all right." He examined the envelope. "Looks like it's been to Madison, Georgia; Madison, Connecticut; and someplace in Idaho."

Time had erased the sharp edges of the memory, and Vicky was able to laugh. "You know, I've always wondered why you never got one."

Justin ripped the letter and the envelope into tiny pieces and dropped them in the litter bag behind the seat. Then he slid into the driver's seat. "So now we know. The U.S. postal service was behind it all the time." He leaned over and kissed his new wife. "Is there anything else you're still worried about?"

She wrapped her arms lovingly around his neck. "There's just one little thing. It's about your passport, the one you forged..."

Take 4 books & a surprise gift FREE

SPECIAL LIMITED-TIME OFFER

Mail to   **Harlequin Reader Service®**

In the U.S.   In Canada
901 Fuhrmann Blvd.   P.O. Box 609
P.O. Box 1867   Fort Erie, Ontario
Buffalo, N.Y. 14269-1867   L2A 5X3

YES!   Please send me 4 free Harlequin Superromance® novels and my free surprise gift. Then send me 4 brand-new novels every month as they come off the presses. Bill me at the low price of $2.74 each*—a 7% saving off the retail price. There are no shipping, handling or other hidden costs. There is no minimum number of books I must purchase. I can always return a shipment and cancel at any time. Even if I never buy another book from Harlequin, the 4 free novels and the surprise gift are mine to keep forever.   134 BPS BP7F

*Plus 49¢ postage and handling per shipment in Canada.

Name   (PLEASE PRINT)

Address   Apt. No.

City   State/Prov.   Zip/Postal Code

This offer is limited to one order per household and not valid to present subscribers. Price is subject to change.   DOSR-SUB-1C

CAROLE MORTIMER

JUST ONE NIGHT

Hawk Sinclair—Texas millionaire and owner of the exclusive
Sinclair hotels, determined to protect his son's inheritance.
Leonie Spencer—desperate to protect her sister's happiness.

They were together for just one night.
The night their daughter was conceived.

Blackmail, kidnapping and attempted murder add suspense
to passion in this exciting bestseller.

The success story of Carole Mortimer continues with *Just
One Night*, a captivating romance from the author of the
bestselling novels, *Gypsy* and *Merlyn's Magic*.

★

**Available in March
wherever paperbacks are sold.**

GIFTS FROM THE HEART

MAIL-IN-OFFER
OFFER CERTIFICATE ✂

I have enclosed the required number of proofs of purchase from any specially marked "Gifts From The Heart" Harlequin romance book, plus cash register receipts and a check or money order payable to Harlequin Gifts From The Heart Offer, to cover postage and handling.

002

CHECK ONE	ITEM	# OF PROOFS OF PURCHASE	POSTAGE & HANDLING FEE
	01 Brass Picture Frame	2	$ 1.00
	02 Heart-Shaped Candle Holders with Candles	3	$ 1.00
	03 Heart-Shaped Keepsake Box	4	$ 1.00
	04 Gold-Plated Heart Pendant	5	$ 1.00
	05 Collectors' Doll Limited quantities available	12	$ 2.75

NAME _____

STREET ADDRESS _____ APT. # _____

CITY _____ STATE _____ ZIP _____

Mail this certificate, designated number of proofs of purchase (inside back page) and check or money order for postage and handling to:

Gifts From The Heart, P.O. Box 4814
Reidsville, N. Carolina 27322-4814

NOTE THIS IMPORTANT OFFER'S TERMS

Requests must be postmarked by May 31, 1988. Only proofs of purchase from specially marked "Gifts From The Heart" Harlequin books will be accepted. This certificate plus cash register receipts and a check or money order to cover postage and handling must accompany your request and may not be reproduced in any manner. Offer void where prohibited, taxed or restricted by law. LIMIT ONE REQUEST PER NAME, FAMILY, GROUP, ORGANIZATION OR ADDRESS. Please allow up to 8 weeks after receipt of order for shipment. Offer only good in the U.S.A. Hurry—Limited quantities of collectors' doll available. Collectors' dolls will be mailed to first 15,000 qualifying submitters. All other submitters will receive 12 free previously unpublished Harlequin books and a postage & handling refund.   OFFER-1RR

PAMELA BROWNING

...is fireworks on the green at the Fourth of July and prayers said around the Thanksgiving table. It is the dream of freedom realized in thousands of small towns across this great nation.

But mostly, the Heartland is its people. People who care about and help one another. People who cherish traditional values and give to their children the greatest gift, the gift of love.

American Romance presents HEARTLAND, an emotional trilogy about people whose memories, hopes and dreams are bound up in the acres they farm.

HEARTLAND...the story of America.

Don't miss these heartfelt stories: American Romance #237 SIMPLE GIFTS (March), #241 FLY AWAY (April), and #245 HARVEST HOME (May).

HRT-1

GIFTS FROM THE HEART
from *Harlequin*

FREE BY MAIL — With proofs of purchase plus postage and handling

A. Hand-polished solid brass picture frame 1-5/8″ × 1-3/8″ with 2 proofs of purchase.

B. Individually handworked, pair of heart-shaped glass candle holders (2″ diameter), 6″ candles included, with 3 proofs of purchase.

C. Heart-shaped porcelain keepsake box (1″ high) with delicate flower motif with 4 proofs of purchase.

D. Radiant gold-plated heart pendant on 16″ chain with complimentary satin pouch with 5 proofs of purchase.

E. Beautiful collectors' doll with genuine porcelain face, hands and feet, and a charming heart appliqué on dress with 12 proofs of purchase. Limited quantities available. See offer terms.

HERE IS HOW TO GET YOUR FREE GIFTS

Send us the required number of proofs of purchase (below) of specially marked ''Gifts From The Heart'' Harlequin books and cash register receipts with the Offer Certificate (available in the back pages) properly completed, plus a check or money order (do not send cash) payable to Harlequin Gifts From The Heart Offer. We'll RUSH you your specified gift. Hurry—Limited quantities of collectors' doll available. See offer terms.

602R

GIFTS FROM THE HEART
ONE PROOF
OF PROOF OF PURCHASE

To collect your free gift by mail you must include the necessary number of proofs of purchase with order certificate.